"McFerrin's writing is strong and beautiful."
—*Library Journal*

Praise for *Namako: Sea Cucumber*

" . . . this vivid, often humorous novel offers a winning young heroine, a complex family and memorable vignettes of a year spent betwixt and between."—
Publishers Weekly

"*Namako* is a novel about a child's virgin dance with the truth with lies and secrets. Each new violation of trust is like a footprint on the tundra, refining the way the child walks through life."—*Los Angeles Times*

"McFerrin's writing is thoughtful and smooth as she captures ever-changing images of the world . . . successfully filtering those images through the eyes of her youthful characters."—*Library Journal*

"McFerrin's prose is subtle and unpretentious, filled with beautifully imagined, just-ripe metaphors. She adeptly captures the heartbreakingly bitter-sweet sensitivity of a child, and paints a touching picture of human relationship."—
Inside Asian America

"This finely-crafted first novel by an accomplished young writer fairly radiates with light and life. And, as it grows into its final crescendo of insight and enlightenment, it also radiates with power . . . a joy, each word perfectly accurate, yet not at all abstract or remote, but relaxed and informal enough to deal with a house full of rough-and-tumble children."—*ForeWord Magazine*

"Haunting in its incidents and mood and beautiful, precise, almost crystalline, in style."—*Multicultural Review*

"Watanabe McFerrin injects Namako with a quirky sensibility that makes it seem freshly minted."—*San Francisco Metropolitan*

"Quite astonishing—beautiful, touching and altogether original."—Jan Morris, author of *Conundrum, Pleasures of a Tangled Life, Fisher's Face* and *Pax Britannica*

Praise for *The Hand of Buddha*

"Women struggle to make sense of their lives in this warm-hearted collection from novelist and poet McFerrin . . . inspirational fodder for spiritually inclined readers."—*Publishers Weekly*

"McFerrin is adept at describing the concerns of women of various ethnic backgrounds, from different geographic regions of America and showing that despite race, country of origin, or physical location, some feelings and difficulties are universal. The stories, written with either puckish charm or an airy elegance, depending on the subject matter, are simply just well told. Although many characters stumble upon bad situations or dark epiphanies, McFerrin's wry and quiet sense of humor shines through and balances light and shadow."—*ForeWord Magazine*

"McFerrin is a travel writer, and it shows: the richest passages deal with locations, places . . . This collection is both promising and accomplished in its vivid and unblinking look at women in the throes of life."—*Ms. Magazine*

"McFerrin's writing is strong and beautiful, almost like poetry, and the result is a provocative, sometimes humorous, and always colorful collection about women from a variety of generations, cultures, and backgrounds."—*Library Journal*

" . . . compassion, humor and a tenderness that sometimes erupts into joy. Magic shines through these stories."—*Pioneer Press*

"The underlying matrix in McFerrin's smart, sexy, and magical tales is her belief in 'embracing possibilities' and accepting the chaos of life, a message well worth imparting."—*Booklist*

" . . . concise, moving, even a bit chilling."—*Pacific Reader*

DEAD LOVE

LINDA WATANABE McFERRIN

Stone Bridge Press ✦ Berkeley, California

Published by
Stone Bridge Press
P.O. Box 8208
Berkeley, CA 94707
TEL 510-524-8732 ◆ sbp@stonebridge.com ◆ www.stonebridge.com

For comments and more about the characters and the world of *Dead Love*, visit
www.deadlovebook.com.

Cover and text design by Linda Ronan.

Text © 2010 Linda Watanabe McFerrin.

First edition 2010.

Printed in the United States of America.

2015 2014 2013 2012 2011 2010   10 9 8 7 6 5 4 3 2 1

LIBRARY OF CONGRESS CATALOGING-IN-PUBLICATION DATA
McFerrin, Linda Watanabe.
   Dead love / Linda Watanabe Mcferrin.—1st ed.
      p. cm.
   Includes bibliographical references.
   ISBN 978-1-933330-90-7 (paperbound); ISBN 978-1-933330-91-4 (casebound).
   1. Supernatural—Fiction. 2. Conspiracies—Fiction. 3. Zombies—Fiction. I. Title.
PS3573.A7987D43 2010
813'.54—dc22
                        2010029248

In memory of Marissa Erin McFerrin

And so, all the night-tide, I lie down by the side
Of my darling, my darling, my life and my bride
In her sepulcher there by the sea—
In her tomb by the sounding sea.

EDGAR ALLAN POE

CONTENTS

THE TRUTH ABOUT ZOMBIES

My name is Erin and I am *not* a zombie, though my boyfriend, the gangster, Ryu, and the ghoul, Clément, tried to make one of me. They nearly succeeded, too, but Clément blew it—as he usually does—and although I no longer speak, appear to be totally apathetic, and exhibit other zombie-like behaviors, I was not really "made" in the traditional sense. I still have my will.

If you read the official accounts, you'll find that Erin Orison, the talented and rebellious only daughter of American ambassador Christian Orison, died in a Tokyo hospital shortly after her eighteenth birthday. But there is so much more to the story.

First, let me assure you that zombies are REAL. Most people know zombies only as the decomposing corpses that paw hungrily and rather ineffectively at the living in trashy books and B-movies. Some would have you believe that zombies are born of disease or that they come from another planet. Haven't you noticed how the truth, especially when it is dangerous, is hidden in a pack of lies? That's how they fool you. They make you laugh. You relax as the magician entertains you and his assistants rob you blind.

But maybe you are different. Perhaps you are a student of history and culture and are a bit more familiar with the truth about zombies. Maybe you've read some of the great works on the subject, have heard of the substances that create them. Maybe you know something about the beliefs that rode to the New World in the cargo hulls of ships packed with the bodies of *living* slaves.

If you have traveled to Haiti, you may even have seen them— these poor, abstracted creatures whose identities have been stolen by an unscrupulous Vodoun witchdoctor or bokor.[1] There are those who, for one reason or another, want to possess a creature. Through various methods, which I'll explain later, these wicked individuals administer a sophisticated "poison." The victim sickens and dies. But here is the trick: The victim is not really dead at all; though the symptoms that mimic death and a premature burial in a lightless box are enough to make them think they have breathed their last. Or could their loss of identity be a result of an actual change in body chemistry precipitated by the bokor's dreadful concoction? Whatever the reason, when the bokor, who is waiting, digs the person up, the poor creature believes it has passed from the realm of the living. Confused, perhaps even mentally damaged, it clings to the bokor. The murderer becomes the liberator, and the victim becomes a slave.

In my case this didn't happen as planned. Ryu's Japanese gangster bosses, the yakuza,[2] wanted to kill me; Clément wanted a slave; but I proved extremely resistant. At the time, however, even *I* thought I had died and that I'd been reborn as a zombie, a creature come back from the dead. Since then I've discovered quite a lot about zombies, about bokors, hounfours,[3] Vodou, and the Loa.[4] I know that I didn't actually die, though I came very close to being possessed and to truly losing my soul.

It all sounds fantastic, I know. "Pure fiction," you might say, for you might not be buying any of this. I understand. Zombies? Really!

Like you, I never take things on faith. My mind cries out for objective straws. All right, let me justify what I am saying with research, with facts.

Please consider the strange case of Felicia Felix-Mentor.

In 1907, Felicia, a native of a small Haitian village where she and her husband owned a grocery store, suddenly became very ill. No one knew what was wrong, but she grew gradually worse until, in the end, she died. Felicia was given a peaceful burial. But that's hardly the end of the story. Twenty-nine years after her burial, on November 8, 1936, this supposedly dead woman was seen walking along the road—naked—on her way to a farm where her brother worked as a foreman. The farm's tenants tried to drive her away, but her brother recognized her at once as the sister he'd buried over two decades before. Dr. Rulx Leon, Director-General of the Service d'Hygiene in Haiti, reported the bizarre story of her reappearance to the authorities. Well-known American writer Zora Neale Hurston actually tracked Felicia to a hospital at Gonaives in southern Haiti.[5]

In her book, *Tell My Horse*, Ms. Hurston writes:

> We found the Zombie in the hospital yard. They
> had just set her dinner before her, but she was not
> eating. The moment she sensed our approach, she
> broke off a limb of a shrub and began to use it to
> dust and clean the ground and the table, which bore
> her food. The two doctors made kindly noises and
> tried to reassure her. She seemed to hear nothing.
> The doctor uncovered her head for a moment
> (she had covered it with a cloth) but she promptly
> clapped her arms and hands over it to shut out
> the things she dreaded. Finally the doctor forcibly

uncovered her and held her . . . and the sight was dreadful. The blank face with the dead eyes.

Ms. Hurston photographed Felicia. You can check it out. The photos of the zombie are in her book.

Then there are the mysterious circumstances surrounding the deaths of Clairvius Narcisse and Ti Femme. These were documented by Dr. Lamarque Douyon, Director of the Centre de Psychiatrie et Neurologie in Port-au-Prince and recorded by celebrated ethnobotanist Wade Davis.[6] Clairvius was declared dead at Albert Schweitzer Hospital at Deschapelles in the Arbonite Valley in Haiti on May 2, 1962. He was buried the next morning. His sister, Angelina, was present at the funeral. Eighteen years later, Angelina was shocked when her long-dead brother approached her in the marketplace. He claimed he'd been resurrected, beaten, bound, and enslaved. For two years, he said, he had worked in the company of other zombies. When their "master" was finally murdered, he escaped and wandered for sixteen years.

Another zombie, Ti Femme, died at home on February 23, 1976, at the age of thirty. There was nothing unusual about her burial except that she was discovered three years later—quite alive but disoriented and completely withdrawn—by her mother. Talk about a cold case! To verify that this was indeed Ti Femme, her grave was reopened and her casket exhumed. The coffin was full of rocks.

And what of Natagette Joseph, who was killed in a dispute in 1966 and recognized wandering around her village by the very same police officer who had pronounced her dead fourteen years before?

More recently, in February 1988, a young man by the name of Wilfred Doricent, a native of the town of Roche-a-Bateau at the tip of Haiti's southernmost peninsula, fell victim to a mysterious illness.

He succumbed to the "sickness," died, and was buried. On September 11, 1989, a former girlfriend recognized him wandering around in a nearby village. On March 12, 1990, a jury dispensed true justice, sentencing Doricent's uncle, Belavoix Doricent, to life imprisonment for the crime of zombification.[7]

And finally there are the seventeen Haitian zombies discovered living in squalid conditions in a dilapidated compound near Jacmel just three years ago. Perhaps you read about them? All were traced to lives and families that confirmed their deaths in the decades prior. Of the seventeen, two—Joceline Relufe and Elitan Danfourer—produced evidence that led to the 2007 apprehension of their "murderer." Investigators in Jacmel believe that the same individual was responsible for all seventeen of the cases.

Then, of course, there is my situation. The consciousness of the girl, Erin Orison, went into hiding on the evening of August 10, 2009. In the days that followed she would materialize in a greatly abstracted state in the streets of Tokyo, Amsterdam, and Kuala Lumpur and in villages in parts of Malaysia until she would appear to be critically injured in a twenty-foot fall from a trapeze (there was, oddly, no net) from which she would rise seemingly unaffected and in one piece.

These are the facts.

THE MEN BEHIND THE CURTAIN

I'm not sure how Clément got the idea to make a zombie, but he surely came across these monsters in his meanderings around the world because he, too, is a creature of darkness. He certainly knew just where to go to get the infernal recipe. I was unfortunate in that he chose me as his victim, though I have known all along that he was my nemesis. It was a feeling I had from the first time I met him in Narita Airport upon my arrival in Tokyo. It was odd that my father, who resided in Tokyo much of the year, had sent for me, since he'd spent all eighteen years of my life pretending I didn't exist. I should have suspected something was up. Perhaps I didn't want to believe that.

To me, Christian Orison is the collegiate young man in my mother's old photos. Stiff-postured and well dressed, he is fair-haired, handsome, and he looks insufferably arrogant. This is the way I know of him. I also know of him through my mother's broken heart and a drug habit that sent her to an early grave and me to a series of very formal boarding schools perched on the slopes of mountains or on desolate coasts. We have never met, this father and I. He is the bankroll behind many of the things I despise, and there is no way in hell I would have responded to his summons except for the perfect hook.

Baiting a trap, I've come to discover, is one of my father's talents. My lure was no less than an audition with Hiroshi Nakamura, a man I believed to be the greatest choreographer to have walked, danced, or glided upon the face of the planet. I sometimes wonder how the disinterested Christian, who knew so little about me, could have come up with so perfect a snare. Did he actually read the reports penned by my dutiful educators? Did he know about my successes in dance? I'm sure his spies were informed, even if he was not. In my heart, I think, there was a tiny place that hoped that he actually wanted to see me. Hope is a treacherous thing. It can make such a fool out of anyone.

So, there I was at Narita Airport, exiting customs, staring at a white card with my name on it in English: "Erin Orison." Naturally, my father was not there.

The man holding the card looked like a skinny Asian Pinocchio dressed in a chauffeur's uniform, but I took little notice of him because the two men standing next to him—one, a good-looking Japanese man talking into a cell phone; the other a tall, white-haired Caucasian man who had pulled his trouser leg up past his bony old shin and was carefully examining his knee—were such an unusual pair. They stood quite apart from the rest of the crowd, not because they were keeping their distance, but because everyone else was keeping theirs. Both stopped what they were doing and stared as soon as I walked through the sliding doors. They weren't the only ones staring. I'm not terribly tall—just five foot seven, actually—but in my short, jade-green sheath and six-inch stiletto heels, I towered over virtually everyone in the hall. I'd swept my purplish-brown hair up in a French twist that made me look still more dramatic, and I made it a point to pause, with a model's instinct for angles and light, in a brief but expressive pose. I've always been bold. The cruel crowd of my school days had little tolerance for the shy or withdrawn.

Both men were impeccably, if idiosyncratically dressed. The Japanese man, who was handsome, wore a pewter-gray silk suit, teal-blue tie, and snow-white shirt with French cuffs secured by cuff links in the shape of attacking dragons. I noticed as I approached that his wrists, where the French cuffs allowed them to be slightly exposed, were marked by the swirling tattoos that cover the bodies of Japan's gangster caste—the yakuza. The older man wore no jacket, a starched white shirt with thin red and blue stripes, navy trousers, dark gray braces, and a bright red bowtie. He dropped his trouser leg and straightened up as I drew nearer, and when he moved, I caught a too-powerful whiff of Armani masking a subcurrent sourness with definite back-alley notes. Quite a potent aroma. Phew. No wonder the crowd gave them a wide berth.

Erect now, he collected himself into a more distinguished posture. He extended an icy, yellowish-green hand. I was instantly uncomfortable.

"Carlyle," he drawled. "Your father's lawyer. I've been dyin' to meet-cha."

I let him take my hand and regretted it at once. His hand, cold though it was, slid around mine in a way that could only be described as salacious. I wanted to pull mine back, but he wouldn't let go.

"Erin." He lingered over my name. It made me shiver to hear him say it. "I'd know you anywhere. Such a pretty, pretty girl." His icy hand tightened around mine.

"You sent the letter?" I managed to squeak, recollecting the letterhead on the formal communiqué that had brought me to Tokyo.

"Yes, yes, I did," he responded, spittle seeming to gather in the corners of his mouth, "And I am glad, so glad of it."

His eyes, which were so vacant, so pale a blue as to be almost white, had pupils no bigger than pinpricks, and they bored into me with an intensity that was a little frightening. His hand held mine in a vice grip, as if he would never release me, and I thought I sensed inquisition, perhaps recognition in the mirror of his dot-like pupils. But maybe I was mistaken.

Then his hand relaxed and his mouth twisted into a crooked leer. "Well, I'm off," he said quickly, turning to the Japanese man with the cell phone. "Ryu, she's all yours. Precious cargo, you know. Take good care of her." Then he let go of my hand and turned away and limped off toward the door.

Ryu—his name means dragon in Japanese—the yakuza into whose hands I'd been delivered, had also not taken his eyes off me. His were beautiful eyes: thin-lidded, black as onyx, set in a face that looked like it was chiseled in alabaster. And he had a smile that flashed swiftly, like lightning, sudden and impossibly bright. Then it was gone. He gave a quick nod.

"*Hajimemashite.* How do you do," I said, extending my hand. "*Dozo yoroshiku.* Pleased to meet you."

"Oh, you speak Japanese."

"Yes, and French and Italian and Chinese."

Lightning flashed across his face again. He took my hand. His hand was not what I expected in a man. It was satiny, cool, smooth, and perspiration-free. His nails were pink as rose petals and perfectly manicured.

"So that is Carlyle," I said. Then under my breath, "I dislike him."

Another great flash of smile and a peal of laughter like thunder. "You don't like him? Then, he is a dead man," said Ryu, unaware that someone else had already beaten him to the punch.

"Ah, a dead man," I whispered as I slipped out of my six-inch heels to stand in my bare feet and gaze, eye to eye, with the beautiful yakuza, with Ryu.

"A snake," he said briskly, pocketing the cell phone. "Snip-snap," he said, and pantomimed breaking something in two. Then he took my arm in a proprietary way that I mistakenly interpreted as attraction. I picked up my shoes. The chauffeur grabbed the bags and followed us out of the terminal.

ASHES TO ASHES

Narita Airport is located around sixty-six clicks east of Tokyo. To get to the city you have to race through a quasi-industrial wasteland blighted with giant apartment blocks composed of thousands of cramped little dwellings occupied by Tokyo workers and their families. Laundry draped like prayer flags festoons the narrow iron balconies that climb up the faces of tower after tower, and on a hot August day the seamy tableau swelters under a thick mask of grit.

Alone, in the back seat of the air-conditioned sedan, I hunched by the door, my face pressed to the window, at once excited and apprehensive about the upcoming meeting with my dad. Would I be able to forgive him for abandoning us, for my mother's drift into madness and death?

Ryu sat in the front seat with the driver. He was on his cell phone again, arguing with someone named Miura. "Fool," he snarled into the phone. "It is business."

Yakuza business, I suspected, which had to be nothing worthwhile. I had to remind myself that, handsome as he was, this was no knight in armor, but a yakuza in tattoos. Why in the world would my father send a gangster to fetch me? An uneasy feeling made me squirm in my seat. I tapped Ryu's broad, suited shoulder. He turned to me, his black eyes narrow and, for a moment, almost cruel.

"Ryu," I asked warily, "why did my father send you to meet me?"

"Bodyguard," he said, lips stretching over his teeth in a long gondola of a smile, dark eyes turning squinty with pleasure.

His smile was ominous, but disarming. A flutter of excitement kicked its way into my chest and drifted down into my lap. "Mmmm," I nodded, still wary, more distracted than appeased.

He turned back to his phone, speaking quietly now. I leaned back in the seat and resumed surveying the scenery. By the time we reached the Rainbow Bridge, the magnificent span that arcs from Odaiba Beach to Tokyo, the dirty haze had thinned. Sunlight did a spangled dance on the waters of Tokyo Bay. I was Dorothy first setting foot in Oz.

Soon enough we were crawling through the crowded Tokyo streets where pedestrians and vehicles vie for purchase. Large signs looming far overhead promised colorful nights ablaze in a neon extravaganza. Intersections bustled with life. Ancient, modern, wooded, high-tech— Tokyo was a city of contrasts. Ryu seemed to draw energy from the surroundings. I watched his body react physically to them, his movements quickening, his neck and jaw muscles tightening in a way that was almost electric.

My father's apartment was in the Roppongi district of Tokyo. If the city has a foreign heart, this is it. It's an international compound, the home of many an expat, a neighborhood full of Japanese antique stores, Western-style restaurants, swank hotels, and fabulous Roppongi Hills, a high-end, sky-high "village" for the terminally trendy. Dad's place was on a tree-lined residential street with a park nearby in which a handful of noisy Western kids were scooting around on their Razors.

"We are here," announced Ryu, easing out of the car. He held the front door for me and we stepped from the sidewalk into the cool, marble lobby. We took the elevator to the third floor. The chauffeur brought up my bags. The walls on the third floor were covered in ash-colored silk. At #3 Homat Higashi, Ryu pulled out a platinum key ring with two keys upon it. He took off one of the keys and handed me the ring with only one key upon it.

"There," he said. "Go ahead. Open it."

"My father is here?"

Ryu nodded toward the door.

The apartment, grand by any standards, was enormous for Tokyo, where space is at a premium. From the vestibule, three steps led down into a sweeping double chamber. Two huge windows, through which sunlight streamed, stretched across the living room and dining room walls. The carpet was white, the furniture dark, the sofas a rough bronze silk. Door-sized abstract canvases by well-known painters covered vast expanses of wall. I recognized Pollock, de Kooning, Diebenkorn. To the left of the entrance, on higher ground, a long hall reached past a guestroom and bath toward a cavernous master bedroom. To the right of the vestibule was the kitchen entrance through which I could see a room full of gleaming black granite counters and stainless steel. Perfectly appointed, spotlessly clean. Just the kind of soulless environment I'd expect from my father. I stepped down into the living room, examined the books that had been so carefully placed on the tables. My father, framed and caught under the glass in a series of photos, looked very much like the man in my mother's old pictures. There he stood with heads of state, with presidents past, present, and possibly future. Much heavier now, his hair not blond but gray, he still had the arrogant look, though time had hardened his smirk.

Ryu watched me coolly. He took out a cigarette, lit it, and leaned back against the front door. "Put the bags in the first room," he instructed the chauffeur.

I stood by the window, gazing down at the children racing around in the park below. "Ryu," I asked cautiously, "where is my dad?"

"Oh," said Ryu. "He's not here. He told me to give you this." He reached into his suit jacket and held out an envelope with my name on it. The note inside was handwritten in the same scrawl that appeared on my father's checks.

> Erin,
>
> This will cover your needs for as long as you are in Tokyo. I leave you to Ryu. He will take care of you. Just do as he says.
>
> Christian

There was, of course, a check. That, at least, I could count on. I glanced at the photos of my father again. His face had the pinched look of a man with a mean little heart.

Ryu sensed my mood.

"Look," he said, taking the note and holding his cigarette to it until the corner caught fire. I watched as it writhed under the lash of heat, curled into flaky gray cinders. Ryu laughed as the note fell apart, the bits of ash fluttering toward the floor. "Look," he began again, "you can't just sit here." He looked at his watch. "Come with me. I'm going to introduce you to Tokyo."

THE PACHINKO PALACE

Ryu's Tokyo was exciting. It was Shibuya[8] with its game rooms, pachinko parlors, love hotels and its boys and girls with torn clothes and bleached hair. His Tokyo was Shinjuku with its high-end Western restaurants, Roppongi's smoking jazz clubs and Ikebukuro with its sleazy hostess bars. On the weekend it was the racetrack at Tokyo Keibajo and Oi Keibajo. Sometimes it was the little boutiques, the fancy clothiers, and the jewelry stores where he liked to shop. At night it was especially thrilling: clubs full of young people not much older than I, where I could dance to techno or trance or trip-hop or ambient riffs, while he chatted with his unsavory pals.

For the next week or so I spent plenty of time with Ryu. Christian's fat check kept the carnival rolling, and I was determined to have a good time, to forget my father and the miserable childhood to which he'd condemned me, a childhood spent marooned in prison-like schools. Ryu and Tokyo complied. So did opportunity. Three days after I arrived I had my audition with Hiroshi Nakamura, in his famous dance studio, and I was accepted as one of his students. I'd gone to meet my idol, nervous and distraught, with all the enthusiasm of someone headed for execution. I left on a cloud of euphoria.

My new teacher, my *sensei* watched me dance—ballet, butoh, modern jazz. It was exhilarating. I did my best. He said, "You have a talent I have not seen for a very long time." Then he bowed. "I have a part in my new ballet. You will dance for me?" he asked gently.

"I would be so honored," I managed to reply in faltering Japanese, my heart beating a wild conga rhythm.

"We should celebrate," said Ryu with a sly smile when I told him the news.

That was the first night I slept with him. After too many sakes and whiskies *onzarokku* (on the rocks), I succumbed to his fatal charms, though I thought that I was the seductress.

"Are you tattooed all over?" I teased, loosening his tie, sliding my hand down his torso.

"Wanna see?"

He grinned through his teeth, like a wolf, and unbuttoned his shirt. Tattoos rippled over muscle. He had the most beautiful body I'd ever seen. I was soon to learn that Ryu's sexual tastes were . . . how shall I put it? . . . unusual. I was no virgin, but all of my previous experiences were hasty encounters grabbed when my friends and I could break from the manic surveillance of our teachers and guardians long enough to create an "adventure." These were quick, clumsy trysts designed merely to thwart the authorities. Sex with Ryu was nothing like this.

It was a dance, a tango over ice in a midnight-blue sea. In this, as in many things, Ryu was an artist, his satisfaction apparent in the performance of the act. Ryu used various methods to take his partners to the very brink of annihilation and drown them in sweltering salvation.

"Ryu, that was amazing," I murmured, collapsed upon the tatami mats, my dress a violet puddle beside me.

We were in the private room of a teahouse; our forms, wicked by candlelight, almost phosphorescent in the darkness; the rice paper screens broken from the force of his body and mine.

Ryu pursed his lips, raised his eyebrows, and silently buttoned his shirt.

After that we were inseparable, my bodyguard and I. He was very good at his job. And I was happy at last. I thought nothing could disrupt the mad paradise I had stumbled into. But one night, an odd incident disturbed my reckless tumble into the watery world of pleasure. I mark it for you and for myself as the beginning of the end . . .

We were in Shinjuku at one of Ryu's favorite clubs. I was chatting with Lou Lou, a very pretty, young, platinum-blonde cocktail waitress and an acquaintance of Ryu's. Ryu was smoking, drinking whisky, and playing liars' dice with the owner of the establishment. The two men were preoccupied with their game and paid little attention to their surroundings.

I actually noticed Miura while he was still on the stairs that led from the street down to the dungeon-deep interior of the club. I'd never met him before, but he was hard to miss. He was extremely tall—around six foot six—and would have been very handsome, but his nose, it seemed, had been severely broken and never properly set. This man, who could have looked like a prince, had the fearsome appearance of an ogre. Like Ryu, he was yakuza; but where Ryu was particular and precise, Miura was slovenly, his shirt rumpled, jacket open, skinny tie askew. He swaggered, almost staggered, across the dance floor, bumping into dancers without apology. And he was loud.

"Ryu," he shouted over the music. "Ryu."

Ryu looked up from his conversation. "Miura," he muttered under his breath.

Miura fought his way toward our table. It was clear he was terribly drunk. He swayed over the table and glared down at the proprietor, then shook his head and gave a dismissive snort. The club owner rose quickly, offered Miura his seat, and left. Miura threw himself into the brightly colored chair. Beneath the large broken nose, his thin lips curled into a smile.

"You think you're pretty smart, don't you?" slurred Miura.

Ryu's eyes became slit-like. It was the only sign of a reaction. "You're drunk, Miura," he said.

"No. No, I know what I'm talking about." Miura looked drunkenly over at me and belched. "You have the chip, don't you, Ryu? The one that unlocks all the secrets of the *Consortium*." He whispered that last word. "I just wanna . . . I just wanna know how you got it before I did.

"Come on, *tomodachi*, Orison's piss-ant lawyer gave it to you, didn't he?" Miura glanced over at me, then looked back at Ryu. "How did you know he had information for sale? Don't act surprised. I know all about it. That chip. . . it's the key to every illegal activity funded by that filthy-rich gang of mucky-mucks. And right there . . . right at the top, with a meticulous record of every crime, every assassination, every dollar spent on making the world a hellhole, sits Orison."

From the moment I heard my father's name I was listening. So my father was involved in some dastardly business. Well, that was no surprise, but the yakuza too? Ryu?

Miura burped again. "Oh, the Consortium will pay plenty to get that record back." He laughed. "I got the whole story out of Carlyle. He sang like a sick cat when I broke that knee. Then I gutted the snitch. Lights out for Carlyle."

"Liar," said Ryu. "I saw him eight days ago."

"Impossible," Miura roared. "He's been dead for lots longer than that. He gave you the chip. I gave him his last rites. Fair is fair."

Lou Lou let out a quick gasp. Her hand covered mine.

"By the time I saw him, Orison already knew about the betrayal. Carlyle offered me lotsa yen to get that chip back for Orison," muttered Miura, "but, I wouldn't turn on my yakuza brothers, wouldn't ruin their blackmail scheme. But you . . . you Ryu, you're up to something, eh? Come on. Where is it? Are you making a deal of your own?"

Miura slapped the table with a large, hammy hand, startling both Lou Lou and me and making us jump.

Ryu looked over at us, then back at Miura. "You talk too much, Miura," snarled Ryu.

"Oh, yeah? I don't think so. Anyway, who's listening? You're not giving the chip back to the Consortium. You've made some kind of side deal with Orison. How much? I want a cut."

Ryu's fair face had actually turned scarlet. His eyes were incendiary. If they could set Miura afire, they would have. Miura shook his big head as if to clear it and turned his smashed nose toward me.

"Oh, what a pretty girl," he sneered. "Pretty as her picture. You know, little lady, you have a very bad dad." He laughed. His fat hand reached across the table and toward me. I looked at Ryu.

"Oh, what?" laughed Miura. "What? You think *he* will protect you? Ryu? Yakuza number one hit man? Ha, that's funny. Think again. That's the guy you should watch out for."

"That's enough. *Yamero!*" barked Ryu and he grabbed Miura's hand, twisting it behind the yakuza's back and escorting the huge man, with surprising ease, across the dance floor, up the stairs, and out of the club.

I was speechless.

"Ryu," whistled Lou Lou, shaking her head.

"I don't understand," I murmured. "How does Ryu manage to put so much muscle on Miura?"

"Well, the knife that he had at Miura's back helped," whispered Lou Lou. "Ryu's known for that knife, and he likes to use it."

"Oh," I said simply.

"Here, Erin," said Lou Lou. "Let it go. Have another drink."

I nodded and lifted the cocktail to my lips: a cosmopolitan—very sweet, very pink. How did Miura know so much about my father? What was the Consortium and what did they have to do with me? Miura claimed he had killed Carlyle a week and a half ago. Impossible. We'd seen him just eight days ago at the airport. What was this chip he was talking about and what, exactly, did Miura mean when he said I should be worrying about Ryu?

I could see Ryu again, in my mind's eye, moving Miura up the stairs, his knife at the big man's back. Lou Lou rested a protective hand on my shoulder; then she slipped back into the crowd. I'd discover later that Miura was right. The men I most had to fear were those upon whom I depended. But what neither Miura nor Ryu could imagine was the wanton spirit behind the cabal. That awareness would come later for Ryu, too late for Miura, and far too quickly for me. I took another sip of my cosmo and waited for Ryu to return.

BE MINE

The Japanese gangster, Ryu, appeared to be dead. He lay naked, face-up on the heart-shaped bed of the Shakayama Love Hotel. I could see Miura, or what was left of him, a giant looming over the bed, leaning ominously over my lover's inert form. Both men were reflected in the mirror above the bed. Ryu, spread eagle, his well-muscled body dressed only in the tattoos that the yakuza fancy, was partially hidden by Miura's massive, white-shirted back, upon which a red stain bloomed, bright and fat, like a large cabbage rose. Miura seemed impervious to whatever had caused him his injury, and he was obviously up to no good. That is how I'd found them when I opened the bathroom door.

Love hotels are a quirky Japanese institution. Like capsule hotels, which are the size of small coffins and a great place to "sleep it off" after a wild night out, love hotels serve a particular purpose—that purpose is "quickies," a hot snatch of love midday or mid-marriage. Some of these hotels are outrageous, with facades capped by turrets and spires reminiscent of tacky fairytale castles, ersatz Middle Eastern seraglios, or one of those corny miniature golf courses. The hotels Ryu favored were far more discreet, their tree-shadowed entrances tucked behind stone walls, the parking underground so that patrons can duck in and out without fear of observation. They are no-tell hotels where guests select rooms from a series of illuminated photos on the wall: the harem, perhaps, or maybe the S&M suite. There is no one to judge you as you slide your thousands of yen through a slot in the wall for your one- to two-hour "rest" or *kyukei* or your *tomari* the overnight stay.

This was the second time I'd been to a love hotel with Ryu. He liked the drama of the surroundings. He liked the privacy, and I liked anything that involved him. This particular room had a black-leather wet-bar stocked with expensive whiskies and a heart-shaped bed with red satin sheets. It also had a very large, well-appointed black-and white-tiled bathroom, and this is where I must have been when Miura snuck into the room.

"What am I going to do about you, Ryu?"

I watched Miura fuss over my unconscious lover. He adjusted the pillow beneath his fellow gangster's head, sniffed at the glass by the bedside and ruffled Ryu's dark hair." Now Miura will vanish with the chip and you are going to be blamed."

"What are you doing here?" I stood, wearing not a stitch, in the threshold between bedroom and bath.

Miura straightened and turned a haggard face toward me. "Allow me to introduce myself . . . " he began.

"I know you. You're Miura."

"Oh. So it would seem. Well, maybe I am, and then, maybe not."

I knew instinctively that there was something to the assertion. It was true; the man in front of me looked like Miura, but there was something terribly wrong with him and, at the same time, something diabolically familiar. I did not yet fully understand the peculiar abilities of Clément, his techniques for reanimating the dead, the way corpses became his disguises. But this was no time for riddles. I said, "What have you done to Ryu?"

"Oh, don't worry," said Miura. "Nothing he can't sleep off. I wouldn't hurt a hair on his head." His eyes, which were devouring in spite of their frightening opacity, moved hungrily from my face down the length of my body. He threw back his head in pleasure. "Look at you," he gushed. "I can't believe we are meeting again . . . like this."

I tried to ignore the fact that I was standing there naked. "What, at a love hotel?" I snapped.

"Yes. Love," he sighed. "You look lovely. So . . . fresh."

I noticed at that point that the rose-colored stain was on both sides of his shirt. It was starting to turn brown. It was blood. He smoothed the fabric and tucked in his shirttail. "Gad, I'm a mess . . . I know your father," he announced suddenly.

"Really?" I said. "Then I suppose you are no friend of mine."

"On the contrary, Erin."

So familiar—my stomach turned when he said my name.

"My father and I don't get along," I fired back.

"No one gets along with him—except maybe Carlyle, who betrayed him and is now dead and gone, and . . . me . . . sometimes . . . when he needs me and when he has something I need. But you don't really get along with anyone either, do you? Though you've been doing a good job of trying with Ryu." There was a hint of anger in his voice, a definite note of contempt.

"How do you know so much about me? Are you one of my father's spies? Where is he? How did you find us here?"

"But you recognize me, don't you?"

"Yes, of course, you are Miura."

"Right. Miura. And . . . ? You know. Guess again." He winked and held out a yellow-green hand.

I remembered Carlyle and his slimy handshake. A terrible, choking feeling rose in my throat. Already, I think, I was beginning to recognize Clément in spite of his many guises. I was beginning to understand his dark secret, though not yet his obsession with me. "Ryu will kill you," I muttered.

"Ryu's not going to kill me and neither are you. And I'm not going to kill him, either. We are partners of a sort, Ryu and I, though he doesn't know it yet. I'm actually taking good care of him."

"Oh, that's why you've poisoned him, why you're terrorizing his girl."

"You're not his girl. You are mine, little fool; and I am trying to save you."

"Save me? From what?"

"From Ryu. From your father. From men who mean you great harm. Why do you think you were summoned to Tokyo? Why would your father turn you over to *him?*" He pointed at Ryu, who was knocked out on the bed.

"Ryu is my bodyguard."

"And then some, I see. Think what you like. Pretend that there is no ominous intent beneath all of this lust. Whatever. Ryu will do no damage tonight and," he added, "I have this."

He held up a tiny black box.

"Looks like a ring box, doesn't it?" he said. "Oh, Erin, won't you be mine? Well, it isn't. This," he said with a flourish, "is the coveted microchip, the one that could put your dad and his cohorts away for a very, very long time."

Miura was raving. *He is mad*, I thought. I looked at his broken face, the dreadfully discolored visage. "What are you talking about?" I said.

"Does it really matter?" he asked sorrowfully. "I am talking about a plot, a nasty blackmail plot that threatens the Consortium and involves a huge payoff that demands your demise. And only I—not Ryu, not Miura, not Carlyle, and certainly not your father—will save you.

"Still, your trust in Ryu, however misplaced, is so very appealing. I only wish you would direct it toward me." He hung his head. "My desire is to save you, Erin. And to that purpose I'm going on a journey—a treasure hunt, a Caribbean fling—but I do want to tell you that I'll be back."

"I don't care," I said. "You are horrible."

"Oh, don't say that. It wounds me deeply," he said. Then: "Take care of your boyfriend. That mickey is going to give him one hell of a headache."

HIDE AND SEEK

Ryu did have a headache. The headache was Miura, or what was left of him. Miura, who Ryu would later discover was not really Miura at all, now had the key to the Consortium's caustic, money-fueled, geopolitical nervous system in microchip form. It was the proof that they had, in reality, created every enemy they professed to deplore. Christian had created it. It was his insurance policy, his ace-in-the-hole. Carlyle had removed it from my father's possession, sold it to the yakuza for a pittance, and they were trading it back to the Consortium for a fortune. Ryu was to supposed to handle the drop, a drop that—as I later discovered—involved Christian's top-dog hold on the organization, a family trust, and a very dead me. But the ersatz Miura had interrupted that plan, and Ryu, who had fumbled the ball, was in trouble with his yakuza brethren. His only way out was to find Miura, whom he'd thought he had killed and recover the chip. Fortunately, or unfortunately for Ryu, Miura left a very big trail. That trail led to the Republic of Haiti, of all places, home of Vodou and hounfours and zombies.

Though Ryu was a member of the Japanese underworld, nothing had prepared him for Haiti—for the poverty and the inconvenience, for the dark faces shut tight against inquiry. The theft, Miura's flight—

all these were embarrassing things. And there was me. Ryu was supposed to kill me that night at the love hotel. He had made a mistake. He had dallied, and Miura had stopped him before he'd achieved his purpose. At this point, I'm sure Ryu was very confused. He'd killed Miura in the alley behind the club. But the big yakuza was clearly still in business . . . interfering, wrecking the plan. He had to find Miura.

They speak French and Creole in Haiti. Ryu spoke Japanese and some English. When he found a translator, the fellow, who was not at all fluent in Japanese, had trouble understanding him.

"I need to find this man," said Ryu in Japanese. He handed the translator a photo of Miura. The translator nodded furiously and stuck out his hand for more money. Together, they showed the photo to Haitians, who looked at it with glazed eyes and no recognition until they found an old woman in Jacmel in the southernmost part of the island.

"Theese man is dead," said the woman at last as she examined the battered photograph of Miura. "You must look for Arnotine Ferucand. He keeled him."

Then the search began for Arnotine Ferucand.

Arnotine Ferucand was not easy to track. The mere mention of his name provoked silence. Arnotine, the translator explained with some difficulty, was a bokor, a Vodoun witch doctor, a sorcerer who knew how to steal a man's body and dispose of his soul. More money exchanged hands. "He is Guedeh,"[9] whispered some of the interviewees. "He is Death."

Whatever his real identity, his name loosened a few tongues.

"What do you know of Arnotine Ferucand?" sneered a tall young man on the second day of their investigation in the vicinity of Jacmel. He regarded Ryu with suspicion. Then he looked at the photo of Miura and chuckled. "Oh, yes this man is dead. Talk to Ronan Duras," he added, looking down with disdain at the rumpled form of the translator. "Ronan will tell you about Arnotine. Tell Ronan I sent you."

There was no laughter in Ronan Duras. He was a wizened old man with pencil-thin limbs and hair like white spun glass. "I hate him," he said simply when asked about Arnotine. "He is a monster. He makes a mockery of our sacred rites. We punished him. But Arnotine Ferucand is not dead. I can show you the rock under which you can find him," he said and spat. Then he handed the translator a handmade business card. "Come to this hounfour," said Ronan Duras. "Come tonight."

What an invitation! A hounfour is a gathering of a Vodou société, a secret gathering to which strangers are rarely admitted. This one took place the next night in a room in a boarded-up factory, a low-slung concrete bunker of a building with a roof of corrugated tin. Ryu went alone. He almost got into a fight at the door. He had a hand on his knife, a fine Kyoto blade the size and width of a letter opener, and was ready to slit the throats of four angry men who'd put rough hands on him, when Ronan Duras intervened.

"Let heem in," said Ronan Duras. "Theese man is my guest." The four men stepped aside.

Old Ronan escorted Ryu into the candlelit den where a gargantuan woman lay on a table in the center of a swaying and shuffling crowd. "She is sick," whispered Ronan, his voice thin and dry. "I will heal her."

Drumbeats and low chanting, almost a crooning, rocked the room. Then a woman in the crowd, a thin woman in a sheer white cotton blouse and green skirt, began to twirl. She was whirling around and pulling at her blouse as if something were crawling all over her.

The rest of the men and women in the room were also moving faster. They were stamping their feet in a kind of dance, singing and occasionally yelling. The drums got louder, wilder and the woman continued to spin, colliding with people, staggering, twirling on and on.

Ryu hated it. He hated the dark, close, sticky, smelly mass of humanity that surrounded him. Two men bumped into Ryu hard—he thought on purpose. His hand went to his knife. He tried to move out of the woman's way, tried to press himself into the crowd, but the crowd parted so that in the middle of the floor it was only the woman and him. Then, the woman threw herself upon him, her skinny breasts mashed up against him, rubbing and pushing in a sickening way, arms flailing, slapping his head and his face, reaching—as he had reached— for the knife.

She was quick, and the element of surprise was in her favor. She grabbed the knife, waved it aloft and squealed. The sharp blade glinted magically in the rheumy quarter-light. White teeth flashed in all the dark faces. Screams broke out. Brandishing the knife the woman charged at Ryu and pounced . . . on the squawking chicken that someone threw into the air between them. The blade worked swiftly. It severed the chicken's head while the decapitated body continued to flap and fly, flinging blood on the whole congregation. Ryu, who was closest, was completely bespattered. But now the woman dropped the knife and lunged for the chicken. Soon enough she had stuffed part of it—the squirting part—into her mouth, feathers and all. Now white feathers flew out over the crowd, a snowfall of death in the sweaty room. Then quick hands, Ronan's hands, grabbed what was left of the twitching bird and placed it upon the ample breasts of the big woman on the table. The enormous woman writhed as he pressed it into her bosom.

"This sick woman will live," said Ronan Duras. "Arnotine Ferucand will die."

Meanwhile, the skinny woman had thrown herself onto the floor where she squirmed and spasmed, her green skirt thrown over her head—just an ordinary evening at the old hounfour. Ryu recovered his knife and pushed his way out to the door while the rest of the société kept up the frenzied dancing. Dancing, drumming, dancing (from the place in the shadows where he waited, Ryu could hear them) long, long into the night.

The next day, advised by Ronan Duras, Ryu went out, alone, to look for the sick woman. She was seated in a shack at a kitchen table upon which was displayed the head of a pig, flies ecstatically spinning around it.

"Come in," she responded gaily to Ryu's knock on the frame of the rag-draped lintel.

"So, you have found me, Ryu," she guffawed when the yakuza stepped gingerly inside, careful not to let his clothes brush up against the filth in the kitchen. It stank. It smelled like death. Ryu sniffed and forced himself to look away from the pig.

The big woman was beaming at him. She had short frizzy hair, a broad face peppered with tiny black moles, two missing front teeth, and breath that could, and should, clear a room. Still there was something disturbingly familiar about her.

"Oooh, you are a smart one," she cooed. "You track me all the way to Arnotine Ferucand. Witch doctor, you see. Arnotine is a bokor, a witch doctor, and he helped me. Old Ronan, he wouldn't help me. But Arnotine, he did. He gave me the recipe I was looking for. But he's dead. Old Ronan don't know that. He don't know nothing. Arnotine been dead for a long time. And now I am dead, too. That old fraud couldn't save me. But that's OK. I got Arnotine's secrets, my secrets now . . . and you, you got me."

She babbled along in Creole. Of course, Ryu did not understand a word that she said. He just stared at her, trying to decide what to do, his jet brows knitted, his dark-lashed eyes narrow and observant.

She laughed again. "Haw, haw, haw, Ryu-san. You don't recognize me, do you? But I know you, and I know why you're here. You want to take me back. That's your mission. Me and the chip. And I know who sent you. Those yakuza, yeah? OK, I'm ready," she added holding out her arms; hands palm upward, wrists and fat pinkies touching. "Take me home, Ryu-san. I'm all yours." And she said it in Japanese.

ARNOTINE FERUCAND IS DEAD

Ryu was shocked when the fat woman spoke to him in Japanese. She was a very unpleasant creature. It was not that she was large. In fact, he noted with some pleasure, that this woman would have made quite a sumo wrestler. She was gargantuan, the dark flesh pleating so thickly around her neck that it looked as though she had no neck at all. Her shoulders were as big as a lesser human's buttocks and, being female, she was gifted with a pair of breasts big enough, in Ryu's mind, to subsume a nation. The rest of her shape was mere conjecture, as Ryu could not distinguish what was what beneath the folds of her red tent-sized shift, though he found himself engaged in lurid speculation.

No, it wasn't her size he found so appalling. And it wasn't the face pimpled with moles or the missing teeth. It was her smell. At first he'd thought it was the pig's head, crowned in flies, upon the table before her, its snout thrust ceilingward. But soon enough his nose, that sensitive and judgmental Japanese member, determined that the smell was emanating not from the pig's head, but from the woman and from a certain spot just to the left of the stove. Every time she spoke a foul wind wafted toward him, a foul Creole wind that he had trouble understanding. Determined, he caught his breath and held his ground. He had a job to do. He must bring back the microchip that Miura had stolen, and he was certain that this woman was the latest link to that valuable asset. He would get to the bottom of things.

The bottom of things—at this point the fat woman raised her enormous bottom from a chair that looked as small as a bicycle seat beneath the grand expanse of her haunches. Standing on what seemed to be a pair of ridiculously small and inappropriately sized feet clad in red tennis shoes, she waddled the few steps over to a corner next to the stove where an orange polyethylene tarp lay in a mound on the floor.

"Arnotine Ferucand," she grunted, pulling back the cover.

The long-boned man lay upon the floor curled into a fetal position beneath the waxy orange tarpaulin. He was definitely dead and there were parts of him missing: one hand and a forearm, half a buttock and thigh. But the most unusual thing about the corpse tucked next to the stove was the expression it wore on its face. The dead Arnotine had a bright and deliriously silly look on his countenance. He looked happy and drunk, and Ryu found this shameful and vaguely upsetting.

"Yes," said the large woman, poking at the body with her surprisingly tiny foot, "that is Arnotine. Ah, Ryu," she continued in Creole, "you are disappointed, eh, and maybe a little confused?"

"You speak Japanese," Ryu reminded, hoping to persuade her into his language.

"Sometimes, when I want to," she rasped back in perfect Nihongo. Now she was speaking Japanese and Ryu very quickly noted both her thorough understanding of his situation and a disturbing familiarity in her temper and style of address.

"Where is Miura? Where's the microchip?" the big woman continued. "Trust me, my friend, your search ends with me. As for your precious chip, I know just where it is, and that's back in Japan, naturally. I came here for other things, for a certain formula, a love potion of sorts.

And old Arnotine obliged. But don't tell me you didn't enjoy our short junket. Traveling can be so enlightening." The woman patted her large belly and laughed. "I return a much wiser and happier being. Let's call it a learning adventure."

She started to hum a dark little tune as she rustled around in a stack of plastic bags, retrieving a large one with several items inside.

"I've packed a few things," she rumbled and ambled to the threshold, pushing herself through sideways, the tattered curtain tearing and exiting with her.

"*Ann ale*. Well, come on," she insisted in Creole, wiping her hands on her dress on the other side of the threshold. "Take me to your leader," she commanded in Japanese.

The drive back to Port-au-Prince was repugnant. It was almost impossible to get the large woman into the car. Upon seeing her, the translator had crossed himself once, crossed himself again, and deserted at the first opportunity, leaving Ryu alone with the human hippopotamus for the drive back to Port-au-Prince.

She filled the entire back seat of the automobile, her oily flesh pressing softly, like well-yeasted dough, against the back of the driver. He could not help noting, as she settled into the capacious back seat, that the tires of the Mercedes were seriously compromised by her weight and he worried for the whole length of the trip about losing one or all of those tires. Ryu cranked up the air conditioner, but it wasn't enough to keep the creature from disintegrating. He was drowning in the humid miasma of her breath and perspiration, in a rank, primordial swill. He was grateful when they arrived, at last, at his hotel and escaped from the confines of the car, but his gratitude evaporated in the hotel lobby.

The hotel was located on the corner of Rue Pinchinat and Rue Lamarre just next to Place St. Pierre in the slightly upscale suburb of

Pétionville. The large woman by now smelled far worse than before and, upon entering the hotel, took to making antics and carrying on. The hotel clerk, whom Ryu had disliked instantly, stopped Ryu on his way to the elevator. He was a tall, thin, young man with full lips, curly black hair, honey-colored skin, and just enough femininity about him to tickle the yakuza's cruel streak.

"No, I'm sorry," simpered the hotel clerk. "This dirty woman cannot come in here. *Elle ne peut pas entrer. Rete!*" he repeated loudly, first in French then in Creole, as if raising the volume would help Ryu understand. If Ryu already disliked the clerk, this feeling changed quickly to loathing. He hated being spoken to in the slow and exaggerated style that supercilious foreigners use on visitors. The fat woman, sensing Ryu's discomfort, decided to make matters worse.

"You shut up," she said loudly in a deep basso voice. "He's my lover. He just wants some pussy."

Ryu had no idea what the woman had said, but he could tell by the hotel clerk's reaction that it was something altogether unseemly.

"Oh, we don't allow that," squealed the clerk.

"Oh, what do you know?" bellowed the woman, and she started to waddle toward a quiet little man who sat hunched in his lobby chair, trying to ignore the scene.

By this time the clerk had decided that the woman was crazy and, seeing that there was no stopping her without assistance, he looked to Ryu for help. Ryu stood as if he were carved of stone, jaw set, no trace of a smile on the thin line of his lips. He pulled out his wallet and peeled off thirty-four 500-gourde notes, around $1,000. The clerk looked at the bills and at the fat woman on an intercept course with one of the residents. The clerk took the money with a smirk that Ryu told himself he would punish. Ryu walked briskly over to his guest, clamped an iron-tight hand around her gargantuan forearm, and pushed her into the elevator.

He had booked a room on the third and top floor of the bal-conied and turreted building and this, in light of the weight of his guest, proved to be a significant error. Not as large an error, however, as getting into a rickety old elevator with a five-hundred-plus-pound woman. The elevator, instead of ascending, whirred and clicked and wheezed and whined and then fell suddenly and swiftly to the base-ment where it came to rest with a staggering thunk. If there had been room in the elevator, both Ryu and his charge would have fallen to their knees. As it was, they were packed in like a pair of sardines in a straw, and the shock simply drove straight up through their feet and rattled them from tarsal to mandible.

Ryu, squashed up against the elevator door by his travel compan-ion's girth, pushed one button after the next, including the red one that set off a bell, but he could not get the elevator to budge. Finally, realiz-ing that he was not going to get the machine to rise to the occasion, he yanked open the door and was popped from the cage. It took an enor-mous effort to get the big woman out of the elevator, up the basement stairs, and back into the lobby, where clerk and guests waited, faces contorted in a kind of shock that threatened to erupt into laughter.

"A ground floor room?" asked the unpleasant clerk with a sneer.

Ryu accepted the key to room number one, a dark chamber adja-cent to the pool, in the very back of the hotel.

"This is a dive," said the woman when Ryu finally got her to the room.

"*Yamenoka-yo.* Enough!" the yakuza exploded and slapped her across the face.

"Oh, now you're in trouble," roared the woman rubbing her blub-bery jaw. "I'm gonna tell on you." She settled herself onto the bed, which sagged wearily beneath her. "Turn on the air conditioning," she ordered. "It's hot in here."

It was 2:45 p.m. Ryu had already telephoned his Japanese contacts from Jacmel the night before with the news that he'd captured his quarry, explaining that she wasn't what he had expected but the microchip was almost within his grasp. They'd book him on the next flight out of Port-Au-Prince, but it didn't leave until 6:05 p.m. Ryu turned on the air conditioner and went to the bathroom to wash up. He stood for a long time looking at his reflection in the bathroom mirror. As always, the face that looked back was impassive though no longer perfectly groomed. A blue-black shadow ghosted his jaw and the area between nose and lip. Other signs of exhaustion revealed themselves on his fair, well-sculpted visage. What was he doing here, in this hellhole of a country, with an ill-smelling behemoth? She was disgusting. Was he making a mistake in taking her back? She did know about Miura and she seemed the only link to the whereabouts of the valuable chip.

Stripping, he stepped into the shower, letting the cool, clear water tumble over his tattooed flesh, washing the decadence and dirt of Hispaniola's westward claw from his thickly muscled body. I believe Ryu thought about me then . . . about my short but meaningful future. Love is such a complicated emotion, one that this man experienced as short blips on the flatline of detachment, a feeling that he had made a point of not clinging to. When he reentered the room, the fat woman lay stretched out on the bed, snoring loudly.

Involuntarily and altogether uncharacteristically, Ryu shuddered. The fat woman made his skin crawl. He called the clerk and asked him to confirm his airline reservations. Then he called the bar and ordered a cold beer and something to eat: *lambi* and *diri blan*, conch and white rice. He drank the beer, but the whistling, snorting, malodorous form of his slumbering roommate ruined his appetite, so he didn't eat. He had room service deliver a bottle of whiskey. Then he sat in the chair and drank it, watching the fat woman snore.

They were ready to leave at five p.m. Two first-class seats had been reserved and that was a good thing, since the fat woman would not have fit into a coach seat. Ryu was worried, in fact, about getting her onto the plane. The desk clerk, whose name was Clément, was getting ready for a change of shift when Ryu and his oversized guest re-entered the lobby. Clément grudgingly checked them out. Ryu had just steered the large woman out the front door to where the rental car waited when he paused and turned back to the lobby. He had forgotten something. Leaving his charge for a moment—she seemed somnambulant under the low-slung sun—he headed back into the hotel, a new bounce in his step. He squinted at Clément when he returned to the front desk to alert the clerk to the oversight. Reaching into his pocket—Clément thought for a tip—Ryu withdrew the knife that he'd retrieved at the hounfour—he wanted to use it at least once in Haiti—and thrust it into the desk clerk.

The knife, handmade for Ryu in Kyoto, was special. It was long and thin like a letter opener and therefore left only the smallest of entrance wounds. Unless there was a scuffle Ryu's victims generally didn't bleed, made no mess—at least not on the outside. But inside, oh, that was a different story. In Ryu's superbly trained hand that narrow blade angled up and around like a skinny whisk, scrambling various organs. Hemorrhaging internally, his victims died quickly. When he pulled the knife from the desk clerk, Ryu finally smiled. He wiped the blade on a pocket-handkerchief kept crisp and white for that purpose. He felt happier, lighter, as he left the lobby the second time, but that joyful feeling did not last.

The hippopotamus was nowhere near the car. For a moment,

the sickening feeling of failure gathered and coiled in the pit of Ryu's stomach, but he thrust it away, redirecting himself into action. He backtracked, and for a third time, Ryu entered the lobby.

They were the first thing he saw when he walked through the door—the angle was perfect and it would have been impossible not to see them—the tiny feet in the red tennis shoes. They were peeking out from behind the front desk. Ryu walked over to the feet to find their possessor recumbent, a beatific smile on her face. And leaning over her, quite alive, a tiny red stain just next to a button right where the stiletto had entered, was Clément.

"Time for a change of apparel," said the insuperable desk clerk in perfect Japanese. A dazzling smile piano-keyed its way across the bottom half of his face. He brushed himself off and straightened, noting the nametag pinned to his chest. To Ryu's credit, he did not even flinch, though a dark curtain seemed to have fallen before him.

"Wouldn't want our trip home to be as unpleasant as the ride to Port-au-Prince." Clément looked down at his shirt where the knife wound had left a bloody dot the size of a ladybug. "Eeew," he said as he buttoned his blue blazer over it. "Nasty stain. A gin and tonic in First Class will get that right out. Well, come on Ryu, we don't want to miss our plane."

GHUL-ISH THOUGHTS

At his point I think I should tell you a thing or two about ghouls . . . or ghuls, as they are known in some parts of the world. I know about them from my mother's books—the only part of her sizable estate that my father managed to miss. There were three small books on this particular subject, tucked away in a bottom drawer of her bureau, which is probably why Christian overlooked them. I first set eyes on them on the very day of her funeral. As I mentioned earlier, I was six when she died. We were living, at the time, in Switzerland near Lausanne where Mother owned a large summer house.

It was November, a depressing time to be in Lausanne. The house was very cold when we returned from the funeral. Mother's coffin had been in a parlor near the terrace. The French doors, which had been opened, were still ajar when we returned. I remember one of my mother's friends, a few men in suits, a gardener. I don't remember my father. Of course not, Christian wasn't there.

"You, skulking out there on the terrace, shut that door," Mother's friend said to the gardener. The friend was thin, pale and dark-haired like my mother. She wore a black suit, black hat, sheer black stockings, black heels. The gardener, a bony little man, nodded respectfully and complied—I remember him because he frightened me. I had night-mares about him standing under the elms for months after I was sent to Geneva, to the first of my many boarding schools.

"And you, poor child," said the friend turning to me, "put on some warm clothes. Lizette would be horrified by the chill in this place."

Later I heard her talking to the men in suits. "So Christian is the executor? Oh, even in death she keeps trying to please him. And Erin becomes the new victim of his neglect."

The new victim of his neglect—I have played those words over again and again in my head: those words and the cold, the wet garden smell, the aroma of coffee, the voices murmuring in the parlor, and what I did after that.

I tiptoed into Lizette's darkened bedroom, my mother's room, one more chamber where she wrote and slept and wept away day after day of sorrow. I opened the bottom drawer of the dresser and pulled out one of her sweaters. It was wine-red, not black like the short-sleeved crepe shift I was wearing. That's when I saw them: three slim, little leather-bound volumes, their gold-printed covers worn ragged, their pages nearly transparent. They were old and musty, but as I held them up to my face, I smelled the faint scent of my mother's perfume . . . just as the sweater had her smell upon it. I thrust my arms into the scratchy wine-dark sleeves of the sweater, tucked the three books under its ample folds, and transported them to my room where I slid them into one of the drawers of my nightstand.

The books would go with me to Geneva, then to France, then to Ireland, from one school to the next, until they would be forgotten somewhere in the long succession of moves. By then I would know them, not by the content, which was dull, but by a few curious entries and my mother's penciled notes in the margins. Of these the most provocative were a few passages on the Djinn, *from the Arabic junna, meaning angry or possessed.* Some of the text was complex, full of fragments from the Qur´an[10] and other mystical references. They spoke of the Djinn as creatures of smoke and fire that preceded humans in creation but who were without material form, though they could assume a shape or identity if desired. These were the first beings, creatures of great power, uninhibited by physical constraints and invested with vast energies, sentience, and ferocity. Like humans, they possessed free will. Among the choices they were allowed to make was whether or not to serve mankind. Some agreed; others did not, and some, fascinated by humankind, found ways to dominate, succor, or suppress us.

Next to one of the passages, Lizette had penciled what read like a poem. Her handwriting was shaky, the spidery letters so hard to read: *Human or Djinn? One is love, the other life. I choose love. I am forsaken.* The passage next to which my mother had written these lines explained the six major tribes of Djinn: the Jinn (this is where the term, genie, comes from; they chose to serve); the Jann; the Marid; the Shaitan (non-servers, enemies, in fact, and the tribe that gives us the serpent, Satan); the Ifrit; and finally, that stalker of the necropolis, ghost of the graveyard, irreverent and decidedly unsubservient low-life lover of the dead, the Ghul.

LET'S MAKE A DEAL

It was a short flight to Miami. Ryu wasn't drunk, but he had another spectacular headache brought on by persistent confusion and an uncomfortable sense of being in way over his head. In an extraordinary change of personality and behavior, Clément fussed over Ryu, insisting that the flight attendant bring aspirin and water and hot towels and ice. The flight attendant was a handsome, fair-haired young man and Clément flirted shamelessly with him.

"Oh, I do love to fly," gushed the desk clerk. "I'm only really at ease when I'm at 30,000 feet. You know all those things that bother other people—engine failure, equipment failure, control system failure, fuel shortage, wind shear, thunderstorms, microbursts, ice, snow, fog, sudden drops in altitude, stalls, pilot error, hijackers, terrorists—well, they don't bother me." He recited his list loudly, so that the other passengers could hear him, and between this catastrophic possibility and that, he'd pat Ryu's knee in a possessive way.

"By the way, Ryu," he said, "you haven't mentioned my little trick at the hotel. You really do know how to take things in stride, don't you? No wonder you're such a hotshot with the yakuza higher-ups. But you lost it with good old Clément, didn't you? You punished him for his insolence. So aren't you rather surprised that I'm sitting here next to you?"

Ryu was more than surprised. He was mystified . . . and he was furious. But being a man of few words and much experience, with a job to complete, he smiled a superior smile as if to say, maybe he was and then, maybe he was not.

"Well, aren't you the smug one?" continued the gabby Clément. "I suppose you've guessed at the truth. You're not dealing with Miura or Arnotine Ferucand or that big bag of blubber you picked up in Jacmel; it's me you must contend with, and I don't mean the desk clerk. Miura, Arnotine, the cow, even our dear friend, Carlyle—these are only disguises. They are covers temporarily assumed for the purpose of . . . well, you'll find out why soon enough. I am all of these and none. I am a master of camouflage, a veritable chameleon. I am something that exists only in your wildest imaginings: a lovable, fun-loving ghoul, or ghul,[11] depending upon your cultural affiliations, with connections in the highest places. Orison, the Consortium—they all need my help. Oh, they all want me. I am 007-and-then-some, the James Bond of the supernatural set. I have the inside track and the talent to play a starring role in their dirty little games. They think I serve them. Not this ghoul. Remember this, Ryu: I play because I choose to play and although they all think it's their game, the game really is mine."

In view of what he had witnessed already, farfetched as this seemed, it must have sounded to Ryu like this grandiose claim was a very real possibility. A sour knot formed in his throat. Discomforted by it, he looked quickly away.

The clerk prattled on. "Too bad about Erin, isn't it? Now, there's an *assignment*. She's really quite lovely, isn't she?" He grew suddenly quiet and pensive. Then he made a face.

"Too bad she believed in you. She has no idea what you are up to. You were going to kill her that night in that stupid hotel. That was the arrangement between the Consortium and the yakuza, between Orison and your avaricious clan. A microchip delivered in the body of Orison's dead daughter: the perfect drop! Ah, but I put a stop to that, didn't I? Poor Erin, just another girl trying to get her father's attention. And her 'protector' and his kind only mean to exploit her. How sad. How tragic. What chance does she have?"

The talk about me, the references to that night at the Shakayama, no doubt upset Ryu. It was supposed to be simple, straightforward. Instead it had become such a messy business. How did Clément know about all of this? Why couldn't Ryu kill him? This one talked and talked. Ryu hated that. Clément's talk would make a long rope and then Ryu would wrap it around his skinny neck and strangle him with it.

Ryu looked at the clerk and smiled and imagined slipping the knife into his side again. But his pleasure turned quickly to irritation. Why hadn't the desk clerk died? Did he really believe Clément's "explanation?" The thought of having some kind of goblin or ghost or ghoul or whatever on his hands was deeply troubling. Ryu did believe in the supernatural, and he wanted no truck with it.

Ryu squeezed his eyes closed, trying to shut out the babble and the image of the clerk's smooth, thin, lightly tanned face, trying to squelch the frustration that he felt rising up inside him. Mostly he tried to shut out the unpleasant and all-too-familiar smell that had begun to wreathe itself around Clément. By the time they reached Narita, after a layover and another long flight, he knew he was going to be sick.

Ryu's colleagues had set things up at arrival. He had no trouble getting Clément through passport control, though by this time the desk clerk's smell was more than unpleasant. There was a large black Daimler waiting for them at the curb. Clément's light-hearted attitude evaporated the minute they stepped from the airport. A completely different personality seemed to take over. This one was silent, almost brooding. Ryu felt off balance and perplexed. It was like watching an actor move from one role to the next.

Clément said not a word on the long ride from the airport to the Uguisu Ryokan. And Ryu also said nothing. Sitting, side by side in the back seat, behind bullet-proof, sound-proof glass, in the sedan's plush, dove-gray interior, they temporarily holstered their hostilities and withdrew into the profound centers of their very private worlds.

They were headed for Ishikawa-ken, the prefecture southeast of Tokyo at the base of the beautiful Noto Peninsula that was once the power center of the influential Maeda clan, their destination a 1,200-year-old inn steeped in tradition and Old World elegance. Uguisu Ryokan—Ryu loved the place. He felt soothed by its tatami-matted suites, its graceful dimensions, its beautiful gardens. Uguisu Ryokan was constructed like a great walled castle, the lobby level laid out like a village.

Beyond the front desk and the jasper-floored entrance were curving halls floored in pebble-framed flagstones that wound past slatted walls of white pine. Little lanterns lit the way and, here and there, a doorway would signal the entrance to a fine sushi restaurant or nightclub. There were five restaurants in Uguisu Ryokan—five restaurants; three nightclubs; six little shops at which guests could buy clothing or sundries or gifts or jewelry or china; three swimming pools; innumerable private whirlpools; four viewing gardens; and two spas.

It was a favorite yakuza meeting place, one for celebrations and settlements. To some it was the last stop, a place of unpleasant reckoning. Ryu had known it in the past as a perk, the reward for a job well done. And now, here he was, headed to Uguisu again, but this time he was no hero. He was arriving with this disgusting baggage and a hoped-for, but not guaranteed, answer as to the whereabouts of the microchip, the one he had lost. He was hung over, unshaven, sick to his stomach and surely in for the worst form of reproach.

The hours in the car with ill-smelling Clément did not make Ryu feel any better. He was still nauseated when the limo pulled up to the inn and parked. Before them, the ryokan rose, a towering, multi-tiered structure. Its various floors floated, or seemed to, like the staggered branches of a red maple or an elaborately sculpted pine from the forested grounds.

Two maids in fancy green- and gold-threaded kimono and white tabi socks minced up to the doorway, bowed, and helped them out of their shoes. If they noticed Clément's unpleasant smell, they gave no indication, their faces as serenely set as a pair of Noh theater masks.

"*Irasshaimase.* Welcome," they chanted in unison. "*Dozo.* Please, come in."

They offered slippers and indicated the way, shepherding the men across the broad lobby, down a winding flagstone path, through a series of softly lit corridors to stop at the pair of frosted glass doors that led to Hagi Spa.

"*Dozo,*" the two women smiled, their open palms drifting doorward in invitation.

Ryu and Clément stepped inside.

They entered a large foyer walled in white pine and floored in granite-colored tile. Dark gray carpet, pale walls—beyond the entrance to the spa was a maze of halls and doors. The receptionist greeted them, handed them each a *yukata* or summer kimono, and guided them through the maze to another pair of frosted glass doors.

"*Dozo, kochira-desu.* This way please," she said, indicating the door, and left them.

On the other side of the door was a dressing room. Long wooden lockers rose along two of the walls. One wall consisted of six panel doors of frosted glass made to look like shoji screens. The fourth wall was all mirror. Clément was already shedding his clothes, not bothering to pick them up from the floor where he dropped them: the navy blue blazer, the white shirt, the dark pants, and an outlandishly bright pair of red, cotton briefs. Naked, he walked over to the mirrored wall and posed, flexing and relaxing the muscles in his skinny arms, thighs, and calves, sliding a hand slowly and affectionately down his torso from his chest to his belly. Ryu noted that his café au lait complexion had turned sallow. The wound that Ryu had inflicted was a purple dot on his abdomen. It radiated out in concentric bruises like a target. Clément saw Ryu's assessment in the mirror. He looked over his shoulder, down in the direction of his abdomen and winked. Then, disregarding the yukata, he sauntered into the bath. The thought of Clément stepping into a yakuza gathering without him gave Ryu speed. Doffing his clothes quickly, he, too, ignored the yukata, grabbed a small washcloth, and followed the clerk into the bath, dressed only in the *tenugui* and his tattoos.

The sight that greeted Ryu when he entered the bath was as dramatic as a scene from any Kabuki play—a death scene shrouded in mist. The room into which he stepped was curtained in steam. Clouds of it rose from the floor and drifted up to the very high ceiling. On three sides of the room was a low band of sweating mirror with a granite ledge that ran around its base broken every six feet or so with silver spigots and low pine stools. In the center of the room was a bath of Olympic proportions. Steps led into its shallow heart and the water lapped up and over the steps, moving in a desultory way. Between Ryu and that pool was a huge expanse of slippery-looking granite-colored floor and standing in the middle of it, his arms outstretched, was Clément. He had a hand each on the chests of two fire-plug-shaped yakuza, both tattooed, in diaper-like *mawashi*, holding what looked like classic *aragoto*[12] poses, their mouths turned downward, their eyes almost crossed in frustration.

Clément had eyes for neither of them. His gaze was set on the steamy far wall, which was made entirely of glass. The naked men, armored in tattoos, looked like brightly colored demons. All of this smacked Ryu as a frieze, a still photo that would remain emblazoned in his mind like an *ukiyoe*, an old woodcut, and he thought it strange that the most extraordinary images in life are transient. Transient indeed, for the poses couldn't hold. It was Clément who broke the spell.

"*Dame-desuyo.* Stop it," he said in womanly, singsong Japanese. "They are waiting for me. Let's get on with it."

The yakuza relaxed. Turning quickly, they marched their visitors to the far wall, which was faced with large, glass sliding doors. They opened them. The cool night air gushed in. Ryu and Clément stepped out to meet it. The yakuza followed them out.

It was immediately apparent that they were in a designer grotto. A high wall of bamboo ran around its perimeter and in the center was a series of natural pools the largest of which was fed by a vigorous waterfall. A wall of stone extended from the waterfall in this largest pool to the edge of another pool of much smaller dimensions. In front of the smaller pool was a grassy bank. Ensconced upon that bank were three throne-like chairs, and upon these sat three old men swaddled in thick terrycloth robes.

Ryu grunted, clasped his hands together, and bowed. Clément assumed a most casual posture, slouching onto one hip and looking over at Ryu with contempt.

One of the old men leaned forward. "Ryu, what is this?"

"Don't ask him," snapped Clément. "You must ask me. I am the one with the chip. And you must ask me nicely," he concluded, his voice honeyed and low.

The old man looked shocked.

Ryu was mortified, like a dog that had fetched a piece of shit and dropped it at the feet of its disgusted owner.

"Very well," said the old man irritably. "Where is the microchip?"

"Well, that's a secret," drawled Clément.

"Fool," growled the old fellow in the middle. "If you have the chip you will give it to us. Grab him," he commanded.

The two yakuza stepped forward, each taking hold of an arm.

"Oh, what are you going to do? Kill me?" sneered the clerk. He looked over at Ryu and smiled. "Yes, kill me," he urged. "I'd love to see you try."

"There are other ways to get answers," said the first old man.

"Oh, really, and how is that? Torture? Something like this?" asked Clément, as he twisted away from the yakuza on his left.

They all heard it: the terrible popping sound of a joint being pulled from its socket. Clément kept pulling his body to the right until the arm had come completely away from the shoulder. It hung, useless, the skin stretched like a hammock between the yakuza's grip and his torso. "Oh, no, please don't hurt me," he laughed. His pleasure was palpable. He met every man's eyes and grinned.

The faces of the three old men darkened. The two yakuza lackeys released him and stepped back.

Clément's hollow eyes narrowed. "Now, keep your goons off me," he commanded in guttural Osaka-style Japanese.

"So, what have we here? A trickster?" asked the first old man, having regained his composure.

The two stocky yakuza took a step back toward the clerk as if to lay hands on him again.

"Oh, it's easy to bully an unarmed man," sneered Clément, contempt in his voice. With the hand on his good right arm, he reached under his right rib and drew a long knife up and out from the fleshy sheath of his abdomen. Ryu recognized the knife. It was his. His mind flashed back on the clerk in front of the mirrors in the dressing room fondly stroking his belly. The five other men in the grotto gasped.

Clément had a terrible smile on his face. "Oh, don't worry. I'm not going to put up a fight. I am a ghoul of peace. Here," he teased, handing one of the yakuza the knife, handle first, knowing he'd drawn the trump card—a knife pulled from his own naked body. "Go ahead. Torture me. Martyr me. Kill me . . . if you can."

"Take it," shouted the second old man.

Like a man in a trance the yakuza reached for the knife. Ryu's knife—Ryu felt himself cringe.

Clément didn't let go of the weapon at once. He held onto the blade tightly so that the steel bit into his palm, and then he released it slowly. One, two, three, four—his fingers fell to the floor. "Kill me," he said breezily. "Do it now. Otherwise let's get down to business," he hissed. He turned to the three robed figures. "Kill me or let's make a deal."

GIRL CRAZY

"*Gomen.* So sorry," said the third old man, his small head pushed forward, neck elongated, like a turtle peering out of its shell. "We apologize for our rudeness. "You are . . . ?"

"Clément," sniffed Clément with a toss of his head full of dark curls.

"Ah, Clément," the old man repeated. Reaching toward one of the yakuza henchmen with a hand towel and nodding toward the clerk.

Clément grabbed the towel between thumb and palm and twisted it around what was left of his hand.

"And you work for . . . ?"

"No one."

"Ah, but I have heard rumors," the old man whispered, eyes squinting as he studied the creature self-destructing before him. "They say that Orison has an *oni*, a devil, in his garrison—a powerful demon with supernatural powers. And now we seem to have a goblin in our midst, for your performance is certainly inhuman. So has Ryu brought us Orison's infernal henchman? Are you that devil . . . Clément?"

"Do I fascinate you?" asked Clément. "It's invariably the clever ones who find me exciting."

"I'm simply being polite, since other methods proved somewhat . . . ineffectual."

The ghoul sighed. "Let me ask you this," he said tiredly, "given my capabilities, if I were in league with Orison and the Consortium and I already had the microchip, why would I be here?"

"Because we have something you want?"

"Now you're talking."

"We want the microchip. What do you want from us?"

"It's a secret," the ghoul said with a smile. "Just know that it will not cost you a penny."

"He *is* a devil and he wants our souls," warned the second old man.

"Oh, don't be ridiculous," scoffed Clément. "Can we put aside these absurd suppositions? What I want is for the drop to commence as planned. I want Ryu, here, to handle it. He will be working with me."

"Perhaps you two are in cahoots," said the first old man.

"Hardly," spat Clément. "He's absurdly loyal to the yakuza, but he's the only man for the job." He nodded toward Ryu. "After all," the ghoul added, "he's already 'made friends' with Orison's daughter."

"What? We still kill the girl?" said Ryu.

"Yes. What did you expect? The old plan, the one you all agreed to, remember?" Clément replied quickly.

"Why should we trust you?" asked the third old man.

"Tell me," said Clément, "what choice do you have?"

Of course, it was obvious. None. The creature had the microchip. He was clearly beyond intimidation. They must go along for a while.

"And what is it that you want?" asked the second old man.

"Nothing that belongs to you," snapped Clément. "My reward lies in resuming the game."

"Alright," said the third old man. "We're agreed." He looked at the other two. They both bowed their heads in assent.

"Excellent," said Clément with a gleeful leap. "I will let the Consortium know that your organization definitely has possession of the chip. They'll prepare the money for transfer and Ryu will proceed with our unusual drop. We will all get what we want."

The three old men nodded, began talking amongst themselves.

Clément sauntered toward Ryu, took a stand at his side.

"I've won this round. You're mine, now," he whispered and put his right arm, the one with the fingerless hand, around the yakuza's shoulders; the other arm hung limp at his side. His smell had become overwhelming. Ryu's head was throbbing. Clément had shamed him in front of his clan. He was furious—furious and exhausted and on the verge of a foul sickness. Ryu turned away to keep from retching.

Later, heading back to Tokyo in the same car they'd arrived in, Ryu sat, whey-faced and upset, next to the quarry that had somehow become the keeper. He couldn't help pondering how quickly the tables had turned. Here he was, in a car befouled by Clément's dreadful odor, only this time it was clearly Clément who was in charge. They traveled for a long while in silence. Then Clément turned to him, his face not sallow, but ashen.

"You work for me, now, Ryu," he rasped. "I have a plan and I need you to help me execute it. It involves your pretty girlfriend, Erin, the one you were supposed to deliver."

The yakuza narrowed his eyes. "She's not my girlfriend," he said.

First, there was silence. Then, Ryu watched the mercurial Clément change once again.

"Look," he spat, his thin gray face becoming rock hard, like something carved out of stone. "Look, I'm tired. You dragged me back here and I came along. Do you think I had to come back with you? Think about it. Think about *ME* and what I am capable of. Don't you think that at any moment I could have given you the slip? Why do you think I let you bring me back? For power? I already have that. For Orison? He's a fool blinded by his lust for power and the possibility of harnessing the supernatural—as if that were possible. For money? Would I come here for that? Or maybe you think I came back to do you a personal favor?"

Ryu felt as if a snake were uncoiling before his very eyes, a cobra rising up. It was a feeling that started at the root of his groin and drove up through his entrails filling his chest, his throat, threatening to choke him. It ended in heat and flame at the very top of his head. He felt like a volcano. He felt like his head would blow off.

Clément regarded him pityingly. "You don't understand do you?" he whispered. "You, with your soulless efficiency, your pathetic devotion to the yakuza organization: a collection of thieves and whoremongers and murderers—you have no concept of what I am in it for. Of course you don't. You are no more than a puppet.

"Why do you think I let you bring me back? I want only one thing from you, Ryu," he said. "And it isn't money or power or loyalty or respect. In fact, there's only one thing I want in all the world." He paused. "In this world and the next, actually," he added dramatically. "One thing only, Ryu, and you are going to help me get it.

"I want the girl."

BLAME IT ON THE FUGU

Those who eat fugu soup are stupid.
But those who don't eat fugu soup are also stupid.
—old Japanese proverb

Ryu was back and I, stupidly, was excited. He'd been gone for a little less than a week, but to me it seemed like forever. Tokyo is a bizarrely beautiful city where every step seems to take you deeper and deeper into a rabbit hole of adventure, but I was so lonely. I felt as if I'd been set adrift like the little shrines that the Japanese carry to the sea and launch. I missed my bodyguard, but when he returned I knew that something had changed. His careless, exquisitely intimate, and possessive manner had disappeared to be replaced by something slick, detached, and extremely professional. He was still attentive and protective, but I sensed that a great and insurmountable wall had risen unaccountably up between us. It was evident at once. I tried hard not to feel hurt by it, and when he asked me to dinner the night after he returned, I was certain that I had been mistaken. I wore a yellow silk dress, silk stockings, orange lipstick, and, because I wasn't sure how he felt about me, very high heels. The extra height made me feel more secure. We were going to have fugu[13] in the one restaurant in Tokyo that Ryu believed truly understood how to prepare it. The restaurant was in the Ginza, Tokyo's elegant, though somewhat old-fashioned "downtown." Ryu had on a dark teal-blue suit and a silver-gray tie, the French cuffs of his shirt fastened by small ivory castles reminiscent of the pieces one uses in chess.

"Ryu-san, this fish, this fugu, is poison, isn't it?" I asked in Japanese.

Ryu laughed awkwardly and answered in less-than-perfect English.

"No, Elin," (he could never seem to say "Erin"). "It is only poison-ous if it is prepared incorrectly. Yamada-san knows exactly what to do with this fish. *Honto.*"

All right. I believed him. I nodded and put my hand on his chest, right over his heart. I let it rest there, unmoving. Ryu smiled tightly, took my hand from his breast and let it go. If he'd looked into my eyes, he would have seen the questions flickering in them, perhaps the unhappiness and doubt. But he didn't. We entered the restaurant.

The restaurant was one of those places that you'd never find unless you were looking for it, unless you were Japanese. When Ryu entered, heads turned. Of course, Ryu had been to Yamada's restaurant many times, though never with me, and I certainly had little in common with the usual clientele. Mrs. Yamada, the owner's wife, rushed up to greet us.

"Matsuda-san, good evening," she said, glancing sideways at me. "We are so honored to have you here tonight."

Ryu's narrow, dark-lashed eyes darted sideways. He grunted a response.

"We're here for fugu," I whispered to the matron, conspiratorially.

"Oh, yes-u," she said in English and smiled. Our eyes met and I think she understood my excitement, the thrill of having fugu for the very first time.

"This way. *Dozo,*" she said kindly, directing us to a small blue booth.

"Yamada's wife loves to dance," observed Ryu. "If she knew you were going to perform in one of Nakamura's productions she'd ask for your autograph."

"Mmmm, and you? Would you like my autograph, too?" I put my hand over his, unfastened a cuff link, and pushed the stiff white fabric of his sleeve up, revealing the snaking tattoos. The starched cotton folded, almost like paper, over the dark markings on his skin. Ryu's name means dragon, and I liked the way the tail end of this particular dragon had wrapped itself around his arm. With an index finger, I traced the coiling serpent up under his sleeve. *We are like famous lovers,* I thought—*star-crossed, of course.* Then I pushed the thought aside.

Ryu sighed. His white teeth flashed for an instant, then the smile disappeared.

"Ahhh, so we're in a mood tonight, are we? What's wrong Ryu? Are you sad?"

Ryu did look sad. True, I hadn't known him long, but I had never seen him that way.

"What are you doing to me?" he laughed ruefully. "You want to leave your mark on me? There's no room on my body. This flesh belongs to the yakuza."

"Surely, there's a place for me somewhere."

"Like the Americans? A heart with your name: 'Erin Orison, My Girl.'"

"Yes, something like that. And I know just the spot." I tossed my dark hair and leaned back, victorious. His eyes told me that I had left my mark somewhere deep inside him, but he would never admit to this. He laughed instead, roughly and without joy. Then he smiled and looked past me.

Poised for the summons, a waitress hurried over.

Ryu went through the motions. He placed our order. "Hamachi with white radish, octopus, ebi, then the fugu soup, of course, and sake."

The waitress nodded. "*Hai, Matsuda-san,*" and rushed to the kitchen.

"They're all so afraid of you," I observed. That is one of the things I liked most about Ryu—that and the absence of sentiment. Without sentiment there is no pain. There was no room for sentiment in my life.

"But not you, eh?" Ryu raised an eyebrow. "You aren't afraid of me?"

"No, but sometimes, Ryu, I am afraid *for* you. I was worried when you were gone. You run with a dangerous crowd. Men like Miura. Men who, like you, can do great harm."

"And you," he said softly, "you have no reason to be afraid?"

The sake arrived. Ryu seemed relieved. It was cloud-white and cool. He drank deeply.

"I'm not afraid of powerful men," I sighed, thinking of the one man this adjective conjured up, the one with the scalpel that had cut up my heart.

"Like your father?" he asked, replacing the cuff link.

"Like him, of course."

"You should be."

"There's no purpose in fear." My nonchalance was an act, one that I had perfected.

"So Japanese."

"Why, thank you, Ryu." I laughed, raising my glass. "*Kampai.*"

"*Kampai,*" he responded and drained his cup.

The first of many toasts. Ryu relaxed a bit after that. I felt him thawing. Suddenly it seemed he couldn't take his eyes off me. He watched me eat: watched me as I swallowed the shimmering hamachi, as my teeth cut into the coral-pink curl of ebi. We drank more sake, chewed on the octopus. Wanting to amuse him, I told him funny stories about my schools and girlfriends. He leaned into the diversion. I wanted to think he was enjoying himself. Then, the fugu arrived, small fillets adrift in a big bowl of liquid. Ryu passed a hand over my bowl.

"No poison, you're sure?" I asked with a smile, taking a sip of the steaming mixture, not pausing for his response. "Oh, this is delicious."

Unlike me, Ryu did not drink deeply. He merely dipped his lips in the broth. His mouth was glistening, and I wanted to lean toward him and kiss him. Then the noise in the restaurant began to sound like water, like water running, like a brook or a stream. Musical. Hypnotic. And my heart was suddenly racing. It was beating very fast. How warm it was in the restaurant, and all of the lights were twinkling like stars: starry, starry night all around me as I floated on a river of sound.

"Oh, I think I've had too much sake," I whispered, hand to my brow as the first little inkling of danger began to tie down my limbs. What was going on? Not the fugu? Surely, not that.

Ryu still watched me intently. His dark eyes never straying from mine. I tried to say his name, "Ryu," but though my lips puckered slightly, no sound came forth. I felt the room slide sideways. Ryu stood swiftly and caught me before I crumpled forward. I felt my chin come to rest on his shoulder.

The owner's wife noticed, looked worried. Ryu apologized, tried to simplify matters. "Too much to drink, *neh?*" I heard him say.

Mrs. Yamada's smile was strained. She nodded and glanced toward the kitchen.

Ryu gathered me up in his arms. He is very strong. He carried me to the street. A cab was waiting at the curb. The door opened automatically, as cab doors do in Japan. Ryu deposited me in the cab, muttered something to the driver and the cab whisked me away. Ryu stood there, at the curb, and watched the cab disappear. Then he turned and walked back into the restaurant to finish his dinner so that Yamada-san would not worry, so that he'd know everything was ok.

"To throw away life, eat blowfish." That is what the Japanese say. Fugu, blowfish, puffer fish, globefish, swellfish, river pig, *Sphoeroides testudineus*—whatever you call it—it contains in its skin, liver, ovaries, and intestine a neurotoxin that is 160,000 times more powerful than cocaine. One of the most poisonous non-protein substances known to man, tetrodoxin packs a lethal wallop that is 500 times that of cyanide, and yet the water-swallowing, passive-aggressive fish that is infused with it has long been considered a delicacy. That's because fugu is also a powerful stimulant. If properly prepared, and that means in a manner that does not induce death, it provides quite a rush: a warming, a tingling, a sense of euphoria. With luck—and if the chef has been exceedingly careful about his preparations—death will not ensue. But blowfish and nature are capricious. The toxicity of this sea creature depends upon the season, the fish and, most important, the physiology of the individual who consumes it. It is a very dangerous fish. In Japan, only licensed chefs are allowed to prepare it. Still, every year there are deaths caused by blowfish. But people continue to eat it. Why? Because flirting with death is a thrill.

Ryu was especially fond of fugu. He loved the flush that suffused his body as his heart went into overdrive, the slight mist of perspiration that formed on his upper lip and brow, the gentle numbing of his extremities and the way the world around him seemed to soften and bend as he drifted up and above it. Yamada had prepared a dish called *chiri*, in which the delicate fillets of the puffer fish have been simmered in a broth that contains the skin, the liver, and the intestines of the creature. To Ryu, fugu was a beautiful weapon, more like a fine blade than a gun. It gave death or delight; he liked that. It bothered him a little that it was Clément who had suggested the blowfish and given him a powder to add to my portion; that in this, as in other things, he had become Clément's pawn; but no matter. The powder would work with the natural toxins in the fugu to effect the necessary results. To Yamada, his wife, and their scrupulous clientele, I would appear to be nothing more than inebriated. To those who mattered, the aim was achieved. I'd been dispatched, and all involved would be happy.

I had never eaten fugu, but I did like to follow Ryu's lead. It was fun doing things with the yakuza. He was dangerous, too, like the fugu. That excited me. But this particular blowfish dinner had it in for me, and I passed out as I sipped at my cool, milk-colored sake, as I prepared to skewer a small Japanese pickle in my Mingei-style bowl. The cab ferried me through the dark streets of the city to my father's apartment. The driver took my key, carried me upstairs—you can't trace a man who must wear white gloves[14]—and deposited me in the bedroom. He positioned me on the bed, placed the key in my bag and pawed at and smoothed out the wrinkles in my dress. Then he did a curious thing. He leaned over me and kissed me. I could feel the cold lips grazing mine, vaguely recognized the sickly sweet smell that wreathed them—a smell like flowers dying. I knew the smell. Familiar and frightening, *he* had come back.

"Sleep well, princess," he said, and removing one of his gloves, slid it into my handbag. Then he looked for the phone, found it in the kitchen and placed three anonymous calls.

By this time my temperature was subnormal. My corneal reflexes had disappeared. Aphonia, dysphagia, and aphagia had set in, and although I still seemed to be conscious, I couldn't speak or swallow or really understand anything that was going on around me. Medics arrived at that point and I was taken to the hospital where I was pronounced dead.

And then I was born again.

BORN-AGAIN ZOMBIE

After I died, I . . . I woke up. I woke up on a table in the hospital morgue, third in line for an autopsy. I woke up a whole new person . . . or a fragment of an old person. By that I mean I wasn't exactly "myself." Who was I? I'm not sure. It was odd, as if I were on some very weird drug, which I suppose I was. But total understanding wouldn't come till much later. I'd been dropped with head-throbbing ferocity from the disembodied limbo of my apparent demise into . . . life. I belly-flopped back into physical existence with a force that sickened me.

This, as you may have deduced, is a typical reaction to tetrodoxin, the poisonous component in fugu and one of the ingredients in the best zombie powders. Many a mortician has been startled when the "corpse" of a blowfish victim comes to life on the slab. Sadly, some-times the clock doesn't work in the victim's favor and the autopsy or a premature burial takes them all the way to the end. That is, after all, how zombies are made. We are the nearly dead, gone long enough to have lost our way home, our brains effectively scrambled and fried by a bokor's infernal concoction. The poison robs us of coherence, of con-text. It strips us of any shred of personal power. Then the new "Mas-ter" steps in.

What I was aware of at first was pain. The pain came from the light that flashed on the other side of my eyelids. Then the smell of my body rose up around me, sickeningly sweet and cloying. That nearly undid me. I thought I would vomit. I struggled, trying to raise myself up and quickly discovered that this was impossible.

Have you ever watched infants? They have such difficulty managing movement. Their heavy heads loll; their arms and legs flop. It takes practice to coordinate action. My fully-grown body was a nightmare. I was trapped in dead weight. It was as if my physical form were a coffin. My limbs wouldn't budge. I could not even raise my eyelids.

I kept trying, without success, succumbing at last to exhaustion. I—what was left of me—still had a will of my own, though it seemed to be in conflict with the lethargic inclinations of my recently zombied constitution. That's when I discovered the trick! My body, I found, was tuned to its own physical directives. If I struggled to govern the process, I short-circuited this function; my body turned rigid and froze. If I relaxed, movement was easy and unbelievably graceful. It flowed. I did not, however, master the technique immediately.

Like many victims of cerebral trauma, I was reborn with a kind of amnesia. Was it a relief to leave my old "self" with all its sorrow and disappointment behind? In some ways, yes, but I must tell you that I've never felt more isolated than I did when I returned from the dead, though I wouldn't have believed it possible. Overall, it is ghastly. Sometimes I think that I don't exist at all, that I am no more than a miserable little corner of Erin's consciousness locked off from the rest of her mind for reasons I can't fathom, though I'm sure they have something to do with Clément's fugu potion. But that is a one-way ticket to oblivion. More recently I've come to believe that the old Erin and the distracted creature I've become are one and the same, though we are often like dance partners that can't decide who's in charge. Thankfully, the intelligence I am determined to claim as the real me usually fights for the lead . . . and wins.

I finally managed to open my eyes. It seems that my pupils were dilated, so that when my eyelids fluttered up, the incoming brilliance was blinding. There were shapes lurking off in the corners of what seemed to be a very large space. I was laid out on a table without clothing, and it was cold. I settled into my new situation. The icy kiss of steel on my backside finally jolted my body into action. I sat upright quickly—too quickly. I was swimming in nausea. Eventually I managed to stand, coughing and gagging, in the small pool of my own regurgitation, my long hair in my face. An orange eruption ran down my chin, spattered onto my chest and my breasts. An acrid taste filled my mouth.

With one hand I wiped my face clean. I groped toward the wall for support, found none, so I stumbled across the room, bumping into tables, knocking over trays. They clattered to the floor, which was also shockingly cold. Clumsily threading my way through what seemed like an obstacle course, I gained the support of the wall. Leaning into that vertical plane, my vision came clear. I saw how I left a peach-colored handprint on the smooth white surface.

Blink. Turn. Scan.

The room was large and barren, and I wasn't the only one in it. Two men and a woman were with me. But the others were far less animated than I. All three lay, naked, on solo tables. So lovely they were in their blue-gray rigidity, like statues carved by a hand capable of great detail. On the wall behind them were a series of stainless steel sinks and a length of white counter. There were glass containers filled with body parts suspended in fluid on the countertop: a pancreas, a stomach, a brain. Above this were cabinets that took a right turn at the corner and continued along the perpendicular wall. Where they stopped, the space was filled with an absolutely gorgeous image that reached almost from ceiling to floor. It was a beautiful rendition of the human body, its inner secrets—muscle, organ and bone—boldly rendered in reds and blues and small splashes of black and pink ink. It became, instantly, the object of my adoration. I felt myself carried away by the twist of arteries, the fretwork of bone, by the sinuous curve of muscle. Nerves, membranes, cartilage, ligaments, trachea, the thick cloud of the intestines, the lungs spread like a pair of wings behind the chubby pump of the heart. Complicated beyond imagination. Breathtaking. The body. I hadn't been back in the world long, but I had found my God.

My mouth fell open, one hand reached involuntarily toward the wall. I could feel my breath quicken, my heart beating faster, so fast it was dizzying. The image, the beautiful image of the body, began to darken and fade. A thick numbness spread through my legs. I felt them buckle. Unconsciousness was rushing toward me again, and I fought it, fought it impotently. I was losing my grip, drifting back into darkness . . .

Then I smelled it: something new, someone else, another being entering the room. A spicy scent: sweat, warm muscle, and blood. It smashed into me, held me hard, a fist tacking me to the moment just before my collapse. It was electric, vitally charged. Sound followed: words in Japanese also crackling with force.

"Eh, *nani?* What the . . . ? Oh, you Gods, she's alive!"

That voice penetrated the layers of encroaching unconsciousness. I lunged for the sound, the "dead" girl grasping at it like a drowning woman gasping for air. Desperate, my nails found their pothook in flesh, sank like talons into muscle. I had to pull hard to pull myself out from insensibility, so I dug in, clutching at the source of the voice. He was not as large as I, and I climbed all over him, trying to drag myself back. He fought me hard, struggling in an explosion of Japanese: "Stop it. Get off. Get off me. What are you? Some kind of . . . zombie?"

Yes. Absolutely.

I could feel him beneath me trying to crawl across the floor.

"Slobbering corpse," he yelled. "Lemme go. I'm only the jan . . . i . . . torrrrr." He rose to his knees. "Ooh. Get your fingers out of my eyes. You devil! Oh! My face!"

His struggle provoked a strong physical response in me. I could feel my consciousness gaining ground, coming back. What a rush! Clawing at him, I threw my arms around his neck, my legs around his waist, rode him like a pony as he careened toward the door. He stumbled and twirled, trying to unclasp me, but I clung like a lamprey to the back of a fish, like a cutworm to a tomato, a fluke to a liver, like a kid to his seat on a carnival ride. It felt good, much better, at least, than a tumble into oblivion.

Together, we crashed through the door and into to the corridor.

"Help," he managed to choke out from the collar of my forearms. "Heeeelp!"

Feet running, sprinting toward us; hands pawing, trying to pry me away. Two, four, six—I could feel them tugging at my arms, my legs. Their pinching and pulling finally delivered me from darkness. I could breathe again. Sputtering, I filled my lungs with air and I surfaced. I'd managed to hold onto existence. I was safe. And I was alive—a creature of warm flesh and blood, not some dead, rotting thing.

Now there were four of us riding the pony. "I've got her," screamed one of them, his voice lusty with victory, arms clasped hard around my waist.

Yes, you do.

I relaxed completely.

He pulled, and we all fell over—two nurses, an intern, a janitor, and I. We lay there for a moment or two, without moving, like the severed appendages of a butchered starfish, all pointing in different directions on the shiny lemon-colored linoleum in the rank spew of my birth.

"Are you ok?"

The four started helping one another to their feet. I was sitting up on the floor—exhilarated, high—heart racing, limbs thrumming delightfully from the exertion. Someone pushed my hair out of my face. I felt a big hand on my jaw, turning my head first to one side then the next. My neck was stiff like I'd slept on it wrong, and it didn't feel good to have my head moved from side to side. The hand that cupped my chin was soft, warm, large, and pleasantly meaty. I felt my lids flutter up. I opened my eyes and stared into the face of the man who was examining me. I looked at him and I smiled.

My first smile, and not well done, I imagine. The young physician could not help but recoil. I saw the nurses' eyes widen. One let her hand move involuntarily to her throat.

"She's supposed to be dead," the janitor grunted.

He had crawled to the wall, where he sat, propped up like a marionette, patting at his wounds with a white cotton handkerchief. The nurses were straightening their dresses and hats.

I couldn't stop smiling my lockjaw-like leer because I couldn't seem to get control over my face. This agitated me and succeeded in ratcheting up the tension in my jaw so that my jack-o-lantern grin actually widened.

By this time, the doctor had recovered some of his aplomb. "This is amazing," he whispered, his eyes running the length of my body, pausing at my breasts slick with apricot-colored puke. "This girl was pronounced dead two days ago. She was scheduled for autopsy this evening. I know who she is. I worked on her case. It's astounding.

"Are you all right?" he asked stupidly, staring into my face, which I'm sure looked absurd, plastered as it was with its corn-cob grin.

Do I look all right, moron? I wanted to yell. *I can't move my face or my body.*

Then he began that stupid twisting of my head from side to side again. I gave up trying to change my expression. I let him move my head around, let it go limp. My eyes closed and the idiotic smile fell, thankfully, from my face.

Suddenly, I felt tired, very tired. Not in danger of passing out, as I had before, just exhausted in a slumber-hungry, sleep-heavy way. I don't know exactly what happened next, but I believe I was put on a gurney.

Then there is quiet and darkness and then I remember a man—no, more like a very bad smell, one that I recognized vaguely and found in some way repulsive—fussing over me, pulling up my hospital gown. I am freezing, and the presence from which the smell emanates seems to be stroking the inside of my thighs with something cold. More force, and he spreads my legs and pushes something up deep inside me. I feel a sharp pain in my gut, as if some vicious creature with pinchers has crawled up into my body and set my organs on fire. Then the hovering form puts its face close to mine. A familiar gesture—where have I felt it before? The voice is smooth, sugary and disturbing.

"There. Zombie or not, all ready to go. You now carry the chip that could bring down the juggernaut and stop the monster that has sold you down the river. Not me. Christian. Don't run from me, girl; it will make things much worse. We have a secret, you and I . . . oh, yes, and Ryu, though he knows only part of it. We can all get what we want if you'll do just as I say and be a good girl . . . a good girl . . . a good girl . . ."

I opened my eyes. The dark blob hovering over me withdrew and receded. Now it was nothing but a shadow backlit by a light on the other side of the doorway, wavering tantalizingly, there, on the lintel. As I watched, the form ballooned and distorted, then shrank and grew still. Was it a dream? The pain in my belly subsided, became a dull ache. A delicate darkness engulfed me. I sank into the elastic comforts of sleep.

LIVE DEAD GIRL

When I woke up again, I was not in the morgue. I was in bed in a private hospital room. It was 2:03 in the morning. At least this is what the luminous hands on the face of the bedside clock indicated. The room was dark, its door ajar. The fluorescent light from the corridor made a big, pie-shaped wedge on the floor. There was a table not far from the bedside. On it was a tray full of plastic-covered dishes and plates full of food. That's what my nose told me.

Suddenly I felt famished. But I didn't want food. My hunger was of an entirely different nature. I could feel it racing with this pulse, my pulse, in the silent dark. I could feel the blood pumping through my body—faster, as my excitement rose. I pushed aside the covers and sat up.

The hall, at 2:06 a.m., was a jumble of movement and sound, but with the door nearly closed, it was not too painfully bright. There was a window in the room to the right of the bed, but the curtains were drawn. The space became gradually clearer, the eyes—my eyes—adjusting. Unadorned walls, the rolling table, two plastic chairs, linoleum of the same lemon yellow—I could see from the hall light—as the corridor floor. I noticed my hands were trembling. I gave my body its lead. I got up. I crossed the room, slid my bare feet over the cold linoleum, dragged my fingers across the Formica top of the table. The surface was cool and smooth. I leaned over and pressed my hot cheek against it.

From that odd angle, I noticed a cotton bag on the corner chair. I raised my head, straightened, walked over and picked it up. It was tied shut and labeled: "Orison/deceased." I opened the bag and sorted though its contents: a yellow silk dress, high-heeled shoes, sheer hose, a beaded evening bag and a cab driver's white glove. I gave an involuntary shiver. I dropped the clothes and moved on. There were medical supplies in a tub near the door—bottles and tubes, a box of sterile gauze, rubber gloves. I didn't stop to examine them. Something far more important was pulling at me, moving my bare feet over the floor.

A mirror hung on one wall. I approached it as one might approach a window, trying to look out onto a landscape, objective reality: physical, solid. The mirror was darkness framed in gloom, and the door to the room did not admit enough light to brighten it. I crossed to the window. I pushed back the drapes. I turned back to the mirror. A weak wash of moonlight invaded the chamber, animating the face there. I looked at a stranger, myself, for a brand new first time.

My eyes were dark, but they had a surreal brilliance, like a couple of coals suddenly ignited. Under each eye floated a blue thumbprint of shadow. These two bruise-like marks never vanished. They were the result of my near extermination. They are also the mark of a zombie.

I pushed back my hair. It kept falling over my eyes. I could not see all that I wanted to see because of the thin cotton hospital gown in which someone had dressed me. It was a short, apron-like gown that the moonlight vaguely illuminated. I noted, upon closer inspection that it was covered with tiny blue flowers that had faded almost to white. I liked it, but it was in the way, so I removed it, pulling it over my head in a movement that slid the well-worn fabric deliciously over my skin. The muscles of my arms and back grew tense, then relaxed, stretching and reaching pleasurably after the long, drawn-out sleep. Still I could not see well enough.

I fetched and dragged over one of the chairs. I climbed shakily up on it. Then, standing before the mirror, I took a good look at myself. Wide shoulders and large breasts, soft globes eerily lit by the moonlight, the nipples erect; flat white expanse of belly, subtly curved; a wedge of jet where the legs joined; long pale legs of a nacreous opalescence; they ended in marvelous feet. I loved the feet, preferring them to the hands because the toes were so delicate, like long buds—tender and rose-tipped—and because unlike the rough fingertips, those toes felt everything intensely: the cold linoleum floor, its uneven texture, the way I stretched and spread them.

Those toes and the mouth were the parts of the body that I liked the most—the mouth because it was full of itself, full of provocative tastes. But I also liked my ears, so perfect, as though they'd been crafted of porcelain. I would have liked, almost, to remove them—the better to see them—to enjoy their delicate shell-shape, so nearly sheer. I moved the dark mass of hair behind one of them, turning ever so slightly to the side for a better view.

This movement brought the door into my line of vision. Open a sliver, through it light sliced into the room, and I thought at first that I was seeing phantoms. But no, my eyes, accustomed to the near darkness, adjusted—the dilated pupils wrestling with and juggling the light to let in a backlit image.

He stood in the doorway, his hand placed palm-downward over his heart in a histrionic gesture. *Dramatic,* I thought. He looked like an actor at the cathartic moment of a play: an antique actor, one with great pathos. He wore a blue-flowered hospital gown, like mine, and his hair, which was long and wispy, was combed rather carelessly to one side of his head, which he'd cocked so that it looked like the limp locks had somehow managed to unbalance him. From his nostrils trailed two thin tubes of translucent plastic that ended in nothing just short of his knees. With his left hand he was playing with another clear tube, this one dangling from his right wrist, where a blood-encrusted sterile gauze bandage held it in place.

It's funny how living moments can become friezes, stiff, like the past caught in the flash of a camera, like photographs.

What a fright, I thought.

Then I saw myself as he saw me: the girl—a once-dead one—standing naked upon a chair in front of her mirror.

So, I looked straight at him and I started to smile, but something about him disturbed me. I could feel the sides of my mouth drawing up and my lips pulling over my wet teeth in a feral expression. And then I heard it—the hiss. Where had it come from? My mouth, I think. And before I knew it, it happened again—another snake-shaped, spittle-soaked explosion of sibilants directed at the man in the doorway. He leered back at me then, leaned his skinny right shoulder into the jamb. Then, he smiled, a big purple-lipped, open-mouthed smile.

"You are in trouble," he said. "Bad. Bad. Very naughty." He spat the words at me, filled them with venom. "You're supposed to act dead. Shame on you."

What was he talking about? I had no idea, but something about him seemed familiar, upset me, made me want to leap from the chair and throttle him. I wanted to tighten my hands around his windpipe, feel it collapse, a flaccid tube under my grip. I wanted to shut him up, to destroy him.

"What's the matter?" he rasped. "Cat got your tongue?" He leaned into the room, his head swiveling around till he saw the bag on the chair, the contents scattered around it. "Oh, too late." He chuckled. "I came for the glove, but I see you've already found it."

There was a racket in the hall.

"There he is," screamed a nurse. "Mr. Takashita. Mr. Takashita, you must get off your feet."

"My fan club," he confided. "They just won't leave me alone. Just as I won't leave you alone," he tittered. Then he tried, with a furious twitching, to wink.

By this time the nurse and two orderlies had arrived. They lifted the skinny little man as if he weighed no more than a sack of white rice. A third orderly arrived with a gurney and the other two slid him onto it. I watched all of this from my perch on the chair in the darkened room, but nobody noticed me. They were preoccupied with the old man.

"Get his oxygen," barked a nurse. "How did he get out of bed? Can somebody read his vitals?"

She had hospital staff running this way and that, but Mr. Takashita was not phased. He lay on the gurney, his head turned toward my room. He was laughing at me, mouthing warnings.

"You can call me Clément," he rasped. "Remember that, girl. You're mine. You can't just go taking things into your own hands anymore. No, I call the shots now. I own you. You'll see. Hee, hee, hee," he laughed. "Hee, hee, hee."

The tangle of hospital personnel closed around him.

"What's he talking about?" asked an orderly.

"He's delirious. Get his oxygen going. Get him back into bed."

They fussed over the gurney and they wheeled him away, presumably back to his room.

"Ok, let's go," yelled the nurse. "*Haya-ku*. Hurry. Hurry."

The shapes left the doorway, rushed off down the hall. I stood on my chair in the darkness. It didn't matter if they hurried, if they fussed. I knew this because I could see what they couldn't, had known it from the minute he'd appeared in my doorway dragging his tubes and snickering at me. Nothing they did could help him now. This was not the man they were trying to save. It was another creature entirely. Mr. Takashita was already dead.

THREE-DAYS-DEAD

The phone was ringing and ringing and the apartment looked like a typhoon had blown through it. The intern delivered me to my father's residence while insisting that I should actually have stayed at St. Luke's Hospital.

"You've been through a major physical trauma," he insisted. "You have not recovered completely." He was already quite upset long before we got to the door.

"It's not our fault. The hospital caters to a population of seven million. The wards are all full. Patients sometimes get lost in the shuffle." He paused. "Still, it's very strange that they released you. I lobbied to keep you there, but to no avail. Someone—I don't know who—must have wanted you out. I really don't understand it."

We'd come up in the elevator. I did not know where I was, but it felt familiar. I went immediately to the door and waited, mouth open, panting, like a stray that has found its way home. From behind the door emanated a most unpleasant smell. The young physician appeared not to have noticed. He thrust his large hand into the small mouth of a beaded handbag and pulled out a key ring with one key on it, which he shoved toward me. I backed away, so he took it upon himself to open the door. What did he think when the smell hit him full in the face? He didn't even flinch. It's strange how people manage to shut that sense down.

The apartment must have been beautiful once, but it was in ruins. In the huge living room, sunlight tumbled through two huge picture windows. Fancy furniture was upended, silk upholstery slashed, the whole mess feathered in down. Bright and fluffy and warm it was, but in massive and stinking disarray. I remember feeling an odd little thrill at the sight of all of that destruction.

"Oh my, what has happened here?" gasped my companion. He made his way through the apartment, drawn, no doubt, by a fascination with despoiled opulence.

The hall, which stretched from the left side of the entrance toward a distant back wall, was flanked by a series of doors that opened onto various rooms. They were all in the same state: beds taken apart, mattresses slit; cupboards thrown open; wardrobes and closets eviscerated, the contents dumped onto the floor, creating a chaotic topography. Table-sized contemporary canvases hung in shreds on the walls, slick surfaces breached, their abstract iconography reduced to tatters. The bathrooms were cluttered with opened boxes and bottles—all emptied into sinks and sunken tubs. In the guestroom, torn clothing lay strewn in large piles. Heels had been removed from the shoes. Books had been pulled from the shelves, spines cut and pages ripped. Draperies had been yanked from the rods, broad hems sliced open, and every electronic device in the place, including the phones, had been completely dismantled and carelessly cast aside. Mixed in with the mess were pieces of jewelry, the gemstones removed. But the precious stones hadn't been stolen. They were scattered about. Someone had been looking for something.

"Oh," stammered my lame-brained escort, "Someone has broken

in," stating what he thought was the obvious. If he'd been more observant, he'd have noticed that though the place had been ransacked, there were no signs of forced entry. The vandals, whoever they were, had let themselves in . . . with a key.

The intern stooped to pick up a shoe with his well-padded hands. I'd seen those large hands squeezed into latex gloves and was thinking that he should be wearing them now. He was covering things with his fingerprints.

"We must call the police," he declared as he continued his sloppy contamination of the crime scene.

In the kitchen—a shiny black granite and stainless steel room— all the plates and silverware had been thrown to the floor. Someone had picked through the contents of the refrigerator and the trash, which consisted largely of plastic and Styrofoam take-out containers and putrid bits of food. There were Japanese pastries strewn all over the floor. They had been broken open, red bean paste smeared on the slate-colored floor along with what appeared to be steak sauce.

"Oh," said my self-appointed guardian, his face losing color. "I think that is blood."

There were "bloody" footprints all over the kitchen and clear signs of a scuffle. Of course we couldn't help but notice the hand, severed and foul looking, next to a dirty white glove in a putrefying puddle on one side of the large kitchen counter.

The intern reached into his pocket for his cell phone. "We shouldn't touch anything," he cautioned needlessly. "We should wait for the police."

I did not wait for the police. While he was calling I slipped out the door, down the elevator and out into the street—confused, three-days-dead, just getting away from it all.

HIS STALKING FEET

It doesn't take long to disappear in a city like Tokyo. Exiting the building, I turned left, heading up Roppongi-dori away from the crossroads. I continued along Roppongi-dori until I came to a series of multi-story towers that caught the glint of the setting sun in their steel and glass ramparts and flashed it back to the ant-like pedestrians like some great, indecipherable semaphore. Tokyo gleamed all around me. I was seeing it as though for the first time, and as before, its shimmer was entrancing. I stopped in my tracks, heart pounding, head back, spinning slowly. I believe, for a moment, surrounded by that glory, I was happy. It couldn't last. That's when I felt it: something, something very close . . . something sly and slippery . . . something I'd encountered before, something I needed to flee.

I took off, weaving through the side streets, then backtracked to Roppongi-dori and turned left on Gaien Higashi-dori. Twilight had unobtrusively draped itself over the city. Lights began to wink on. My pace slowed to a walk as darkness crept over the town. But the darkness offered no cover. I could still feel something following me in the gathering gloom. And I recognized it. Bad, ominous, so unpleasantly familiar: It was Takashita, the cabbie, Miura, Carlyle; it was *him*.

I scooted around a corner, crossed the street, moving quickly past closed shops, skirting the western perimeter of giant Aoyama Cemetery. Things became deadly quiet, the gentle purr of the twilit city gobbled up by a black hole of silence, my panting trail through the ink-webbed streets devoured breath by breath by the death-dealing creature that stalked me. I looked back over my shoulder. My eye caught swift movement—shadows bumping into each other, colliding—that vanished. Murky stillness swam into the breach.

Then it was back: my pursuer, heavy, suffocating, and certain. And there were others! I could feel them, three maybe four others, just like the first. A low growl rose involuntarily in my throat. No response, not even the sound of footsteps on the sidewalk—I was alone. I picked up my pace. Again, the phantoms fell in behind me. I heard a feverish tittering.

A sick feeling uncurled in my gut. It rose from my abdomen and crawled into my throat where it lodged and threatened to choke me. My disgust had a smell: the smell from the hospital, from the apartment—the telltale odor of death. My heart raced. I could feel them behind me: a thirsty pack, their hunger a thick tongue of horror, snatching at my back, creeping greedily up my spine.

I was back on the main thoroughfare, sprinting, afraid to look behind me. I pushed my way past the pedestrians streaming down Aoyama-dori and into the Tokyo subway. Step, step, step, step, step— I raced down into the luminous underground: crowds, noise, people pushing and shoving, their faces fluorescent, a bruisy yellow-green.

I stepped into the current, slipping in past the turnstile, let it sweep me along as the next train rushed up, doors sliding open, blank-faced people falling out, blank-faced people crowding in. It was an underground full of zombies! I winced at the irony. Huddled in a corner by the silver seats, I stood with my back to the door, electrified, every hair on my body at attention. A girl with bad skin and long bangs that curtained her eyes looked sheepishly up at me. I glared down at her and around the train, trying to spot my pursuers. Everywhere I looked I thought I saw them, but the characters around me looked innocuous, tired and uncomfortable, maybe even a little afraid. Still, I felt *they* were on the train.

Omotesando Station. Meiji-Jingumae. I switched lines from Chiyoda to Yamanote. Harajuku Station, Yoyogi—the crowd shrank and expanded at every stop like an enormous amoeba. We were nearing Shinjuku Station, and that is where I knew I'd alight. Somehow Shinjuku station signaled safety.

When we pulled up to the platform, the crowd spat me from the train. I reeled into the river of three million souls that flows daily through Tokyo's biggest station. No ticket, I pushed my way through one of the turnstiles, a surprised commuter stranded in my wake. Up stairs, through corridors, past crowded shops, down passageways greased in noise and food smells: quickly, quickly, until the fast-moving stream of humanity burped me up and into the high-rise glitter of the roiling Shinjuku district. The crowd thinned as I jogged away from the station. Quiet night closed in around me. I had lost them, lost them somewhere in the teeming subterranean city. A feeling of joy rippled through me. I slowed to a walk, breathing deeply and let myself be dazzled by sparkling Shinjuku.

THE COCKTAIL HOUR

All around me skyscrapers rose to the heavens: thirty stories, forty, forty-five, fifty. This is the flashiest, brightest ward in Tokyo, the towering bastion of commerce and government, its seamy back streets lined with nightspots, clip joints, karaoke boxes, and private clubs. I felt comfortable at last, almost happy, gazing up at the checkerboards of windows lit up like marquees, my mouth pulled back in a grin. There was something pleasantly familiar about every crossing, about every straightaway and angle of the road. Zigzagging my way through the maze of tall buildings, I moved further and further from the station toward darker, wildly active streets. Men, lots of men, brushing past me; men on corners, in doorways, raising eyebrows, voices, eyes fixed on me as I passed. I just ambled along till I came to a dark building where two giants in dark blue suits stood like infernal sentries on either side of a doorway. They bowed familiarly. One of them opened the door.

I was at the top of a staircase that led down into a smoky bowl of music and bad light. Descending, I found myself in a large room dominated by an enormous black bar. Behind the bar were two model-handsome bartenders, tattooed and pierced, big hanks of their spiky black hair bleached to bright platinum blond. Behind them was a mirrored wall. On the black metal shelves in front of that mirrored wall were bottles of every shape and description, twinkling like jewels under well-aimed spotlights. Every seat at the bar was occupied, every occupant sitting tall, saying nothing, silently sipping his or her drink. At their backs was a dance floor. The dance floor was fed by another dark stairway on the opposite side of the room from which people descended, in various states of undress. They flowed onto the dance floor, bumping and grinding against one another, caught up in their private erotic fantasies. All around the dance floor was a snarl of small black tables, each surrounded by a host of chairs in colors that looked, in contrast, to be feverishly jolly and gay. Lime-green, electric orange, aqua, lemon-yellow—almost all of the chairs were full, occupied by a battalion of fine young humans wrapped in black, bare shoulders rubbing, eyes ringed in shadow, pale skins as incandescent as lampshades. Some burned from within with a twitchy fluorescence; others were definitely close to lights-out, waiting for the next drug or musical outrage to turn them back on. I felt like a hand slipping into its glove. Still recovering from my short bout with death, I fit right in. I looked for a seat. There was only one empty chair. I threw myself into magenta.

The club was packed. The music bleated out over the crowd, the bass reverberating, pounding with rhythm. It was fantastic. No one bothered me. No one tried to engage me in conversation. No one asked me ridiculous questions for which they really wanted no answers. Everyone seemed as listless as I. A few cocktail waitresses snaked from table to table, slipping across the scarred concrete floor in their heavy black boots, torn dresses and stockings. I was fascinated by their brilliant and inventive colors of makeup. Purple. Silver. Bottle green. I loved watching the way their conversation slipped from their mouths, a kind of voiding. No tedious and unnecessary observations that pretended significance; their talk was empty and blessedly uninflected.

One waitress slid up to my table—the table I now shared with two boys with royal-blue hair and metal bars of surgical steel piercing their pink, kitten-tongues. One of the boys was wearing a green rubber skirt and his bony white knees kept hitting me under the table, so I turned to him and hissed, drawing my mouth into a feline snarl. Then I turned my chair from the two of them. I think he was French, or pretending to be, because he muttered under his breath, "tant pish, meenie shkirt" and stuck his nose up in the air in a gesture of hauteur that I somehow knew to be characteristically French.

A snicker fell from the cocktail waitress's red lips.

"Erin," she scolded. "Where have you *been*? I've missed you. By the way, you look lovely tonight."

I felt a smile stretch over my lips. She was alluding, of course, to the yellow dress, which by now was looking a little bit soiled, to a couple of wrist hematomas, and to the bruises on my knees and arms from my fight with the hospital staff. The bruises had become large mandalas progressing from pale rose to purple. Some displayed faint hints of the yellow and green that would later flower around them. I felt suddenly gay and quite colorful. This girl whose name, I discovered, was Lou Lou, seemed familiar. She made me feel good. Lou Lou was trapped in black. Black dress. Black stockings. Black boots. It wasn't that she lacked imagination. I could see that the problem was that under the hip exterior was a frightened young human who believed too much in everything. She had too much hope. Hope is like a sickening rollercoaster ride that takes you up and down and throws you about. The contemplation of that hope and its repercussions was an abyss more horrifying to me than oblivion. I shut my eyes to close it out, breathing slowly in the reassuring darkness that I created. I looked for the surface and found it again.

Lou Lou was leaning over the table and whispering desperately and conspiratorially, "I have found it, Erin, the perfect space. It's a fine little cottage in a complex of cottages in Yanaka: old-style Tokyo, so hard to come by—you'll love it. Move in with me. Pleeease. You can finally ditch your dad." With one feather-light finger she traced a small cross on the top of my hand. I opened my eyes and looked up into her pale round face, so like the face of a cherub except that it was thickly covered with makeup. Her short, spiky hair, bleached to a yellowy-white, stood up around her head. I looked into her blue eyes, which the darkness in my own eyes cancelled out. I looked straight into her hope. I said nothing.

"Just come by," she urged, wrapping one of her beautiful marble-white hands around mine. She was working; her hand was warm. Mine were like ice. "Leave your father's apartment. You don't need him. He's not good to you, Erin. Leave Ryu," she said breathlessly as if the mere saying would cause an invisible ax to fall. Then she took a deep breath and straightened. "Just come by."

I watched her inch away, wriggling through a crowd that had grown viscous, a thick knot of bodies and smoke around the bar. I was edgy and tired. The two French boys had gone. They'd forgotten their smokes—Gitanes—and a book of matches from the Park Hyatt Hotel. Those boys were quickly replaced by a couple of immature salary rats who should have remained on whatever treadmill they'd jumped from. They were like a pair of giant hamsters gorging themselves on fake freedom.

I lit one of the cigarettes. Fascinated, I watched the way the cigarette burned, studying how the match opened a little orange mouth at the tip as I sucked on one bitter end. A thin taper of smoke rose up like a prayer. I opened my mouth and filled the air around me with what I refused to swallow. The girl coughed. Her date watched me warily. I took the rest of the cigarette, which was all but that one puff, and tossed it into his beer.

The girl's eyes narrowed ominously. "No smoking, bitch!" she spat, staring at me. Her shiny black hair looked evergreen under the fluorescent lights. Her face looked very nearly purple.

They got up to leave, and her date cast a sly glance at me and brushed against my shoulder so seductively that for a moment I wanted to follow him. But I'd also be following *her*. I didn't move. Fatigue slammed down on me again.

That's when a skinny cocktail waitress slid up to my table. She looked like a skeleton in black underclothes. Susan. Susan was her name, and she knew me. "Hi, Erin," she said. "Never see you here without Ryu. Where is he?"

When I didn't respond, she just shrugged. "It's your life," she said. "By the way, girl," she added, "that creepy guy at the bar sent this over to you."

On her tray was a single tall blue drink. I peered through the crowd in the direction that she'd pointed a skeletal thumb and saw the guy she was talking about looking back over his shoulder at me with a big grin on his face. One of his front teeth was missing, a little black door in his smile, and from where I sat, it looked like he had two sets of eyebrows. He made my skin crawl. Susan echoed my thoughts, "Pretty creepy, huh?"

She couldn't guess how sick he was making me. My flesh was all goose bumps. There he sat with a whole group of equally hideous guys. I looked from the gang at the bar to the eerie blue drink on the tray. It glowed like a methane-colored flame in the darkness. It looked almost like poison. Susan was already sliding away. I grabbed her arm, which contracted almost to nothing under my grip. My mouth dropped open.

"Wha . . . ?" I managed to stammer, pointing to the drink that she had placed on the table.

"Oh, I don't think you'll like it, Erin," she said. "One part rum, two parts fruit juice, one part curaçao; it's a zombie."

WHAT A GHOUL WANTS

I walked very slowly over to the bar where he sat with his friends. He had turned his back to me and was sipping his drink. I just stood there for a while until he finally turned to face me. His four friends were lounging like lizards their bodies slung lazily half over their chairs, half over the bar.

"Can't think of a thing to say?" he asked. "How about 'thank you?'"

I saw now that what I had thought was a second set of eyebrows was really a jagged cut over his left eyebrow that had scabbed over. On closer inspection I could see that his face was covered with bruises. His lip was swollen and discolored over the lost tooth. He had very short black hair, baggy clothes, and he smelled like a sewer.

"Quit following me," I hissed, surprised to have found a voice— my voice—though it was a cracked and barely audible thing.

"I couldn't help myself," he gushed, pushing his tongue into his cheek. "You know, I am so attracted to you. Always have been. I can't help but pursue you."

His friends were giggling. They, too, had the same disheveled appearances. They also stank. That's when it hit me. I knew exactly who he was and who they were: the darkest and dankest of the beings, supernatural low-life, the bottom rung of the ladder. I felt sick.

"You're a ghoul," I croaked hotly.

"Don't throw stones if you're in a glass house," he answered smartly. "That is a rash accusation. How can you say something like that? In fact, how can you talk at all?"

"I know a ghoul when I see one," I snapped, though I wasn't quite sure how I knew this since he was the first one I'd seen. But a vague memory stirred of a book . . . and a girl . . . and a beautiful woman . . . who had died. My chest and jaw tightened. I squeezed my eyes shut. Takashita, Miura, Carlyle—the curtain of confusion parted at last. Of course, it made perfect sense.

"You're a ghoul, and your friends are ghouls too."

At this point all of the boys slapped their knees and started laughing. One of them almost fell off of his chair. The stench of their breath filled the air. Ghouls are corpse eaters. They stuff themselves on the dead. Some ghoul subcultures, the fringier ones, occupy the dead bodies before eating them. They do not murder people. They take what has been discarded, reanimate it, and when the body is beyond use, they find a new corpse and eat up the old one. If they keep this up, they can hang with the humans, though they don't really need us; they're eternal. These boys had either picked up some pretty stale bodies, or they had been knocking around in the old things for days. They were, by now, pretty rank. All of the bodies looked as though they'd been roughed up, a wound here and there. The deaths must have been violent.

As if guessing my thoughts, the ghoul looked around at his friends with a grin and opened his arms. "Our luck, a windfall," he announced grandly.

"You stink," I said.

"Really?" He seemed genuinely surprised. He sniffed the inside of each of his wrists, as if smelling for perfume. "Oh, my, l'air de la nuit. You're right. It's time for a change. What a shame. I've grown so attached to this old thing." He guffawed and again set up a ruckus among his companions.

"But let's not talk about me, my little miscreant. Let's talk about you. I must say I do find *that* strange. Don't you know that creatures of your ilk are not supposed to be able to speak? But then, you did break my little spell. And that's strictly against the rules. My, I bet it's hard for you, isn't it? Tsk, tsk." He clicked his tongue in mock reproach, shaking his head from side to side. "Yes, I've been following you. I've been following you because I, too, have a keen sense of smell, although you wouldn't guess it from this get-up. I can smell transgression a mile away, and let me tell you, you reek of it. A disobedient zombie—it's an outrage! Now, you may think that a naughty little half-zombie girl like yourself can just go blithely along, quietly ignoring the rules and no one will notice. But I notice. I notice, and that is enough." He leaned forward so that his hot, smelly breath was full in my face. "And," he added, "As a member of a highly evolved ghoul culture that specializes in perverse behavior, I find your dilemma—because I do think of it as a dilemma—highly intriguing. I will, therefore pursue you, have, in fact, been pursuing you for a very long time. You see, I have a stake in the action. I want to know where this will lead. I just hope it leads to my doorstep.

"From my mouth to God's ear," he concluded, attempting to lick my ear and slobbering on the side of my face with his big purple tongue. "Oops," he apologized, "I missed."

His friends fell into an uproarious chorus of laughter, and one of them laughed so hard that two of his teeth fell right out of his mouth tinkling like a couple of dropped cuff links onto the top of the bar. This sent them all into further hysterics.

I was feeling something compelling. The same feeling I'd had in the hospital when I found the white glove, when Takashita appeared at my door, the same feeling I'd had out in the pitchy streets when I'd sensed someone stalking me. There were other memories caught up in it too; memories that flickered just beyond recollection. They were sad. But the strongest feeling was in my gut. It was fear at first, then, a low fire that started to spread. It was anger, a fierce cutting anger that was torquing me out and taking a kind of control over me, and with it, hot and stinging, came a flood of desire: a desire to speak, a desire to act, a desire to tell this atrocious ghoul what a blasted, perverse, stinking fiend he was. And with the desire, more subtly still and most horrifying of all, was an undercurrent excitement.

"Quit following me," I snarled through tightly clenched teeth.

"You have no sense of humor," he retorted. "Never have I heard tell of a zombie so articulate, so—dare I say it—lusty. Now, there is a rare contradiction in terms: a lusty zombie. It's appalling. It's an outrage. What perversity will you not sink to? One would think that you actually had feelings. God, what a radical thought," he exclaimed slamming his shot glass onto the bar. Then he looked at me closely and a wicked grin spread over his bruised face, making it into a ghastly mask. "Maybe you do," he said laughing to himself, softly at first, and then loudly as if at some fabulous joke. "Oh, my, maybe you still do! Such a twist on an ancient experiment! And it is I who will help you uncover and explore them, the nasty little zombie feelings, monstrous, strictly not allowed. I will be like the greedy impresario courting and developing that freakish talent that will forever set you apart, make of you that holy of unholies: the sideshow attraction. So there you have it," he said. "Our destinies are linked. You're mine, you know," he croaked. "I've worked hard for this. I will not leave you alone."

He'd gone on for some time. The rest of the ghouls, bored by his monologue, appeared to have fallen asleep, collapsed on the bar, their heads in their arms. Even he seemed a little disgusted when he looked about and noticed the slovenly picture they made. He pushed at one of the slumbering ghouls and failed to get a rise out of him. That one almost appeared to be dead.

"Ick," he shivered disdainfully, "that's the problem with leftovers. While it may not appear so to you, I do have my pride. Of course, I'll eat myself when it comes to it. No problem. But, to tell you the truth, I'd much rather eat you. Or her," he chirped merrily, quite pleased with himself, as Lou Lou approached the bar.

"Last call," she announced.

"You are adorable," he gushed, grabbing her round little face in one hand and squeezing her cheeks between his bloodied thumb and two equally mangled fingers.

"Well, I must go," he continued, smacking each of the ghouls on the side of the head to wake them. "These costumes are beginning to stink. We don't want to miss breakfast. Ladies, goodbye. Until we next meet. My name is Clément." He bowed. "Erin, my dear," he continued, "We have a date with destiny. I shall come to you in mufti. You will know me by my unquenchable wit. Come along, boys."

The other ghouls were struggling drunkenly to their feet— whether because of the alcohol or for other nightmarish reasons, I couldn't begin to guess—and the whole derelict clan staggered out of the club together.

"Ugh," Lou Lou grunted. "Those are the kind of men I attract. And what's worse, Erin, is that I am actually attracted to them. That beat-up one, for instance, was really sort of charming, wasn't he?"

Hardly. I was too numb to speak. The anger had subsided, leaving me exhausted beyond words, and I hoped that I would never set eyes on that ghoul again. But of course, fate had other plans.

LOVE LETTERS XVIII

Nakamura Hiroshi or Hiroshi Nakamura, as one says in the West, the choreographer with whom I was enamored and whom my father had used to lure me to Tokyo, had an unhealthy obsession with drama and death. He grew up in the theater, the adopted son of a famous *onnagata*,[15] one of the Kabuki actors who play only female roles. She was both father and mother to him. Nakamura's passion for dance was apparent from an early age, as was his attraction to all the enticements of his adoptive parent's artistic world, including a young dancer named Koan. Years ago they'd split up because Koan was keeping secrets from Hiroshi and had broken my mentor's heart. I knew this from Ryu who delivered the information matter-of-factly just before my first audition. It had been quite a blow-up, an enormous and sensational scandal, as the love-sick Hiroshi had penned a scathing letter to Koan, which the press got a hold of and published! Apparently my teacher had a fine way with words. What the unfortunate Hiroshi did not know at the time was that the even less fortunate Koan had AIDS and would eventually be admitted to St. Luke's Hospital where, as I awoke from my death-defying slumber, he was breathing his last.

Nakamura-san only learned about his ex-lover's illness from the scandal sheets and, as expected, reacted dramatically. He was consumed with guilt and became more obsessed with death and its permutations than ever. It colored his work and his frame of mind, driving him into a fearful and ever-darkening humor. But I didn't know any of this when his short note arrived, a note from the man whose name and reputation had brought me to Tokyo: Hiroshi Nakamura.

The envelope was scripted in an elegant hand (not Hiroshi's) and was addressed "Erin Orison." Lou Lou was the courier. She had intercepted the message at her front door. Lou Lou's little cottage at three o'clock in the morning—how could anyone have known I was there?

I didn't hear the knock on the door. I was in bed with Shipu, Lou Lou's Burmese cat, draped, purring, across into my chest. I had remained at the club, sitting at the bar, after Clément and his smelly friends left. Lou Lou clocked out, joined me at the bar, had a few drinks and talked about men and about her new home. "My life is going to change now, Erin," she'd said hopefully. "No more loser boyfriends. I don't care how much I want them. Cold turkey. I'm on the wagon as far as low-life men are concerned. Like Seiji, remember him? *Such* a naughty boy."

She laughed a sweet, slushy laugh and pushed my dark hair back behind my ears. "You have beautiful ears," she murmured as if caught by surprise. And I looked again into the silver-blue orbs that were her eyes, hypnotized by the light shards in her irises, amazed at how they caught the meager illumination of the bar, amplified it, and cast it back in a chaos of brilliance. Her lips, a pair of soft swells meeting and parting, were inches from my cheek. Wetness pooled in my mouth when I looked down at them. She smelled of musk and bruised juniper, of gin and cocktail olives.

"How about that guy, here, in the bar tonight?" Lou Lou continued, her head leaning on mine, her cheek pressed up against my ear.

"He was a piece of work, wasn't he? Whew. Talk about the call of the wild." She laughed into my face. I opened my mouth, wondering if I could swallow her laughter. Her wide eyes opened wider, then closed. "Erin," she slurred, hand in my hair, "you'll come home with me? I hate being alone."

What could I say? At that point I wanted to eat Lou Lou alive. I'd start with her words, her mouth, each perfect eye, her thoughts, her dreams, her fears. I'd swallow her whole, feel her slide down my throat, unfurl like a flower inside me until my fingertips were her fingertips, my voice her voice. Is this how a zombie desires? This was real hunger. Oh, I could begin with her chin, it was right there in front of me, small and smooth and pointed toward my lips. My hands had already found a place on her flesh, each one well up on a leg where her black thigh-high stockings ended and bare skin began. "Come on," she said, sliding from the barstool. My hands fell away like dead leaves. She grabbed my wrist and almost dragged me up the stairs, through the unmanned front doors and into the cool Tokyo night.

If there were stars overhead, we couldn't see them. The eternal shimmer of Shinjuku cancelled them out, but the moon, a thin, scythe-shape, loomed over the sky-high rooftops. The subway was enough to make even the most avid of hungers congeal—whey-colored faces flickering under the jellied fluorescence. Where were we going?

On the train I saw that Lou Lou had changed, morphed back into a yellow-fleshed maiden in a glittery wrapper of too much make-up and pointless expectation. We disembarked at Nezu Station, emerging from the bunker, rushing down Kototoi-dori, hurrying down dreary little streets. Suddenly all I could think about was the ghoul. How he'd followed me. What he'd said to me in the club. The tall blue drink swam before me, a methane-colored accusation. A zombie. "I will be like the greedy impresario courting and developing that freakish talent that will forever set you apart, make of you that holy of unholies: the sideshow attraction. Our destinies are linked. You're mine, you know. I will not leave you alone."

It had been difficult to find Lou Lou's apartment. It was behind a wall of fence, down a skinny path lined with cinder block and azalea. We arrived at a tall wooden fence with a gate, which Lou Lou unlocked, gleefully producing a shiny new key. On the other side of the fence was another world: a city of potted bushes, narrow azalea-lined paths, and tiny wooden bungalows with low wooden porches or genkan. Old Tokyo. Tokyo un-bombed. Lou Lou's place was at the very back of the complex.

"Careful, Erin," Lou Lou had whispered drunkenly as we'd navigated through the garden. Her cool white hand was wrapped around mine, her ginny breath in my ear.

Breathless, Lou Lou opened the wooden door, dropped her shoes on the genkan and scooped Shipu, the Burmese, up in her arms before turning and saying to me, head cocked in a mixture of pleasure and pride, "*Dozo*, Erin. Come in."

More drinks, sake this time. Then, somewhere between the sake and sleep, the message arrived. Odd: its delivery in the middle of the night like that.

"Erin, oh my God, this just came for you."

Lou Lou, black-kimonoed, stood over me in the bedroom, an enormous white envelope dangling from her fingers. Shipu quit purring, meowed in feline irritation and jumped from his perch on my chest. I sat up in bed.

"Yakuza," muttered Lou Lou. "Yakuza delivery boys, I'd guess—two of them. Hoodlums. How did they know you were here?" She pushed the envelope toward me. "For you," she said, raising her eyebrows.

The envelope was extraordinary—the size of a file folder and snowy white with a single inky thumbprint sealing it closed. The paper was thick and softly textured. It looked like creamy white skin. Inside, it was lined. The lining was black and cushioned a single card scripted in black ink brushed in the most beautiful hand. Along the right side of the card, two lines of calligraphy waterfalled from top to bottom. In the center the same message was written in English—one line, perfectly penned. "Hiroshi must see you," it said. Then it gave an address. Hiroshi? The name had a powerful resonance, but on that night hours after my release from St. Luke's, I did not know who Hiroshi was, could not connect the name with a conscious memory. But the note had an imperative quality and the envelope, the card, the penmanship were so mysterious, so exquisite, so alluring, that I'd have to call them . . . well . . . irresistible.

"Yakuza," cautioned Lou Lou, as if reading my mind. "Yakuza brought this. Don't go, Erin. It's late. This feels like a trick. You can always go later today."

I barely heard Lou Lou. I was caught up in the sweep of a brush, the smell of the ink, the beautiful white paper. Kami is the Japanese word for paper. It is also the homonym for god. And, in many ways, the invitation did feel like a heavenly summons. There is something about words written on a blank page, the idea behind them, the intent. There was beauty in the hand that had written this, beauty and urgency. Lou Lou unrolled her bedding next to mine. She slept, Japanese-style, on futons spread out on the tatami mats, the only way with the small space in a Japanese home. Beautiful silk futons, plum-fan-and-orange-hibiscus-patterned, thick as blankets of snow. I tucked the note between the futon and tatami. We took off our clothes and lay naked, side-by-side on the silken pallets. I wrapped myself around Lou Lou, body still aching. But she had fallen deeply, drunkenly and irrevocably asleep.

GRAVE MATTERS

He was dressed like a ninja,[16] wrapped in darkness. And his friends, silent as shadows, were clothed as ninja as well. No one would have seen them in the garden, crouching and creeping among the pots. They cat-footed their way up the paths in their rubber-soled, two-toed, black tabi socks. They knew exactly where we were. It was as if they had GPS, their on-board computers pre-programmed, the address fixed in their minds. Not so much as a board creaked when they set foot on the genkan. They were as invisible as Bunraku puppet masters, as the dressers in a Kabuki play.

He picked the locks—all of them—quickly, moving around the cottage until every door and window could be opened, soundlessly, easily. Then they invaded, the way smoke permeates a room, through cracks and crevices—a door barely opened, a window only slightly raised. Dropping to the tatami floor, one through five, they stole toward the bedroom where Lou Lou and I were dreaming. Cat burglars? Thieves? Assassins? Terrible as assassins, better as cats—they dawdled on their prowl to run gloved hands over objects, to examine photos, look into lacquer bowls. Shipu was awake and uttered a welcoming meow, rushing up to greet them, purring and pushing against one of them, drawn no doubt by the faint aroma of decomposition that floated about them like a cloak. Carefully, inch-by-inch, the gang members made their way toward our beds. Shipu was ahead of them, pleased to be in the vanguard, his tail rising up over his back in punctuation. Exclamation point. Question mark. Slash. Slash. Slash. Shipu hopped up onto the futon first, purring loudly, so loudly that I opened my eyes.

I found myself staring straight into his eyes. Not the cat's, but the burglar's. His face was over mine, his legs straddling me, knees on either side of my hips, his pupils, thin slits ringed in amber in thin-lidded eyes that bored into mine. He pulled down the mask that covered the lower half of his face to reveal a wide nose and cruel mouth.

"We meet again," he said huskily. "Not really the outfit I'd planned."

I knew that voice.

The scab up on his left temple was gone. His face had been altered entirely. New face, new body, but I recognized him at once. I opened my mouth.

"No noise, zombie-girl," he said quickly, covering my mouth with black duct tape. There was a struggle going on next to me. I looked over to my left. Lou Lou was awake, sitting up, a ninja sitting behind her, his legs wrapped like arms around her naked hips, one arm vice-like around her chest, one gloved hand over her mouth. The futon and sheets were pooled about her knees in confusion. Above the black glove, her blue eyes danced, wide, frantic, and signaling, desperately darting right, to the area just over my shoulder.

The ninja ringleader got the message when I did, but I was fast and the brass lamp came crashing down on the side of his head. In the split second after the impact, I wriggled out from under him, trying to get up and head for the front door. He was up and in motion before

I could jump to my feet, somersaulting over my head, like a funereal saltimbanque, landing impossibly on the wall next to the window with his feet planted squarely upon it, his body perpendicular to the floor. I froze and gaped at him jutting straight out from the wall, fiendishly defying gravity like a gargoyle on the spire of a church.

That's when the third ninja pounced. He'd been up on the ceiling, crouched on all fours, watching me like a black spider in the corner of its web. He landed on my back and shoulders, bringing me back down to the bedding with a soft thud. Then he and a fourth went to work on me, wrapping my ankles in more duct tape, binding my wrists with tape behind my back.

For the second time in twenty-four hours I was trapped. It was maddening, and I thrashed about helplessly on the ground, nearly dislocating my arms and neck while three ninja stood above me laughing. The leader, who had by this time descended from the wall, kicked the bedclothes in my direction. "Wrap her up," he commanded, "before she does physical damage."

They moved very quickly, these ninja, and my struggles ended in almost instant mummification. Next to me, Lou Lou, naked and duct-taped, looked on in terror until one of the ninja kneeled down beside her and making an elaborate ritual of it, decorously folding and refolding the blindfold, covered her eyes with a kerchief. Then they made tea.

Two of them sat in the kitchen sipping the steaming green liquid while the other three played their gravity-defying games. They climbed up the wall like flies. On all fours, they walked upside-down on the ceiling, sprang back down to the floor, tumbled across the tatami, then somersaulted back up to the ceiling again. Shipu jumped from chair to chair, delighted, neck craning, crooning in pussy-cat pleasure at their splendid antics. In the process, one of them lost a foot, and this seemed to fill them all with glee, especially when Shipu ran and tried to take a few bites out of it, turning it over and pushing his nose into the foot's tabi sock.

"For God's sake, get your foot," the lead ninja said tiredly, sipping the last of his tea. "And get them. We wouldn't want them to keep this appointment." He walked over to me where I lay on the futon, wrapped tight as a chrysalis in the bed sheet. My face was the only thing not totally covered.

"Your yakuza 'friends' will be here any minute, but you won't be," he sang merrily and he winked. Then he pulled the mask back up over his face. His henchmen hoisted Lou Lou and me and, as soundlessly as they had entered, they soft-footed it back through the garden.

They carried us easily, like very light bags, hopping the five-foot-high fence when we got to it, one of them preceding the others and catching us when they tossed us over the top. I was not blindfolded so I saw the black sedan waiting out on the narrow street, watched the fat driver open the trunk so the ninja could throw us inside. I recoiled when the lead ninja ran a naked finger down the side of my cheek and purred, "Let's see you get out of this one." Then he closed the trunk. I felt as if I were suffocating. Low and constant, I could feel the growl of the engine, feel its vibration against my chest. Then there was a knocking sound; I thought I heard doors opening and someone yanked Lou Lou out of the trunk. . . .

It was not a traditional graveyard, though there were a number of them nearby. It was, instead, one of the tiny Buddhist cemeteries that line some of the narrow streets of the Shitamachi, Tokyo's old downtown. The small yard was chockablock with graves and toba, the tall wooden funerary slats with sacred texts trickling downward in black ink. But we were inside and, I might add, underground, in what could once have been a bomb shelter. It was dank and mildewed and cluttered with paraphernalia: blank markers, small wooden chairs, grass sandals, bits of ceramic, pots of ash, wooden buckets and dippers for cleaning the graves.

The ninja, who you may have guessed were actually ghouls, had deposited us in this basement room, which I suppose I should call their "dorm," although I've since learned that they never sleep. Lou Lou, duct-taped, still nude, but no longer blindfolded, was writhing about. Cocooned in the bed sheet, I couldn't budge and I lay there on the concrete floor, looking like a large white grub or a mummy.

"Booty," sang out the head ninja, who also happened to be Clément. He threw his arms upward and all the ghoul-ninja, even the one with one foot, began prancing around him in a dance. One moment they'd be balancing on the rim of a bucket, the next stumbling drunkenly and clumsily tumbling to the ground. They seemed to ignore Lou Lou's pointless thrashing about though I suspected it was the cause of their very obvious excitement.

"Welcome to our humble home," said Clément. He had plucked a few flowers—carnations—from one of the newer graves and tossed them our way. "You are safe here."

"Boys," he commanded, addressing his slovenly ninja cohorts, who seemed held together by the black rags wrapped around their bodies, "dress them in finery. Show them every comfort."

In response to this order, his fellows dragged forth a bag from one corner of the cellar and began to pull out old clothes: men's shoes, suit jackets, ladies' blouses, a coat, a pink skirt, an aqua-colored beaded cardigan sweater, a short salmon-colored shift. They tossed the pink skirt and aqua sweater at Lou Lou. The garments landed on top of her wriggling form. The colors, so different from her ever-black, must have shocked her. She froze and her blue eyes widened. The ghouls, meanwhile, had started a tug-of-war with the salmon-colored dress. The victor in the tug-of-war held the garment over his head like a flag, then lowered it, and marched solemnly toward me at a ceremonial pace, the other ghouls falling in step behind him. The ghoul with the dress knelt by my side and carefully placed the garment on top of my sheet-bound body as if dressing a paper doll, smoothing out any wrinkles. His eyes, above the mask that covered the lower half of his face, looked momentarily sad: melancholy and rot—not exactly a winning combination. Then he quickly tore the tape from my mouth. I immediately let out a wail that could wake the dead. It rang through the cellar and up into the temple above us, no doubt confirming any lingering graveside superstitions once and for all.

"Enough," yelled Clément. He was beside the kneeling ninja in an instant, cuffing him on the side of the head. The poor creature's temple caved in like the shell of a very old pumpkin. "Just *what* do you think you are doing? Damn you," he growled, slapping the tape back over my mouth.

The other three ghouls started to giggle. Clément towered over the ghoul at my side, his gloved hands in fists, and let out a world-weary sigh. "Well," he said, "I suppose you're already damned . . . as are we all." He touched the head of the kneeling ghoul somewhat tenderly. "Sorry," he mumbled. "We'll get you something new . . . ," his apology interrupted by a rustle on the stair and the appearance of a rather old monk.

The ghouls were not the least bit surprised by the monk's appearance and he, in turn, seemed not at all surprised by theirs. He glanced over at us—the ghouls, the bound women—and shook his head. Then, shuffling over to a corner of the room, he retrieved a pot of black paint and took down a box from a shelf on the wall and extracted a brush. The ghouls watched him. One even waved. The old monk ignored them and carried his supplies back upstairs.

"He thinks we are figments of his imagination," said Clément.

"We can do whatever we like. He pretends we do not exist, though he does seem to chant his prayers with increasing vehemence.

"As for you two, Erin and Lou Lou," the ninja leader added, "I'm sure he sees you as a new wrinkle in his ongoing nightmare. All that matters is that he never interferes and, with caskets arriving regularly, we have a constant supply of new bodies. They come here for a service before heading for the crematorium.

"Well, back to business," he continued. "We do so want you to be comfortable here—comfortable and safe. The yakuza, the Consortium—everyone is looking for you, Erin. They weren't happy to hear that you walked out of the hospital. Believe me, you don't want to fall into their hands since their plans for you end in a coffin sent special delivery to your less than loving father. I am your savior," he crowed. "I care for you. So why, why do you run from me? Got something against ghouls? Seems everyone does, but I thought I could change your perspective. Sadly my little plan didn't work. Hardly a zombie, you are still a willful creature. But I am going to protect you in spite of your aversion to my aid. You will room with us for a bit. At least until I can come up with a better solution. It isn't too bad here. We like it, don't we?" He turned to the other ghouls who violently nodded their heads, except for the one who removed my gag.

"These Japanese are so afraid of mamono—devil beings—taking over their dead. They have all kinds of rituals to keep us away: daggers and sickles on the chests of the expired; sutras, prayers, and vigils. Bah. Superstitious hocus-pocus. None of this works. We get what we want and they get a changeling. An old body burns as well as a new one. As long as they have bones to pick through[17] no one is the wiser. First things first, though," said Clément. "A kaimyo[18] means a corpse and that, to us, means a future. You, my friend," he said to the injured ghoul, "appear to be particularly needy."

This said, he took to the stairs and the other ghouls followed with supernatural stealth, flying toward the upper floor like several black cinders.

No sooner had they disappeared than another figure appeared in the stairwell, this one bent and gray and considerably less agile. It was the monk creeping back into the cellar. He looked around to make sure the coast truly was clear then tiptoed over to where Lou Lou lay writhing. He looked down on her and put his index finger to his lips. "Shhhhhh." She stopped struggling for a moment. The monk removed her gag. Lou Lou squeezed her eyes shut and filled her lungs with air to prepare for a copious scream. The monk slapped his hand quickly over her mouth and shook his head "no." Lou Lou squirmed for a moment before getting the point. He waited till she was calmer and shook his head "no" again. She nodded and then responded with her own slow negative shake of the head. Then she nodded again. The monk uncovered her mouth and Lou Lou was silent, breathing heavily, as he unbound her. Averting his eyes slightly, the old monk handed her the skirt and the cardigan sweater and while Lou Lou dressed, he removed my bonds as well.

Freedom. I closed my eyes for the comfort of darkness. I could feel liberty singing through every fiber of my being. When I opened my eyes, I saw the old monk staring at me with a childlike gaze of profound wonder. So I flashed him one of the wide-mouthed grimaces that I'd been trying to shape into smiles. This made his eyes puddle up and with trembling hands he handed me the salmon-colored chemise. I just sat there, so he pulled the garment over my head, added a pair of socks, even shoes—dressing me as if I were some kind of doll, or maybe a corpse; he was probably much more familiar with those. By now the old man was shaking. He was clearly out on some kind of spiritual-psychological limb, having stepped smack-dab into one of his nightmares. He pulled me to my feet and pushed me to the bottom of the stairs.

"*Iku*. Go," he urged.

By this time Lou Lou was fully clothed and jittery, but no longer hysterical. "Come on, Erin," she whispered, buttoning the last buttons of the aqua-blue cardigan. "We've got to get out of here. *Domo. Domo.* Thank you. Thank you," she said to the old monk and grabbing my hand, she pulled me up the stairs. The old man, eyes misty, stood at the foot of the stairs, one hand on the banister, watching as we made our escape.

We emerged into daylight. Not a ghoul in sight as we huddled against the tall fence in a garden bed on one end of the cluttered cemetery. There was a slight breeze and the crowded graveyard was wrapped in the faint scent of dying flowers threaded with a shrill tongue of incense. I wanted to burrow back into the little curtain of bamboo that lined the fence and sit for a while. It would be lovely to rest here where it was so still and silent. But Lou Lou would have none of it. "Come on, Erin. We have to get out of here," she insisted, dragging me toward the gate.

At the cemetery entrance I pulled away from her. "What?" she asked me, alarmed. She really looked beautiful standing there in confusion in a makeshift and uncharacteristic wardrobe of glowing, baby-soft color.

I might have hesitated for a moment, but surely no more than that before I turned and headed off in my own direction.

"Well, OK, but be *careful*," she called after me as I set out for the only place that mattered, the destination designated on a summons elegantly scripted on a cream-colored card from someone I vaguely remembered: Hiroshi Nakamura.

HOW HE FELL FOR YOU

All roads lead to Shinjuku-ku. 3-7-1-2 Nishi-Shinjuku. That is the address I gave to the cabbie, a kind man who took the card and did not charge me for the ride. Once again I found myself in that high-rise, fast-paced part of town, very close to the station. Why did everything seem to lead back there? Why did it feel so familiar? 3-7-1-2 Nishi-Shinjuku was a hotel—close to 50 stories, one of the tallest in the neighborhood. I walked up the curve of concrete drive that swept up to the front. The entrance was cavernous, a huge lobby of rust-colored marble and wood. On a banquette of creamy oak, a wristwatch sat. Sculpted in brass, it looked meltingly soft and perfectly real where it lay, as if left by someone. Someone. Someone at the entrance. I felt eyes upon me from every direction. Dark squints and scowls. I spun around only to find myself surrounded. They stood and squatted all around me, their heads leaf-shaped, elongated; their haunches thick and powerful; their dark weapons tipped in ivory and gold. Some had long necks and breasts like torpedoes; others had gnashing teeth and fiery raffia hair. All were as black as pitch and filled with fierce power: African fetishes, almost a dozen of them, mounted on five-foot blocks of black marble along the walls of the lobby. I walked up to one of them, reached up a hand to caress wooden knees as sharp as cut glass. "From the collection of Hiroshi Nakamura," read the placard on its marble base.

"Hiroshi must see you." Hiroshi. Hiroshi Nakamura. The name was so very familiar.

"Can I help you with something?" a thin Japanese man in a dark two-piece suit asked in pleasantly accented English.

"Hiroshi," I intoned hypnotically. "Hiroshi Nakamura."

"Ah," he said quickly sucking in air, subjecting me to a quick inspection. What did he see? A very young woman, carelessly clad in a salmon-colored chemise with mismatched socks and out-of-style shoes. I must have satisfied some secret criteria because he closed his eyes and bowed slightly, led me to a bank of elevators and, addressing a brass panel the size of a light switch, inserted a small brass key. One set of doors slid immediately open.

"Hiroshi Nakamura," he confirmed with a nod. "*Dozo.* Please." Then the doors shushed closed.

There were four buttons in the elevator, two pairs of two. The top two were labeled Kozue and #1, the bottom two were labeled Lobby and Gym. Excluding the other buttons was easy. I pushed #1 and zoomed up fifty floors to be deposited on the level between forty-nine and fifty, between the restaurant, and the hotel's rooftop spa: 3-7-1-2 Nishi-Shinjuku, #1.

The doors opened to the baleful music of a shakuhachi flute, solo and hoarse, crying into the white-carpeted foyer. The sound emanated from a monolithic sienna-red door (no doorknob, no visible features) that stood open about fifteen feet away. The great finger of sound found its way into my pelvis and snaked up through the upper half of my body, finding a resting place right behind my eyes, which started to water unaccountably. I opened my mouth as if to answer. No sound came out. But I felt as if my own mouth were a great speaker from which the sound of the flute now emanated. Maybe I was actually moaning when I slipped through the door. I gasped audibly once I was inside.

Before me, black as tar, shiny as oil, the floor stretched like a wide pool of molasses. It was so glassy, so smooth, that I found myself removing first one shoe, then the other, setting my stocking feet directly upon it. It was cool and slippery and I slid along the top of it like a saint walking on water. Rising up from it, like giant piers, were a series of columns identical to those in the lobby, except that they were lower, perhaps two feet from the ground, with more of the horrible statues set upon them like a headhunter's trophies on pikes, and arching over that onyx black substrate, a full two stories overhead, was a roof so white it was blinding.

But I had no time to dwell upon any of this. The flute was disappearing into the hiss and spit of smaller woodwinds and the rumble of kettledrums furiously pounding with a force that nearly floored me. In desperation I looked to my right at a huge, wall-sized window UV-coated and curtained, obscuring the distant face of Mt. Fuji.

That's when I saw him, sitting rigid as a pharaoh on a brown leather armchair, his eyes wide and boring into me with an almost palpable heat. He seemed as startled as I. Then he threw back his head to the roar of the kettledrums, and I half expected the room to ring with loud, saturnine laughter. Instead he pushed himself stiffly to his feet, head thrown back, his eyes never leaving my face, and he walked toward me. He was thin and bald and he slid over the floor like a phantom, with supernaturally feline grace. I, in turn, slid toward him, drawn as irresistibly as an iron shard to a magnet.

Hiroshi Nakamura.

My approach brought a smile to his lips.

"*Naze shitte ta no?* How did you know?" He asked in Japanese first, then in English. He seemed to know me, but seemed to have no knowledge of the summons. His hands flew toward me wrapping around mine like gloves of ice.

"Koan is dead," he said sorrowfully, and I could hear the tone of the shakuhachi flute in the ragged break in his voice. "But I have finished the ballet. Something I couldn't do while he lived. You will dance it," he added. "That is why you are here. It is full of my grief, my guilt, and my regret. How could I know of his illness? He never told me. How could I know that it was the reason he left me? I dealt with him cruelly. When he tried to reconnect, I turned a deaf ear. I was heartless. And now he is dead, and I can't bring him back to ask his forgiveness. How many turnings in the dark of the cave of life are taken through misunderstanding? This ballet is my tribute to him. It is my best work. My only work."

Several samisens "oohed" and "aahed" at this, and again I felt the music take hold of me in the strangest way.

"You know this part," said Hiroshi. "Frivolous, vain, like the flower dance, the hana-odori."

I felt my head swaying from side to side as my body became absorbed by the music. One foot turned in, I took a delicate little step, then another, eyes down so that I could watch mesmerized by my reflection on the onyx mirror of the floor. Lean like a heavy-headed lily, sway, sigh, step, step, step, lean, sway, sigh, then freeze. The high-pitched twang of a single string cut through the other instruments, full of judgment, full of blame. Now the movements were butoh, drawn from the dance that came from war, from the suffering and shame of Nagasaki and Hiroshima. These were the movements of dying and I mimicked them with a bitter exaggeration, balanced on one foot, one hand reaching in an eternity of pain toward Hiroshi.

He staggered backward. He had not yet choreographed this part of the dance. I was improvising. I could feel the movement. My being was reading his mind and inscribing upon the space that surrounded us the exact line of his misery. Twisting sideways now, still balanced, crane-like, on a single stem, chin over my shoulder, I raised my other hand to my face, touching my eyes and mouth, aping the gestures of lovers. Then I turned toward Hiroshi, opened my mouth and snarled. I was an oni now, a devil with no remorse. Hiroshi's hand flew to his heart. I slid slowly to the floor in a Chinese split and, bending from the waist, touched my forehead to the floor. The music ended in whispers—whispers, bits of woodwinds and strings and snare drums, then silence.

It was powerful, potent enough to raise the dead, and indeed, Hiroshi looked as though he had seen a ghost, but this was not a reaction to savor smugly, because I saw at once that Hiroshi was actually looking beyond me, beyond the upside down "T" that I'd settled into on the floor. His eyes were looking out over the expanse of polished black wood to the door, which was now completely ajar. Standing in front of it, gangrene-gray and moribund, like a corpse summoned by my dance or some equally demonical force, was a gaunt, fetid figure.

The creature was smiling. "Hiroshi," it croaked, its head cocked to one side, love shining like beams from its eyes. "Hiroshi," it rasped again. "I forgive you."

Hiroshi, I observed, had, as if mirroring his visitor, turned a similar porridge-gray color. "No," he said, shaking his head furiously. "No, Koan, you are dead."

"No, I'm not," the smelly old corpse insisted. "Would I come here if I were dead? I don't care what they say. I'm alive. And I love you, Hiroshi. I have never loved anyone but you. I couldn't stay with you; I knew I was ill. But you thought I had spurned you and you refused all of my overtures. Now, that was so cruel. You hurt me more than anything I have ever known. I've been so unhappy, felt so wronged."

All the time this nightmare Koan spoke he was inching toward Hiroshi, and Hiroshi was backing away.

"No. No." Hiroshi kept muttering, his fear of ghosts having gotten the better of him, the terror twisting his tongue.

"Hiroshi," said the appalling creature, stepping over me as if I didn't exist. "You love me, don't you, Hiroshi? I know you love beauty, but what does it matter that I look this way? Isn't there still a place for me in your life? Can't you forgive me? Accept me?"

There was one small carpet in Hiroshi's apartment, a stupid thing to have in a place with such slippery floors. It was a red and clay-colored kilim, no doubt from the same dealer as some of the horrible fetishes that the choreographer collected.

Hiroshi backed away far too quickly and his foot caught the edge of it. The kilim, which seemed at this point to have a life of its own, shifted magically, and I wondered, for one brief and terrible moment, if there weren't some dark force at work in the fetishes, in the rug, in the music, in my dance and, most certainly, in Koan.

Hiroshi staggered, tried to balance himself with his other foot and only succeeded in losing his balance completely. Then he fell. He fell like a tree falls when it has been hewn down expertly—straight back and away from the woodcutter. That's how Hiroshi fell—like a tree in the forest. But Hiroshi's head never hit the ground. It was stopped on its floorward trajectory by the gold-tipped spear of a particularly vicious little African fetish. He had the misfortune to catch it on the back of the neck in the area just between the atlas vertebrae and the base of his skull. But he did not hit it straight on. The short spear pierced his neck, severed his carotid artery, and a pillar of blood sprang up and sprayed from the wound. There he lay, or more appropriately, sat, skewered by the fetish, his blood gushing from the spigot in his neck.

I watched it pump and pump, the red puddling on the smooth, black floor. I crawled toward Hiroshi, put my hand in the blood. Yes, he was certainly dead.

"Now, look what you've gone and done," said Koan.

Only it was no longer Koan's voice. It was a voice that I recognized, one I'd heard too many times.

"Yes, it's me," said the ghoul. "You were expecting the dead man? Hiroshi certainly wasn't. Clément . . . oh, I mean karma . . . comes calling."

GO VAN GOGH

"What a mess," he complained, kneeling down next to Hiroshi and feeling his pulse.

"Dead," he asserted. "Lovely." Then: "Oh, you've really complicated things. And I was merely trying to retrieve you in the most playful of ways. Give you both a bit of a scare. Drat! The yakuza are going to be unhappy. Now we'll have more police. You keep screwing things up. You're supposed to be dead," he hissed. "How can I possibly keep you under wraps if you keep flaunting your very live and disreputably lively self all over town?"

I must have looked surprised.

"Oh, don't look so innocent," he scolded. "What do you think you were doing in that hospital morgue? It's actually where you belong. Ryu, in particular, is going to be really pissed off. Bad enough I interrupted your execution at that sordid hotel. Yes, he was supposed to kill you, silly girl. You are, thanks to your father, the object of the yakuza's and the Consortium's very hostile attentions. Not an enviable position. Now you have gone and made matters worse. The yakuza, the Consortium and your dear dad have this in common: They are merciless. And Ryu, in spite of what you may think, is not a nice man. Now,

I, on the other hand, am a gentleman, and while I have actually gotten you out of many a scrape, I can't get you out of this.

"Well, run away! Isn't that what a zombie does? You certainly aren't doing my bidding. Oh, don't give me that smoldering look. I didn't kill Nakamura. I'm just a dead lover. I don't even exist. I can see those headlines though: *Dancer on Murderous Spree: Cabbie and Choreographer in Four Days.* No, you won't be able to hide now. I just knew you'd get caught one day."

He was totally ignoring the fact that I'd had nothing to do with Hiroshi's death. It was his fault the choreographer was dead; he'd shown up in the moldering body of the man's deceased lover. I could see just where this was going.

Clément stood up slowly, blood on his hands. "Yes, you are responsible for all of this. You are a very bad zombie, you know. I went to a lot of trouble to make you and you are supposed to obey me. And I don't like it that you keep running to other men when I have so much to offer."

He twisted off one of Koan's ears and held it toward me on a bloody palm. "Like this," he said. "It's for you." I looked at it in disgust. "Oh, I see," he said sulkily, "a bit too Van Gogh. No one ever appreciates the artist."

He started to toss the ear over his shoulder, considered for a moment, then pocketed it. "Except, maybe, another artist—like your lovely friend, Lou Lou. I'll bet she'd understand me." Clément licked his lips. "Lou Lou," he sneered. "Let's call her, OK? She must be home by now. Let's see if Lou Lou will come to your rescue."

I swallowed hard. Everyone seemed like pawns in Clément's nasty game. And what was the object? I feared it had something to do with me.

"Of course it has to do with you," he said quickly. "It's all about you

. . . and me," he added. "Always has been." He studied his dark purple nails for a moment. Alright, let me see," he said, pulling a cell phone from his pocket and punching in numbers. "Lou Lou?

"Lou Lou, this is a friend of Erin's. It's Clément. We met the other night at the club. Do you remember me? Oh, you remember my voice? How sweet. I told you we'd meet again. Well, Lou Lou, you will have to pick Erin up. She's had an accident. What? No, she didn't tell me about last night. No, no, darling, it isn't serious, but it seems she's gone and bled all over herself. Don't worry, she's all right, but you see, there's been a death. And the yakuza are involved. Yes, you know what that means. You'll find her at this address: 3-7-1-2 Nishi-Shinjuku. Come and get her, please. She'll be in the lobby. That's on the thirty-second floor. Yes, the upstairs lobby. And Lou Lou, better bring a suitcase and a ticket out of the country. That's right. Erin needs to leave town. I'll pay for it, of course: breast pocket of the coat. Oh, no thank you necessary. Me? No, I have a dinner engagement." He laughed. "We'll meet again some other time. We'll do lunch."

It was nearly five p.m. when Lou Lou arrived. I was wearing Koan's overcoat, which, surprisingly, hadn't the least bit of visible blood on it. Clément was gone. He'd left after stuffing the coat's inside pocket with cash. There was a lobby floor manager who watched me with some suspicion as I sat there, waiting. I shoved my hands into the coat pockets. There was an ear in one of them.

Lou Lou entered, dressed in black platform shoes and a short black dress. She carried a large black shoulder bag and a small black suitcase, like a flight attendant's. It had no distinguishing characteristics.

"Erin?" her tone writhed with the questions she dared not ask. "Come on," she said quickly and led me to the ladies' room. She pulled another black dress out of the shoulder bag, and I changed into it while she pocketed the cash and disposed of the topcoat and the bloodstained pink shift. "What happened? Oh, never mind. Don't tell me. Here," she said, handing me an airline ticket. "To Holland, to Amsterdam, actually. I have a . . . relative there. He'll collect you. Take the suitcase," she commanded. "He'll want that."

Minutes later we were out of the hotel and rushing to Narita Airport just as a very private elevator descended to the lobby level and opened to reveal, to the surprise of the lobby manager and the hotel guests, the bloodstained body of a very dead and nearly decapitated choreographer crumpled upon the floor. Hiroshi. Hiroshi Nakamura.

THE WOLF MAN AND THE MULE

It was a first-class ticket to Amsterdam, which meant that the seats were roomy and the food and liquor flowed for the length of the flight, which departed at 9:55 p.m. from Narita Airport and arrived almost fifteen hours later at Charles de Gaulle. Slippered, blanketed, hot toweled, and doted upon, I sat in first class while the flight attendants popped back and forth from their galley like genies. Champagne at take-off, light jazz, more champagne. Then there were hors d'oeuvres: shellfish soup with fennel and sweet onions, garlic mousselines, smoked eel, salmon, caviar and, yes, more champagne. After that came the entrees: lobster and scallop fricassee with Beluga caviar and coriander, sautéed duck breast filled with dried nuts on a nest of carmalized leeks, sturgeon wrapped in phyllo with cognac and garlic butter.

"Would you like to try the Sancerre?" asked the flight attendant cum cocktail waitress cum maitre d' before serving me the salmon. She poured me a glass of the golden stuff.

My appetite had returned with a vengeance. Between that and the insistence of the attendant, I was doomed to overindulge. I became completely absorbed in ingesting. Dessert followed entrees, and after a small plate of cheeses and a tart rhubarb cobbler, I consumed nine or ten Belgian chocolates and, at the insistence of the airline employees, who were intrigued by my surprising capacity, a few glasses of fine Dutch genever.

Then there was a plane and airline change, which I made under the exacting direction of a solicitous flight attendant, and another hour to Amsterdam on KLM Royal Dutch Airlines—the sixty minutes filled with more snacks.

I was fat as a blood-happy tick and skunk-drunk when I arrived at Schiphol Airport in Amsterdam at around nine o'clock in the morning. The flight attendant had mistakenly exchanged bags with me. All those little black bags look exactly alike. She noticed her error, though, and corrected it when I exited customs.

The two men who met me at Schiphol Airport were handsome. They looked like twins, both tall and well muscled. They had light brown eyes and brown hair, though the one called Alain wore his loose and long. The other, Albert, had shorter hair, and it was streaked with gray. Alain, also the slightly broader of the two, was Lou Lou's half-brother. She'd described him to me on the way to Narita almost two days before.

"You'll recognize him easily, Erin. He looks like a wolf, amber-eyed, very calm. Alain can take care of everything." I detected more than sisterly affection in the description. "And he'll probably be with Albert who looks a lot like him, but a bit more, uh, predatory. So the two are really easy to spot."

I wondered what Lou Lou had said about me that made me so easy to identify. The two men walked up to me without hesitation, nearly bumping into the flight attendant, who was saying goodbye with a smile. Alain greeted me by running his hands over my breasts where they lingered for a moment. They swept down over my chest and toward my hips. Then he leaned toward me and whispered, "Safety precaution. Consider yourself frisked." He smiled a wide, white-toothed smile. "Better than a handshake," he added. "You like it?"

I did. And I'd liked the flight and I really liked the airport, but maybe it was the genever and creamy Dutch chocolate that had punctuated the experience; I'd really liked that a lot, too.

Amsterdam smelled delicious. Even there, at the airport, it was full of sugary, yeasty, robust, meaty smells. I could lose myself in them. In Tokyo odors were wasabi-hot and vinegar-thin. They were sometimes so sharp they were piercing. This country smelled different. The smells here were so thick they made my head spin.

I nodded, closed my eyes, inhaled, and let myself be carried away by the surprising olfactory extravaganza. Such a tangle, although one fragrance seemed to muscle out all of the others: licorice. I could smell the sweet-salty scent of licorice drops on Alain's breath just above me, very, very close—so close I felt I would drown in it. "Welcome to Netherlands," he murmured to the top of my head, and I knew I had found my way home.

His friend Albert watched us with disapproving eyes. "Come on, Alain," he said hastily and not quite kindly. "Let's get this little baggage out of here."

Grabbing baggage (me) and bag (the nondescript black carry-on that the flight attendant had returned), they escorted me out of the airport.

"A marvel of engineering, Amsterdam." That is how Alain described the centuries-old settlement bullied up against the ingenious Zeiderzee-turned-Iselmeer as we emerged from the train station and into the klieg-like brilliance of the Stationsplein at ten a.m. It was a city quite unlike Tokyo. In Amsterdam, a chill-laden breeze blew in off the northerly situated "southern sea," carrying with it the saltwater smells that fumed in over the dike and across its freshwater prison. It was a noisy city cobbled in stone and rattled by bicycles. Sunlight leaped in shiny spangles off the water of the canals. The streets were cluttered with a multinational mish-mash of people that gave the community an oddly derelict look. And everywhere, from every nook and cranny in the waterlogged town, emanated a stew of intoxicating aromas. Small cars and canal boats spewed diesel fumes. Indonesian and African eateries released spicy clouds of perfume from behind beaded doorways. There was the smell of coffee, of sugar, of chocolate, the smell of tobacco, of fresh paint and sweat and salt and fish. There was the smell of waterlogged wood, of fries and cologne, the smell of sex and of cannabis.

Darting from the Central Station, Alain and Albert steered me expertly past buskers, through throngs and over bridges spanning the electric surface of the water, then along the wide and populous Damrak, before bearing right for more settled, albeit seedier terrain. In less than a heartbeat we were in Amsterdam's Red Light District, the filter through which all newcomers stream. It is bordered on the west by Warmoesstraat, the oldest street in the city, and sprawls in a clutter of alleys and streets across Oudezijds Voorburgwal and Oudezijds Achterburgwal, the two canals that marked the one-time perimeter of the medieval town. We dashed past one brightly painted doorway after another, past sex shops and peep shows, past glass-windowed rooms in which women primped and posed provocatively in various states of undress, and finally, through the splintered red threshold of a storefront with the word "Tattoos" emblazoned upon its narrow window in yellow and blue enamel.

A haggard blond man looked up from the arm of a young female upon which he was inscribing an enormous blue moth with a needle on the end of a mechanical arm that whirred and sang. He paused in his work and flashed us a gap-toothed smile.

"What's up, mates?" he asked.

"A delivery—airmail," Albert said gaily.

"Marvelous." He gave a quick slap to Albert's hand and went back to his customer. "Pretty girl," he added, nodding toward me. "Want a tattoo?"

I did. I held my arms out in front of me, insides of my wrists turned upward, but Alain grabbed me by the forearm and turned me toward the door.

"No time for that," he said quickly, and we headed back into the street.

Our next stop was a coffee shop, a shadowy place, carpeted in moth-eaten oriental rugs. Again Albert greeted the proprietor. The stocky, brown-haired man gave him a hug and handed him a menu. "Something for you, Albert," he said.

"And we have something for you," answered Albert and the two men knocked fists.

"And who is this?" asked the shopkeeper noticing me for the first time.

"This," said Alain, "is Lou Lou's lovely friend."

"Mmmm," said the man, handing something to Albert with a grin, adding, "You're supposed to smoke it here."

"Since when?" said Albert.

"Since never."

They laughed and we left.

"Bye-bye, Lou Lou's friend," said the man.

Alain was actually whistling as we walked home past ring after ring of canal. Bridges framed canal banks lined with bicycles and festooned with flowers. Skinny dormer-style windows beckoned at the top of narrow canal houses. Tight alleyways boasted murals of elaborate graffiti. Magical little doorways opened up onto inner courtyards with well-groomed rose beds and closely clipped lawns. I was tantalized by the city, ready almost to abandon my hosts, to follow this young girl on her bicycle, that old lady with her dog, but I didn't because we were heading *home*.

Home was a houseboat on the water, not far from Nieuwe Doelenstraat and the mouth of the River Amstel. At one time Amsterdam's outer limit, this was the old home of the Kloveniers Doelen and the city's famous "Nightwatch." The streets in the area were crammed with hotels and boutiques and tourists and noisy little cars, along with the ubiquitous bikes. But the houseboat was strangely quiet inside, a splintery brown and red cradle rocking on the much-trafficked waters of the canal.

I was lifted onto the deck by Albert, who handed me, just like a piece of luggage, over to Alain after he carefully handed over the black suitcase that Lou Lou had given me.

The houseboat smelled of licorice drops and hashish and developing chemicals and was sparsely furnished and crammed with art. In the main room, which held only a table and two rather worn chairs, photographs covered every surface. Matted enlargements of photographs leaned against the walls. Next to the stainless steel sink of the simple galley-style kitchen sat two short crystal glasses, a bottle of a licorice-flavored spirits called absinthe, and a decanter of some kind of red wine. On a clothesline that stretched the length of the kitchen was a long line of prints pinned next to each other like boxcars in a train. The next room was a bedroom. It had a big bed covered in a white tapestry cloth and a few odd antiques half-hidden from where I was standing. Albert and Alain disappeared into this room, shutting the door behind them.

I hardly noticed. I was still studying the pictures that hung from the clothesline in the kitchen. From these photos stared a bold, fashionably suited woman who, frame by frame and with no change in position, attained a greater and greater state of undress until she was finally nude. Then the process reversed itself, except that instead of clothes, tattoo after tattoo was added in the sequential frames. Large brown velvet moths settled upon each of her breasts. An orchid opened on one shoulder, a striped gecko displayed the inside of its mouth on the other. South Sea islands showed up on her belly and disappeared into the shaved split between her legs. A sea serpent slid down her thigh. Constellations unfurled on her right arm. On her left arm, winds chased clouds to the wrist. And so on. In the last picture, she was completely covered in tattoos, including her neck and her face. The tattoos were beautiful, like Japanese woodcuts full of waves and wildlife and fat-petalled flowers. The color in the photos was supernaturally vivid, and I felt myself responding to them with a dry mouth and an odd kind of thirst.

A horn bleated over the water through the window behind me, and I turned my attention again to the black and white prints that littered the room with the table.

On the table were stacks of pictures. These were studies of shadow: women naked behind the lace-like curtain of wrought-iron gates; dark and light-skinned women in Escher-like poses; women peering fearfully from behind the stark black verticals of prison bars. I flipped through image after image. There were studies of objects—everything from eggs to delicate flowers—bearing bar codes; of wraith-thin wrists marked with numbers; of license plates; of signs reflected in windows; of tattoo artists in action; of South Sea islanders, their bodies covered in complicated designs.

The photographs were extraordinary. They were full of conflict and contrast and profound sensuality. Page-turners, you'd call them. I found myself drawn to the next, then the next. Meanwhile Albert and

Alain were in the bedroom examining the contents of the suitcase. I was fascinated with the photographs. They were fascinated with it.

A mule is a beast of burden. Part ass, part horse (generally preferred in the jackass-mare combination), mules are bred for employment, and bred they must be because these hybrid creatures are sterile. They have the lovely, long ears and the delicate little feet of the ass and the strong, well-muscled body of the horse. But their special appeal lies in the way they take to the harness, a tendency attributable to the horse. However, unlike the horse, mules are enduring creatures. They handle hardship well and, like their wild ass ancestors, will stubbornly harbor their strength. Needless to say, these low-maintenance creatures are the darlings of work camps, mines, and military zones. They are, in fact, the beast of choice where requirements dictate that labor be both dependable and expendable. In smugglers' parlance, mules carry drugs—well, contraband of any kind, but in most cases drugs. For example, the suitcase that the stewardess had exchanged with me had heroine in it, shrink-wrapped to defy the dogs.[19] But the more significant and far more valuable item that I carried to Holland was a microchip tucked away, deep inside me. And I, whether I knew it or not, was a mule.

Alain walked out of the bedroom with a big smile. Albert was carrying a tote bag. "Look, Alain," he said, "I'll call you. I'll make the arrangements."

"Fine," said Alain. They were both in a very good mood.

"He's a fabulous photographer isn't he?" Albert said warmly. Then he gave Alain a quick slap on the ass.

When Albert left, Alain walked to the kitchen, poured a glass of absinthe and lit a pipe's worth of hashish. He looked up for a moment to the clothesline strung with photos, studying the succession of images, dissecting them with an artist's eye. "So, Erin," he said over his shoulder, "my sister likes you a lot. She says I should take care of you. Do you need taking care of?"

He turned from the photos and directed his gaze at me—the same studied gaze he'd used on his pictures. I could not bring myself to look away. He was examining me with a photographer's eye, camera eye, eye of the needle. He peered through my little black dress with his x-ray specs. Woman as still life, I did not move. He took a long, deep hit from the pipe and put it down. The weedy smell of hashish filled the room. Then slowly (slow-mo camera moving in for the close-up) he walked toward me, his eyes on my face, on my dress, on my bare legs. At the table he placed his drink in an empty space, carefully moving his precious prints out of harm's way. Then he leaned down and touched one of my legs, running his hand lightly over it: calf, knee, thigh.

"Muscular," he observed. "You're a dancer."

He pushed the black dress up over my hips, belly, and breasts and discovered it was all I had on.

"Hmmm," he said, "yes, I could see that." The man with the x-ray specs pulled my dress up over my head.

It must have been close to noon. Outside, on the canal banks, city noise—voices, autos and bicycles clattering over cobblestone streets—had escalated. Inside Alain's houseboat home the ambient din was reduced to warmish snuffles and murmurs. Sunlight flooded the rooms, bounced off white walls, bleaching black to ghost-gray. Alain had me pinned to the wall, his hands, like his eyes, roaming over every fold and curve of my body.

"Beautiful," he whispered, "compliant. I like that in a woman."

I was far more than compliant. His artist's hands moved over my flesh, and it was like striking a flint. He took off his shirt, stepped out of his jeans. He had a lean body, sinewy, but not thin. Somewhere deep within me a trigger was tripped. Maybe it was the way the houseboat rocked on the water. Maybe it was the smells of absinthe and licorice drops on his breath or red light district pheromones raging across canal after canal along with potato chip and mayonnaise smells and the pungent whiff of cat piss. More likely it was the cheese, the chocolate and the gin, the nakedness of the wolf man and the sweep of his hands. A switch had been flipped. Everything went autopilot.

You might imagine, as I would have if it had not happened to me, that a near-zombie girl would just stand there like a big blow-up doll. Not at all. I am a seemingly will-less creature, and let me tell you, it takes a great deal of will to resist sex. All living things are designed for it. It is their singular purpose. There was no doubt about this in my body. Horny as any bitch in heat, I was down to the basics. I was consumed with a slimy, single-celled reproductive certainty, swamped with a kind of glandular ecstasy. I couldn't fight it. I wanted to crawl up the wall. The world turned hot and juicy.

Imagine that you are eating a peach and it begins eating you back. That's how surprised Alain was when the laconic object of his attentions mounted a counter attack. I wanted to devour him, and I don't mean metaphorically. This is the point at which murder takes place— murder or self-immolation. This is the lust that kills. Remember the praying mantis, the black widow spider, crimes of passion and desire. But, something inside me—some ancient parasitic wisdom—prevented me from devouring him. It did not stop me from trying to swallow his tongue. The drooling thought "deliciousness" popped into my head, and my salivary glands sprang a leak.

Meanwhile, I had become a balloon. All my hormones adjusted their levels and discharged. I was enflamed and unstoppable. My breasts, which I have already explained, were plenty large, seemed to swell. My womb seemed to have opened up like an umbrella, the blood in it beating like a big Vodoun drum. I imagined my lips splitting, oozing blood; breasts spilling milk; innards raining spicy mucilage. I was caught in my own monsoon. I wanted more.

More, it seemed, wanted me, too. I could feel it making a case for itself between my legs at the Ark of the Grand Central Orifice. Taking a deep breath that collapsed our cheeks, I sprang, wrapping my legs around Alain's waist. Like a prizefighter caught by a hard right hook, he staggered and very nearly fell. To his athletic credit, he managed to retain his balance. Then we became a kind of carnival balancing act, a two-torsoed creature waddling into the bedroom where we turned and collapsed onto the bed, which, in turn, collapsed under our weight. Kabooooooom.

Now Alain was beneath me, his face under mine, his lips pink and tasty. I slipped into the saddle, slid onto that brilliantly designed, perfectly sculpted horn. What a ride we had then, my pony and I. Alain was watching me with a mixture of terror and desire. He could no more stop than a male mantis can shake its amorous mate. I was a pole dancer sliding up and down, a jillaroo bouncing along in the outback, a frigate ship tossed on the Cape of Good Horn. Straddling him, both hands on his chest, I rode him into the sea. I was in some kind of organic nirvana. Mandalas and kaleidoscopes were opening up like flowers deep inside me. Waves of purple and pale chartreuse, plumes of iris and swamp grass scrolled past my upturned eyes. Lust flashed giddy tattoos all over my flesh in a rose-red flush. I couldn't actually hear it, but I was wailing like a cat in heat, my caterwauling sailing up and out the window, turning heads all along the canal. The big dopamine hit mushroomed up and into my brain. "Oh, oh, oooooh," I crooned as the dike burst and the waters of the Isslemeer came in, flooding Amsterdam.

I think it was good for him, too. He lay still for a moment, his face in a grimace. "God," he said gazing up at me in a kind of adulation. "God, that was good. What exactly are you on?" he wondered aloud and put his hand over his eyes.

I sat looking down on him, my body suffused by a delirious glow. A silky endorphin parachute was carrying me back to the bed. I was paralyzed and couldn't move. Not unusual for me, but I had also found peace and a strange form of union. In Alain, I'd touched some lost part of myself. I was transformed forever. That's how I became Alain's slave.

Alain, on the other hand, bounced up out of bed. Dressed in the only thing that mattered at this point—his watch. He consulted it for direction.

"Ach," he exclaimed, exploding into action. "Time to go. We'll be late."

Pulling me out of the bed he paused for only a moment to give me a lingering kiss. "I like you," he said. "You're different." Then he slapped my ass and herded me into a tight little washroom where we shared the coffin-sized shower. Before we left the houseboat, he got us both dressed, slicked back my hair and painted a number on my forehead.

"Sit there, just like that," he said, positioning me in front of a mirror. Then he stepped back and snapped a picture. This is the only thing that I have left of Alain: this picture with the grim woman with a number on her forehead, looking into a mirror; the photographer behind her, the camera hiding his face.

I saw the grins and furtive glances in our direction as we stepped from the houseboat.

"How are the cats, Alain?" asked an old neighbor, raising a brow.

"Grrrr," Alain growled back playfully, hurrying us along.

Our destination, he informed me, was the nearby restaurant and café: In de Waag.

"This," said Alain, playing tour guide again as we approached the hulking brown edifice—he was very proud of his city—"is an important historical building. It was built in 1480, or thereabouts, as the city gate. It's the oldest secular building in Amsterdam.[20]

"You see that octagonal turret?" he whispered, leaning provocatively toward me and indicating a corner tower. "That was an anatomical theater. The Surgeons Guild built it in 1691. It housed northern Europe's very first public dissections. You know that painting, *The Anatomical Lesson of Professor Tulp*? Rembrandt painted it here. He lived nearby. Visiting the theater was one of his favorite pastimes. Have you seen it? No? Well, I will take you to see it one day." He added this last remark, absently, for he already had spotted his contact.

Marie sat at one of the Internet stations just inside the door, her long blond hair hanging on either side of her face like lank curtains, her small, monkey ears poking through. She was absorbed in her e-mail. Alain put a hand on her shoulder.

"Marie?"

She looked up and blinked, the real world pouring into the virtual.

"Oh," said Marie and smiled warmly, her small nose wrinkling and rearranging the freckles on her face. Then she saw me and recoiled. "Uh," she exhaled as though stunned. "And who is this?" she demanded in Dutch. I noticed that she was looking at the number that Alain had written upon my forehead.

"Number 421," said Alain with a smile. "Erin, I'd like you to meet Marie."

At this point, Marie rose from her spot at the line of computers. I should say unfolded—she was tall and thin and she wore platform shoes that added another four or five inches to her nearly six-foot height. Obviously one of Alain's models; number 420, I assumed.

"Ummm," she said slowly. "Come let's play a game."

"No time," said Alain.

"Please, please," begged Marie. "There are three of us. Three is the perfect number. Please, Alain. Exquisite Corpse.[21] You never play anymore."

Alain looked besieged. "She's addicted," he laughed. "Not this time, Marie, we must get down to business."

Marie looked down at the floor, then she glanced at me with disdain and wrinkled her nose again in her rabbit-like manner. "Oh, alright," she sighed, folding herself back into her chair. "I found it online, you know."

"What?"

"Exquisite Corpse."

"Marie."

"OK. OK." She looked up at Alain and smiled. "How is Lou Lou?"

"Fine."

"Your 'little sister' Lou Lou should be careful. She hangs out with too many criminals."

"And you don't?"

"Well, it's different for me." Marie tossed her long hair. "I am protected. I have some *very* powerful friends." She had one eye on the screen. "So, have a seat and we'll talk. But what about her? Can she make herself useful? Get some coffee?"

I was not really paying much attention because something, a darting figure silhouetted for a moment in the sunlit café entrance, had caught my eye: a boy—he looked fifteen or sixteen—small, yellow-haired. He beckoned to me, or seemed to. I took a few steps toward him.

"Going somewhere?" asked Alain.

"We have our business," reminded Marie.

"Yes, that's right. Go on, Erin. Marie and I have a few very pleasant exchanges. I will find you when we are finished."

Dismissed like a dog, but I barely heard him. I was already headed toward the door.

My eyes weren't quite ready for the change in light. The café light was soft and creamy. Outside the sunlight was brittle and hard. It crashed into objects and exploded off surfaces. The figure was haloed in and disguised by this brilliance. He was poised at the stairwell, expectantly, energy gathered for an ascent, but he hung back, not yet committed to the climb, waiting, it seemed, on me.

Naturally, I followed, but slowly, dallying on the stairwell, reluctantly entering the little brown door at the top.

He was waiting for me just inside. Very short, this Dutch boy, and I saw now, bedraggled. Oily brown locks streaked through his straw-colored, shoulder length hair.

"Well, here we are," he laughed from a pair of very dark, swollen lips. He was strangely bloated. The length of his thin arms, revealed by the short sleeves of a royal-blue T-shirt, were tracked with needle marks that had turned black. They looked like long tangles of blackberries.

"I'm sorry," he apologized, "I just couldn't resist."

That's all he needed to say. I already knew who he was.

THE ANATOMY LESSON

The boy was looking at me with total lust.

I, in turn, studied him in sheer horror. It had been little more than twenty-four hours since I'd seen him in Tokyo.

"Why so surprised?" he asked. "I got you the ride out. Why wouldn't I follow you here? You should know that clean getaways are a myth."

I backed toward the door, turned. I wanted to get back to Alain.

"Oh, no you don't," he rasped, grabbing my wrist to stop me. His grip was fierce, his hand stringy and strong, more like a talon really. "Sit down," he insisted shoving me into a chair. "I have something to say to you and this time I'm going to make sure that you listen." With that he reached out to where the door stood ajar, slammed it shut, then let go of my wrist. He walked back to the door and locked it.

"At last, we're alone," he sighed. "And here, in the most appropriate of places. Do you know what this room is?"

Of course I knew. We were in the octagonal tower that Alain had so carefully pointed out just a short while ago when we arrived at the restaurant. I didn't move.

"This is an anatomical theater, the first in northern Europe," announced Clément—for that's who the Dutch boy really was—being unwittingly redundant. "It is here that modern man rigorously explored his own composition, read the entrails, probed the mysteries of the human body. Doctors, artists, madmen, voyeurs, omphaloskeptics of every ilk—they all came here for a peek into the old inner sanctum. Knowledge seekers, hah." He spat. "Just a bunch of rubberneckers gawking at an accident. Nothing lofty about that, is there? The crème de la crème of the scientific world, the free thinkers, the wise men, and what do you think they found? A secret? A soul? No. They found . . . they found . . . cadavers. The closet that spirit hangs in. No more, no less. A windfall of flesh and blood and guts and brains." He laughed, and the laughter rang up through the octagonal room clattering against the walls like the clapper of a bell.

"So, here you are, then," he said regaining his aplomb. "Dead bodies. Dead bodies, dead bodies, dead bodies—all earthly roads lead to the corpse," he muttered, lost in his own bitter musing. Then he caught himself again, coughed, mumbled an apology—"sorry, sorry"—took a deep breath and shifted emotional gears.

"Well, things are hot in Tokyo," he said. "Here a yakuza, there a yakuza, everywhere a yakuza. Your flight has caused quite a tempest. Especially now that everyone knows that you aren't actually dead. Damn that intern. How was I to sneak you out of the hospital after he took over like that? And then you run off . . . oh, of all the stupidity. And after that you had to make such a spectacle of yourself. I mean, really, did you have to go right to the club? After that every yakuza in town knew you were alive.

"And then that business with Hiroshi—that was such a mess. Well, yes, I must admit the Koan part was my fault. I just couldn't stop myself. You know Hiroshi was so obsessed with that lover of his. What romance! It was a perfect set-up, and I did so much want to impress you, Erin. As an artist, I mean. Unfortunately it ended badly, but, well . . . so, here I am, you see." He took a little bow. "Once again here to protect you."

I sat, staring up at him, my mouth open.

"What? What? You are judging me, aren't you? How dare *you* judge *me*? Oh, right, just because I'm a low-life, corpse-inhabiting ghoul. Well, at least I have scruples. Yes, I am a very moral creature. For instance, what do I think of Alain? I think he's a criminal, drug-dealing, self-serving bastard. You think he's an artist. I am an artist, too, you know. Take Koan's curtain call. Well choreographed, *neh*? Take my amazing entrances and exits, my relentless curtain calls. I am so much more than your run-of-the-mill ghoul. I am a death artist. Not that I really ever kill anyone. I can't. That's against the ghoul rules, and if anyone bothered to pay any attention they'd see that I don't do murders. I might engineer them, but I never do the killing. No, I give life where it has been taken away. You, for example, you are supposed to be dead. Ryu was supposed to kill you that night in the love hotel. Then your corpse was supposed to be transported back to the U.S., where your father would claim it and the chip . . . before the rest of the Consortium got their hands on it. That's our little secret agreement. It's his chip, after all. You see, no one wants a live you; they want a dead you. But you didn't die. Do you know why? Me. Yes, I am the one who saved you. That's what I learned in Haiti from that old bokor. From Arnotine I learned the secret of raising the dead. I learned about Vodou and sociétés and the *Gros Bon Ange* and the *Ti Bon Ange*. I learned that the *Ti Bon Ange* is the part of the soul that creates character and willpower and personality and that you can demolish this part of the soul, separate it from the *Gros Bon Ange*, and a creature will live, but just barely. Did you know humans have two souls? Well, maybe *you* don't even have one now. That's because of me. I've been obsessed with you ever since I first saw you long ago. And you saw me once, in a garden. Surely you remember. We go back a long way, you and I. Your father was only interested in your mother's money. And he found a way to get it. But it's never been about that for me. For me it was about Lizette—I warned her, but she wouldn't listen. Now it is about you. I want to possess you, Erin."

He paused significantly.

"You know, I've never had anyone of my own," he sniffed. "Not a living, breathing body, just dead ones. I am so damn tired of cadavers. I am sick to death of death! I want to wallow in life for a change. That's why I made a little trip to see old Arnotine. Now there was a bokor for you. He was my instructor in Haiti and my dream was within my grasp. But I've always been a terrible student. Ghouls generally are. I get an "F" in zombification. "F" for fucked up. That's what happened. I fucked up. And now you are not mine or yours or anyone's, except maybe that stupid, drug-smuggling photographer's. But that is not going to last."

I was not really listening to Clément's rant. I had stopped when he mentioned my father. Clément said it was all about my mother's money. Christian controlled her entire estate, an estate that had been left to me, in trust. But when I came of age . . .

"By the way, Haiti is not a bad place. Not for a ghoul, I mean. Ryu hated it, but then he's Japanese. It is paradise for a ghoul. Definitely one of the hot spots. If you had an infrared map that picked up chaos, certain places would glow bright red—lots of death. And I have a kind of radar for death. Call it a survival instinct. There are places, for example, that are glowing bright red as the forests die. But, the most significant hot spots are the ones where people are killing one another. And, oh boy, there are plenty of those.

"But enough about Haiti and hot spots and world travel in

general, let's talk about us, shall we? We have so much in common. Did you know that? You are a young American girl, recently zombied, or nearly. I am an international ghoul, a death-eating machine and the ultimate bon vivant. I've been everywhere, been everyone. Did you know I was Vincent Van Gogh for a while? Oh, there was a sorry character—so conflicted. I was Egon Schiele, too, for a time—after the illness, of course. I've always been fond of artists: high mortality rate, you see. Vienna, in those days was a blast, a very hot-pink little city on a continent that would turn poker-red. I have so much to tell you, Erin."

He was incredible to watch: petite, skeletal, and animated, almost jumping out of his skin, happy as a kid on heroin rushing down a climactic corridor. Was he actually high?

"So, you see, I, too, am an artist. You could say that I freelance. I once worked for Christian. Today I work for the yakuza. They had something I want, and now I have something they want. Well, I have everything actually, or almost everything. It's really all about an exchange—everything is about an exchange—although they don't really know quite what the exchange is. They think it's about money— money in exchange for a chip that follows the movement of money through dirty hands and back to the bloated profits of apparently (but not really) unrelated entities. It's not; it's about *souls*, one soul in particular.

"However, you are not being compliant and that isn't part of my plan. My plan revolves around you—the woman they wanted to murder. Miura killed Carlyle. Ryu killed Miura, Clément, and the cab driver, and he tried to kill you. Arnotine killed the fat woman. Ronan killed Arnotine. Disease killed Takashita and Koan. Fear killed Nakamura. As for me, I am innocent. Innocent.

"You called it, of course. I am a ghoul, a supernatural slave, a peon.

I find form in humanity. Maybe I am a despicable parasite, but I am a parasite with a purpose, a parasite linked forever to mankind.

"Mankind: Let me tell you something about manfuckingkind. Mankind is fucked and fucking perpetually. Humans get a nice good look at the light and what do they do? They aim for darkness, for everything guaranteed to make them feel really bad. Drugs. Murder. War. Now, I ask you, is that stupidity or evil?

"Well, it's stupidity. Mankind is the stupidest creature ever to have any awareness of the supernatural realm. By that I mean of the possibilities. And what are the possibilities? Well, they are endless and extreme. Look at you. You can't run. You basically can't, you shouldn't, be able to initiate a thing. And me? I am will. Pure will. Polar opposites? Perhaps. But I think we could make quite a team. You are Beatrice to my Dante. We are yin and yang, Gable and Lombard, Tracy and Hepburn, up and down. Well, you see what I mean. We were made for each other, Baby, don't you think?"

I didn't think. Every nerve, every muscle, every part of my body was recoiling. He had almost succeeded in rubbing me out or reducing me to no more than a spiritless vessel. So what if he wasn't a murderer. He had been in cahoots with my father, the extent of whose evil intent I was only beginning to grasp, though it did seem to me that the ghoul, with these plots within plots, was actually trying to ruin him. What Clément stood for was death and darkness and the end of all things. He was repellent. I needed Alain.

"So, you know they are all after you now. Ryu will have to fix things. But suppose I prevent it. Suppose I decide to keep you out of their hands. What can they do to me? Keep me away from a body? If the one I've inhabited deconstructs without a replacement, I'm lost to this world. Doomed to circle aimlessly like so many of my silly brethren. You have no concept of how frustrating it is to exist merely as idea; but thus far, no doing. Why? 'Cause those yakuza are always up to their armpits in dead bodies, which makes it hard to keep this cat from the canaries. So, basically, I do what I please. Meanwhile, in the world around us, they bask in destruction. Why?

"Stupid, isn't it? Any man, any woman, who opts for evil is an idiot. I should know. Evil knows itself and doesn't appreciate not being appreciated for how bad it is. But no one has explained to me yet, how bad *good* is. It must be dreadful, eh? Why else would people run from it? Is good really so horrible? I can't say. I haven't tried it. But if I were to give it a face, it would be yours."

While he was talking, he circled behind me, leaning over my shoulder, his cold lips close to my ear. He grabbed my wrist again. I got out of the chair and tried to twist away.

"Come on, Erin," he wheedled, "it would be you and me together. Ricky and Lucy, Taylor and Burton, Bogart and Bacall. We could be such a team."

A team. Right. There was a pretty picture: ghoul and zombie, dead and undead. Certainly not a dream I found attractive. He must have read my mind. There was another sudden shift in his mood. He tightened his hold on my wrist.

"So, maybe I should kill you," he said sourly and reaching behind one of the chairs, he pulled out the kind of knife that you'd use to skin a mule. "And as long as we're breaking the rules, maybe I'll do it, become a killer ghoul—a renegade—like a damned, disobedient zombie. Another abomination. A fuck-up. One I should eliminate. I could do it. Do you know what happens when we break the rules? All hell breaks loose. Tyranny has permission to flourish. And some of us just love that.

"They're smuggling, you know, those new 'friends' of yours. But you have something that makes them look like girl scouts peddling cookies. The secret you carry will change history. Your father thinks he understands power. And the others—all vying for control—they all want to play God. But they haven't a proper résumé. Who would hire a human for that job? Let's talk about qualifications. If anyone has them, it's one of the djinn or, more specifically, me."

His mood seemed to be changing once more. He'd run out of steam. He looked down at the knife and studied it for a long time, as if suddenly aware of its features. It was around a foot long and the blade, which was wide, flat and curved at one end, was also terribly sharp.

"Go," he said suddenly. "Get out of here before I do what they want. Yes, I'm letting you go, you stupid zombie girl. Oh, don't think of this as affection. Think of it as entertainment. You are a little game that I have invented and with which I'm altogether intrigued. Where would I be without you?"

He unlocked the door. I took my chance and ran from the room. He didn't rush to stop me. He was preoccupied. He had one claw-like hand curled over the threshold and he was cutting off his fingers, one after another. "Oh," he said, as the knife came down on each digit in an almost mechanical fashion, removing the pinky, then the ring finger, then the middle finger, then the index, and finally the thumb. "Oh, the yakuza are going to be angry. I've been a bad boy. I've been a bad, bad boy."

SOMETHING TO RAVE ABOUT

Why must people stare? You'd think they'd never seen a five-foot-seven, one hundred and twenty-pound zombie with a number written in black ink on her forehead before. When I found my way back down the stairs and into In de Waag to search for Alain, he seemed to have vanished. I scanned the crowd: milky northern European faces shooting stares, subtle and otherwise, their eyes trying to digest me. I felt like dead meat. This induced an involuntary hiss. I closed my eyes to find the comfort of darkness, a little privacy, and with them closed navigated the room by sense of smell. Smell: It is a wonderful way to avoid eye contact. Stupidly, I felt invisible. Guided by my nose, my ears, the other senses, I almost made it to the door. I was about to exit and plunge into the cesspool of scent that circulated outside when I felt a hand on my arm—a hand with all of its fingers.

"Now, Erin, where do you think you are going?"

How can a touch undo you? The touch ran through my arm like an electric current, as if a thousand slippery little electric eels were slithering quickly through the neural pathways of my body straight through my heart up into my head and then down between my legs to another part of my anatomy, which vibrated like the buzzer on a front door.

"Business finished. Marie is gone."

Alain spun me toward him, his hand sliding possessively down my back.

I was so relieved I wanted to collapse. I let my body go limp and he, with the grace and sensitivity of a dancer and a lover, felt the sudden change, caught me on the drop and held me up.

"What is wrong with you?" he demanded, guiding me outside.

What could I say? Weak knees? Exhaustion? A sickness and disgust, not unlike my first experiences in the morgue, that filled me with horror and threatened to drag me down? Clément, with the noxious stink of death that always surrounded him, had a way of bringing this up in a putrid wave of nausea. But Alain had a way of keeping it at bay. What I felt for Alain, what I experienced when he touched me, seemed to dispel the corruption—a corruption that I was beginning to equate with ideas. His touch took me away to a place that was vital and purely and blessedly physical. I opened my eyes. Alain was at my side, his arm stretched around my back and hooked up under my rib, supporting me. The sun was retreating, the last rivulets of its light sluicing down the narrow shanks of the canal houses, running down into the gutters, splattering on the cobbles, disappearing into the earth. Guard change. The square emptied of the daylight crowd, waiting for the night shift to take its place.

"Late, hmmm?" said Alain. "And where have you been? No matter. We have an invitation, a nice one, from one of Marie's friends."

This did not impress me. Clément was in Amsterdam. Everything would go wrong. I had a sense of imminent disaster.

But Alain was oblivious to this. He had made his delivery. I saw the flash of plenty of cash in his camera bag and knew that his trade had been made. He was ready to celebrate.

"Let's go to this party, shall we?" he said and ushered me out of the square.

We walked along the canals as the day shrank from view. Night oozed in through the city's nooks and crannies, seeped into and over the skinny streets and bridges, crawled up the tall flanks of the buildings, poured ink into the Amstel. Alain stopped at the houseboat to stash the payment. Back aboard the sweet cradle of safety, I fell upon the bed and stared up at the wooden ceiling overhead. I threw a forearm up over my eyes to hide them, to hide myself, although I knew there was really no way to hide. I had traveled thousands of miles and yet he'd found me. In fact, I was probably exactly where he'd expected me to be. I was a pawn in Clément's game, a pawn from which the will had been carefully excised. I'd thought I was a prisoner in a strange girl's body, but I was really the prison and the girl, Erin, the prisoner. What I was, whatever I was, was an abomination, a horror's horror, the botched experiment of an outcast. Such an outcast! Willful, self-absorbed, bloated with ardor—my polar opposite, Clément repulsed me with an indomitable force.

Did you know people have two souls? Well, maybe you don't even have one. That's what he'd said. *I want to possess you, Erin.*

I moaned. Alain walked over to the bed, leaned over me. I did not see where he had sequestered the money.

"You are going out."

I turned my head away.

"Yes, you are, strange girl."

Who was he talking to? The body or the creature that occupied it? The big-breasted girl or the diminishing sentience that desired nothing more than to merge completely with him?

"Up, Erin," he commanded, hands pushing back my thick hair, mouth closing over mine. Resuscitation. My arms clamped around him. He untangled himself.

"Later," he laughed. "We'll do this later, OK?"

I shook my head, no, no, no, no.

"I promise. I promise," he whispered, breathing his reassurances into my mouth and ears. Then he pulled me up and pushed me toward the door and into the cool Amsterdam night.

The restaurant was only a short distance away, on Spuistraat, the entrance tucked in between two rows of brick seventeenth-century buildings. It was gloomy inside and dark. I was shivering when we arrived. A dreamy-looking blonde girl wearing harem pants and a tight, rib-baring bodice greeted us at the foot of a shadowy staircase. Her nose and her brows were pierced. She had a jewel shimmering in her navel and another on her forehead in between her pale brows.

"Bindi?" she asked proffering a glass bowl full of what looked like glittering teardrops. They were the tiny third eyes that Indian women wear on their foreheads. She gazed for a while at my forehead, seeming to study the numbers written on it, blinked, and turned to Alain.

"How about you?" she said in Dutch. "Here is a nice one." She fished out a teardrop that glittered like a fire opal. I thought of the fish that Alain had drawn with the teardrop in its eye, his part of the exquisite corpse, and I wanted to warn him—*Don't put it on*—but the girl had already placed it in the middle of his forehead, right between his dark brows.

"There, now we can find you in the dark," she said, giving him a kiss on the cheek and leading us to the stairs.

We climbed. The staircase was steep and cramped and vibrated with the muffled beat of music on the floors above. The rhythm was hard and fast like a running man's heart. Light swung out onto the stairwell and retreated. It felt like we were ascending in a giant lung, the light inhaling and exhaling.

The old houses of Amsterdam were built with economics in mind. That is why they are tall and thin. Taxes were charged for the street space, so homes were built narrow and deep. The restaurant we'd entered was situated in a nest of five of these buildings and the staircase allowed access to a warren of gloomy wood-paneled, low-beamed rooms. In the first of these rooms a host of exotically attired men and women milled about amid antique chairs and white-clothed tables set with elaborate towers of food. Music rained down on them from speakers sequestered in the beams and this, together with their chatter, created a deep, panting din. There were makeshift altars everywhere, jostled up against northern European finery, upon which little statues of various gods—Shivas and Kalis and Buddhas and Ganeshas and Kuan Yins and Christs—frolicked, prayed, and writhed in perpetual pleasure and pain. The altars were decorated with candles and flowers and fruit and mirrors and jewelry and bits of colored silk. Albert was in this room.

"Alain," he called, no doubt spotting Alain's opaline bindi even as we stood shrouded in the gloom of the stairwell. "Marie said she'd invited you. Come here. Join us. There's someone I want you to meet."

He turned and said something to the tall, gray-haired man standing next to him. The man looked toward us and smiled widely, his white teeth flashing between magenta lips that stretched across the lower half of his face like a long bow. No, not Clément, but I still felt my flesh crawl. Clément didn't have to be there. And he didn't have to make an appearance. I could feel his work all around us.

We crossed the irregular threshold that separated the stairwell from the room. The blonde girl, leaving us there, evaporated into the crowd. I hated Albert, and I could have strangled him right there and then. He was a parasite, a hanger-on, a pimp. What did Alain see in person like him?

The crowd was a one-celled animal pushing and pressing us toward him. "Alain," he exclaimed when it burped us into his vicinity, "here is someone who wants very much to meet you. His name is Gilbert."

"Enchanted," said Gilbert in French, looking searchingly at Alain while extending a limp hand. "And this is your friend?" he asked nodding toward me.

"That's Erin," Albert interjected with distaste.

"Erin," repeated Gilbert. He stepped toward me, put his hand in my hair. "Erin." He rolled my name around in his mouth as if tasting it and looped a lock of my hair around his hand. I felt as though I had met him before, under unpleasant circumstances. Gilbert was suavely handsome. Unlike the other revelers, he was conservatively dressed in a charcoal gray suit, though his tie was a nearly neon red. He did seem vaguely familiar. I didn't know then, that this was the impression he gave to everyone who met him. This was part of his art.

Another girl in a harem-style outfit approached us. This one held a candy dish piled high with small packages and pills.

"Cigars? Cigarettes?" she asked coyly and laughed. Someone bumped up against my arm. I felt a long stab of pain and tried to jump away, but Gilbert held me by the hair, his hand close to my scalp.

"Erin," he said again, this time like a sigh, a shudder—the way a train sighs when it pulls into the station. The name hissed its way into my mind and uncoiled and whatever had been in the needle crawled up the veins in my arm. Fast. It worked fast. With it came a kaleidoscope of images: A Japanese man—Ryu—laughing; Nakamura-san fondling an ebony fetish; Koan performing his dance of death; Lou Lou petting a wildly purring Shipu. It was oddly relaxing, mesmerizing.

I felt quieted and adrift. It had all happened so quickly, magically. A poke and voilà—Gilbert, with his potions and poisons, was a master of diversion.

He turned his attention back to Alain. "We have a mutual friend," said Gilbert.

"Marie?" asked Alain.

"No, someone else."

"That's funny," said Alain. "I wonder who it could be?"

I didn't hear any more of the conversation. Someone came up and asked if I wanted to dance—a large woman. She took my hand and guided me through the crowd. Then, we were in another room, this one exploding with sound and bodies. The music and the light and the bodies were pulsing and I watched as the room expanded and contracted and changed; it took on a new look. It was ragged and dirty, the walls made of corrugated tin. The big woman had disappeared. The other dancers had also disappeared. There was only me in the room, me and a snow-white chicken, a snow-white chicken and a talking head, the head of a dolorous black man suspended in mid air. The head was speaking to me in Creole. It was saying something that I couldn't understand. Like a head on a TV set, it droned on and on. And behind it and above it—in fact, all over the room—a newsreel played.

In the newsreel, black people ran. They ran through the street, some all by themselves, some holding hands, others with babies in their arms. Chickens scattered at their feet. An army of soldiers on horseback gave chase. The head just kept right on talking. It was saying something very important, but I couldn't understand a word. Then, I heard the name, *Erin*, whispered, and finally the head said in profoundly accented English, "Watch out for heem."

At that point a large woman in an orange skirt entered the room.

Her feet were covered with rags of the same color. She stepped onto the dance floor and started to whirl. I felt very dizzy; I closed my eyes. Then I was back in the original room, only the cast of characters had changed. So had the music, but I didn't notice this at first. My head was pounding to the hard techno beat. I felt something trickling out of my nose. I licked my top lip, tasted blood. The music had slowed to a funereal pace and the people around me swayed listlessly to it. A roomful of zombies, no place for me; I fled, climbed the stairs which dead-ended in another dark-paneled chamber. More antique chairs, white-clothed tables set with crystal and silver—in this room the far wall held rows of wooden casks.

A small group of guests was gathered around them, stiff as mannequins, while a fervent, tuxedo-clad fellow tapped wine from a cask, held his ruby glass to the light, sipped the wine, swished it around in his mouth, spat the wine out and tossed the rest of the wine in his glass on the floor before proceeding to the next cask and the next. The crowd nodded politely every time he spat and threw out the wine. He was on his fifth or sixth glass when he looked up from his work and saw me. His response was quick and electric and crackled across the room. He threw back his head, nostrils flaring, pursed his lips, and frowned. Like the dominant beast in a tightly knit pack, he was ready to give the alarm. The other members of his group turned from him at that point and fixed their stares upon me. I was pinned by fourteen pair of menacing eyes. It was clear that they deemed me an intruder and did not wish me well. On my side of the room, a bright light radiated from what I could smell was the kitchen. Making no sudden move, with my eyes on the group, I inched my way toward that door.

In the kitchen two tall women with red hair stood at an enormous industrial stove, stirring soup. They looked like twins. Both wore short black cocktail dresses, chef's toques, and threateningly pointed, six-inch stiletto heels that made them appear taller still. The chef's toques were stiffly starched columns topped with a poof that made them look like they had their red heads up in their respective clouds.

The cook sat at the table, pale as a ghost, his arm out in front of him as if he were giving blood.

"He's tired," said one of the twins as she stirred her soup.

"Yes, yes," laughed the other.

Suddenly it was clear to me: the wine casks, the pale cook, the twins.

"You are all vampires," I said.

"Really, no, I am not a vampire. I am Trekka," said one of the women.

"Yes, ha, ha, ha," laughed the other. "Have a drink. Have some borscht." She pulled a large spoon, full, from the pot. The spoon dripped a hairy mixture of beets and red cabbage.

"Oh, Greta, you have ruined it. You know now I will have to pull the cabbage out of my teeth."

"Critic, then you get no soup, you will have to subsist on wine." Greta winked at me and went back to stirring the soup.

The cook at the table groaned and shook his head.

"Oh, darling, you are exhausted," said one of the twins. "Here have some of this soup that you helped us to make. It's delicious." She walked over to him and spooned the red mixture into his mouth.

To say that he found it energizing would be a gross understatement. The man's eyes opened wide as if he'd been shocked. His hair stood on end and he hopped up and began waving his arms and yelling in high-pitched and unintelligible Dutch.

"Shhh, shhh, quiet darling," said Greta, wrestling him into a headlock. "You'll be fine in a minute. Calm down." She kissed him on the top of his head. Then she looked up at me and smiled. She did indeed have red cabbage stuck between her sharp little teeth. "They always react this way at first. Then they like it. Such an energy burst."

The man continued to struggle, but Greta, the muscles on her wiry arms bulging, had him completely under control. She dragged him over to the stove and shoveled another ladleful of the soup into his mouth. The man spasmed again, but Greta held him tight.

"This will go on for some time," explained Trekka while Greta continued to force the borscht into the man. "Then he will rest. Are you hungry? Do you want some of our soup? Or are you just a voyeur?"

I was hungry, but I didn't want any of their bloody borscht. I backed my way from the threshold.

"Leave the girls alone."

It was Gilbert. He'd found me, and his tone was thick with malice. Then he smiled, his elastic mouth stretching into another ominous bow-like grin.

"They are just playing."

Once again he wound his hand in my hair and he pulled me to him, very close, his wide lips spreading before my eyes, his teeth glistening like a row of tiny white lights. He had removed his suit jacket, loosened his red tie. I could hear the music pounding a few rooms away. I could feel the tempestuous whoosh-whoosh of his heart.

"Ah, Erin, you know about something I want. But you won't talk, will you? I can see that. You listen. How unusual to find a woman who actually listens. It makes me wonder what kind of woman you are. Not a real woman surely. Something else?"

The hand not in my hair moved to my throat, lingered there tapping lightly as his other hand pulled back my head. The wild tattoo of his heartbeat quickened. "I can have anything that I want," he gloated.

Of course he could. He was a vampire, too.

"A vampire, perhaps," he said reading my mind, "but that title is purely metaphorical. I am a banker, a venture capitalist, and a commercial success. I create nothing. I live off the productivity of others. I accept their money, their hopes and their dreams. I invest. I harvest. I suppose in that way I'm a vampire. We are all vampires at root, aren't we? Isn't that why the concept is so enticing? Show me someone, who doesn't eat, who doesn't feast on the living? My crime, if there is one, is in owning up to it.

"Are you listening, Erin? Good. Listen well. I have received a phone call and that is why you and your partner are here. It seems something that I deeply desire is very close at hand, some information, something well worth the investment. Do you know what it is? Of course you don't. I was told you know nothing about it. You thought you were simply carrying drugs. But your partner, Alain, he knows, doesn't he?"

Now my heart was racing. I could feel it rising in tempo, matching his, beat for beat. This was sounding complicated, arcane. There was a hellish signature in it.

"What if I told you that a nest of hypocrites was about to be unmasked, or could be, if certain facts were revealed—facts that implicate them in a greedy plan more destructive and diabolical than any invented devil could devise? What do you suppose such creatures would pay to have that information suppressed? We are in the midst of an interesting moment in history, a moment not unlike the old eras of terror. All rules are about to be broken and new ones made. Walls will come down. The vast plain of possibility will unfurl before us. It is mind and soul-boggling," he said, "and we are in the vanguard of that change." His voice had softened, become something akin to a purr. He drew a finger the length of my windpipe; then he tightened his grip on my hair. "You have a powerful patron—one who precedes both of us—and he insists that I leave you unbroken," he mused and cocked his ear to the music. "Ah, an evening raga, I think—an exquisite evocation of

night." The music, which had softened, laced its way through the restaurant's rooms with soporific results. Gilbert's heart rate had slowed,
was quiet and deep and powerful.

"In the end," he continued, "It all comes down to the truth. Such
a nebulous thing, the truth, easy to twist; some will do anything to
suppress it. And that is where I come in. You see there is a record that
implicates certain men who seem above reproach. A record stored in a
microchip. You did not know it was quite so important, did you?

"It has been sold and is out for delivery. That is where I come in.
I'm here to intercept it. The forwarding agent, your patron, is double-
crossing his blackmailing fellows. He doesn't want much in return: a
paltry sum and . . . you. But now he says he's lost track of the chip. But
he's given us someone who knows: the photographer fellow, Alain. He
says we just need to get him to talk."

Forwarding agent, blackmail, patron, Alain—it was all horribly
clear. If this was about the microchip, it was certainly nothing Alain
could know anything about. This was just another play in Clément's
stupid game, but to what end? What was really at stake?

"What's at stake?" asked Gilbert, surprised, as he meddled around
in my thoughts. "For us, the very nature of reality is at stake, the safety
of the world, the illusion around which everything else revolves. The
truth will blow the lid off the concept of good men and bad. And if
we get beyond that, there is no fact, no fiction. No truth or lies. Then
every creature consigned to the world of imagination—demon, vampire, angel, djinn—can truly exist—in this one. We will step from the
pages of books, from the recesses of the mind, and onto the stage of
life. It is revolutionary. And we—my dear friends and I—are the first
creatures of the new revolution."

Gilbert's dark eyes turned nocturnal, his black pupils slitting like
a cat's. Still holding my hair fast in one fist, he pulled at my arm. Very

quickly, expertly, he stabbed a needle into a vein. Then that stretchy mouth of his opened onto my neck, formed a rubber-tight seal, and he bit me.

The next seconds, minutes, hours, days melt away. There is only this dream:

I am in a dark place. The light comes from one source only: a small window at the top of a wall. There is a dissonant music playing somewhere. Gongs and symbols and pings and plinks, and there are shadows on the walls. The shadows have human forms. They are dancing and interacting. The dance turns into a fight. Many fights. The shadows are dancing and fighting. I am in the middle of this. I am lying down. There is a man bent over me. He pushes a long tool down my throat and pulls something out. He holds it up to the light. I think for a minute, *oh, oh, that is what a soul looks like.* He holds it up and it flashes like a gem. The shadows disappear. Then I am walking in a quiet garden, and I am alone. There is a doctor there, too. And he looks like Alain. I want to touch him. If I can just reach out . . . Then, he changes. He turns chalky gray, then white. Only his lips are vivid. They are red. My nose is running. I taste blood. Then the shadowy images return and start dancing again. Wildly. And I feel someone clawing at me, pushing me away. It is Gilbert. He pushes me away, choking and gasping for air. "Ach, horrible, what are you?" He spits blood. "You've made me sick."

I feel light-headed, dizzy. Without his support, I tumble to the floor and lie there looking up at the ceiling, the broken end of a needle stuck in my arm. Gilbert is still coughing and spitting up blood. That is the last I see of him. I can't keep my eyes open. I sink into sleep.

When I wake up it is quiet in the restaurant. No one is there. I poke my head into the kitchen. Utensils are strewn everywhere. The sink is full of dishes. There is borscht on the walls. The twins and the chef are gone.

There is no longer a crowd in front of the casks. They stand empty and abandoned, the white-clothed tables covered with wine stains and crumbs. I make my way down the stairs. The room filled with dancers is empty, too, deserted except for one wooden chair in the corner. Sitting on the chair is a man. He looks like he is sleeping. I can't move. I think I recognize him. Slowly, reluctantly, I make my way across the room. Yes, I recognize the man in the chair in the corner. The man in the chair is Alain.

Alain is tied to the chair. His arms are behind him, his hands bound at the wrists. His legs are also tied to the chair. His head slumps forward. It looks as though he's asleep. But he isn't. I know this when I try to wake him. I poke at him. I raise his chin. No, this isn't really Alain. The face is chalk white. It is ghastly. This poor creature looks as though it has been drained of all the blood in its body. The dun-colored eyes are dull and lifeless. I let go of the chin. The head slumps back down. Around the chair are bottles and jars. There is blood in them. Alain's blood. I wish I could pour it back into him.

I wander back through the morning to the houseboat, but I can't get near it. There is a crowd.

"Someone blew it up," says a woman next to me. "Can't imagine why. First they threw out photos and furniture. They must have been looking for something. Then they blew it up, and do you know what happened? It rained money on the canal."

DEAD GIRLS DON'T LIE

Nakamura Murdered!

Front page news in the *Sports Mainichi*. Ryu folded the paper and tossed it onto the table with a look of disgust. He already knew the story. Not the one printed in the paper, not the one that named me, Erin, a girl who was supposed to be dead, as the probable killer. He knew the real story. The one that involved a creature by the name of Clément or whomever he was masquerading as now. But the evidence, of course, pointed to me. According to the article, a girl had been seen on the first floor of the building at precisely 10:15 a.m. She introduced herself to the floor manager. He let her up to the choreographer's penthouse apartment. He said he had seen her with Nakamura before. She was difficult to forget: tall, theatrical, beautiful—dangerously beautiful. But that morning her behavior had been strange, distracted, laconic, as though she were on drugs. No, the floor manager asserted, he had not been suspicious. Many beautiful women visited Nakamura-san . . . and many men.

The floor manager's shift was over at noon. His colleague was on duty in the lobby on the thirty-second floor when the elevator descended at precisely at 5:15 p.m. and disgorged the body of the practically decapitated choreographer. The manager remembered seeing the same woman—he identified her from photos—in the lobby. She'd been wearing a tan-colored overcoat. *Odd*, he recollected thinking; it was an ill-fitting garment. She stood, as though mesmerized, in one corner of the hall. Someone asked him a question. When he looked again, she was gone. Then the elevator arrived and all attention was directed to Nakamura, Hiroshi.

There was no proof of a murder, but detectives found the topcoat and a bloodstained shift in a trash receptacle in the thirty-second floor bathroom. They also found—and here the speculation turned grisly—an ear. Yes, a human ear—in one of the overcoat's pockets. They were not yet sure whose, but that would soon be revealed. And there had been another earlier murder—this one in the young woman's apartment. She had been in St. Luke's Hospital only a day before, released to the care of an intern who didn't want her discharged, who claimed she was seriously disturbed. Her name was Erin Orison. She was American, eighteen years old, a dancer, and there was a bit of a scandal. Her father was a diplomat of impeccable reputation. She, on the other hand, had a record of misbehavior, and she and her father were reportedly estranged. The article was not clear on the reason she'd been admitted to St. Luke's, but it was clear on the time of release, on the fact that she had run from her apartment, which was a crime scene, and on the eyewitness reports that placed her at a popular yakuza watering hole on the night preceding the murder.

Ryu stepped away from the table. A mess. He hated messes. There was the blackmail scheme, the girl's botched elimination, all these dead bodies and a runaway chip. Glancing down one last time at the paper, an item in the racing news caught his eye and he smiled, his thin lips curling into a grimace, the counterfeit of a smile that had earned him the name oni-Buddha (devil-Buddha) from his cohorts. His pale, handsome face could look almost wooden, like a Noh mask or like the laughing twin in the Western theater duo, the one called Comedy. He had, in fact, two favorite modes of facial expression—this, his comic face or the down-turned tragic version where his mouth formed the shape of a horseshoe, upside down, with all the luck running out. Smiling or not, he could be frightening, his unhappy face only slightly more disturbing than his gay one. And that is the face he made next, as he forgot about his win at the races and remembered he had a problem with a runaway girl and the still missing chip.

Moving to the kitchen in his tiny but fashionably modern apartment, Ryu mixed a drink: raw egg, rice milk, cod liver oil, protein powder. In three gulps it was gone, its mildly unpleasant flavor somehow reassuring. He placed the glass on the counter, chased the first drink with a half beer, and toyed, unconsciously, with his pinky finger.

He had been drunk when he arrived home to find Clément waiting for him in the early hours of the morning. Liquored up and whored out, trying to forget how he'd been persuaded to hand Orison's daughter over to the disgusting thing he'd fetched back from its miasmic Haitian detour. I don't think it troubled him to kill me, as he had been ordered. After all, executions were among his stock and trade, and he had little room in his life for love. What did disturb him was giving me to Clément. Everything about the witchdoctor-fat-woman-clerk made him sick. It was an instinctive response, a gag reflex kind of thing.

It was around three a.m. He'd come home from an evening of women and cards, his pockets fat with cash. He'd been cheating and, as usual, he had not been caught. Ryu made it a practice to win and lose. He actually preferred losing; it was far less demanding and it made him very popular with his cohorts—a funny way to buy love. That evening, feeling the loser already for so many reasons, he'd made the decision to win. That didn't ease his distress, nor did the booze and the girls. He was doubtless feeling generally disgusted when he pushed open his front door. The disgust turned to revulsion when the smell smacked him hard in the face.

He didn't turn on the light. He could not see a thing, but he was on alert.

"Do us both a favor, don't turn on the light."

"You."

"Yes, moi, or a version thereof. I'm uncomfortable, Ryu. I don't like this disease-riddled corpse."

"Clément?"

"No, not Clément, idiot. I dumped that identity long ago. Let's see . . . cab driver, hospital patient, bar boy, ninja and . . . oh yes, AIDS victim, that's who I am now. The name is Koan. Forgive me if I don't get up."

Ryu's eyes adjusted to the darkness. He could just make out the silhouette of what appeared to be a horrifically skeletal man, seated in his leather armchair.

"What are you doing here? How did you get in?"

"Grand Inquisitor, you aren't," snapped Clément. "I'm here to see you. I came in through the window. Why don't you ask me what I've been up to?"

Ryu did not ask.

"All right, I'll tell you." Clément repositioned himself in the chair. "First I went to visit our little friend, Erin. You know, the dead girl, the one you murdered, the one you gave to me. Everything seemed fine. Met her in the morgue. Gave her a wake-up kiss and our 'gift.' Got her quickly released, in spite of an interfering intern who, incidentally, decided to escort her home. Too bad for me, I wanted to welcome her properly, but the damn zombie girl got away.

"Oh, I'm sorry. I didn't tell you our gal isn't actually dead. It's a little trick I picked up in Haiti from a dying Arnotine, though, at first, he was reluctant to share. So while Erin was actually DOA at St. Luke's, I revived her. Technically speaking, our girl is a zombie. Sorry. I thought she'd be completely compliant, and we'd all get what we wanted. But something didn't quite work. Erin isn't listening. Worse yet, she's running away: from me—her Mentor, her Creator, her Lord and Master. Well, she thinks she's running away. Let's just say the girl and the microchip are on the move. They are on their way to Holland."

Through the smokescreen of his visitor's truncated narrative Ryu was able to discern a few facts: a) The necrotic creature seated in his favorite chair was indeed the latest incarnation of the peevish and much-despised Clément; b) Erin was not dead, at least not in the usual sense; c) Erin and the chip were no longer in Tokyo. The revelations came as something of a surprise to Ryu's intoxicant-muddled brain. It was like a very bad dream, one he had hoped was over.

"Poor Ryu. Come here. Sit down next to me. Let me tell you a bedtime story."

Ryu didn't obey. He slumped instead onto the back of the couch.

"Have it your way," said Clément. "But the tale must be told. There once was a ghul . . ."

And the story spilled out—long, convoluted, grave-gorged, and fetid—Clément's whole perfidious history, which had something to do with creatures of fire and smoke and djinn and an entity by the name of Saitan. It was a hunter's tale, a story about searching and finding and losing and searching again. Body after body, the dead rose—one after another—in a carrion-stink across borders and years. Clément rambled on, philosophized, rhapsodized, waxed histrionic until Ryu's head fell onto his chest and he collapsed into the soft leather pull of the couch. Then he dreamed about goblins and ghosts and ghouls, about graveyards, ghats and gutters, about epidemics and war zones and the clean-up crew of the necropolis. And finally he dreamed about a beautiful zombie: Erin—the girl who got away.

That was last night. The news about Nakamura's death was in the paper by morning. Clément was long gone, no doubt to the Netherlands, and Ryu was quickly on his way there as well.

LIMBO XXVI

All of that is another lifetime ago, she thinks. Then she wakes up.

Who is the man sleeping beside her? A banker, he'd said, a Belgian banker—just a man who has taken her in.

Who is the woman in bed with him? It must be her.

When she gets out of bed, the other woman stays there. Is she a ghost, then? Or is the woman in bed, who looks so much like her, only a body? The two of them, man and woman, are curled toward one another like the petals of a tulip. They do appear to be dead. They are sleeping. Tulips are beautiful flowers.

The house is cold. She moves her hand to her cheek. This is accomplished without hands really, only the feeling of moving one's hand. There is no cheek to meet the hand. There is only the cold. The cheek is cold.

She performs the usual movements gratuitously since they have no physical counterparts. Just as she dresses, eats out of habit. None of it has any basis in physical reality. She has begun to think of herself as a ghost. The body that follows her around, vaguely attached, annoys her. She makes an attempt to ignore it, to pretend it doesn't exist.

Perhaps it is the overwhelming sense that a certain thing is spoiled or tainted and should be thrown out. She meets herself occasionally, a shudder down the other woman's spine. How long can she go on in this way, in a kind of limbo? How long has it been? Months.

The early morning hours are quietest. Quiet before the household gets up. She roams the yard, then, and climbs down to the creek to sit under the huge bole of a tree. The mosquitoes move away.

Her most vigorous action is, once, to collect an armful of rushes from the soft bank, but, as with all things, she grows listless, leaves them strewn all over the yard. No, she does not feel pointless; that would assume a point.

Sometimes she wanders out from the gates. She is looking for graveyards. Sometimes she loiters along the roadside, staring at stones, reading invisible names as though from some checklist. She is looking for one name really. One name. She forgets what it is. The only thing she recollects is a number. "I am number 421," she says sadly. There was a time when the dam broke in Amsterdam. The houseboat exploded, too. It rained money. They were all so surprised by that.

Sometimes she finds a nice stone and stops, as though reflecting upon something. This is silly because she is reflecting on nothing. Not even searching her mind. There's nothing there. Oh, yes, a number.

"I am number 421," she says and she sighs. There was a time when the dam broke in Amsterdam. The houseboat rained money. Everyone was surprised about that.

The housekeeper assigned to watch her finds her disturbing.

"What is she doing out there in her nightdress?"

In this, as in other things, there is no connection between the outward appearance and what is actually going on.

That is when *he* appears in her garden. Or, maybe it is in the graveyard. One way or another, he is digging. She knows him—a trickle like ice water down her spine.

"I am your savior," he says. He is the gardener maybe. Perhaps he is the undertaker. He smells bad. She looks into his wheelbarrow. It's full of worms. Worms.

Someone is calling. She shivers. She goes back to the house. Worms.

When she returns to the garden, he is back. This time he is wearing a shin-length tweed coat and a cap. He looks as if he has grown a beard. The beard keeps growing after you die. The lower half of his face is in shadow.

"Nice dress," he says when she approaches. She sees she is wearing a white satin nightgown. The hem is covered with creek mud.

"How long can you hide?" he asks.

She does not know how to answer that.

"They'll find you here. Run away," he says.

"Go away," she slurs back.

The defiance exhausts her. She is in bed for a long time after that. When she rises, she goes to the window. He is still there, in the garden. Worms.

She realizes that she hates him.

The man in the bed has become the man at the breakfast table. He ignores her mostly. He calls this tenderness.

Everyone in the house ignores her. That is what she sees. But there is the man in the garden. He watches her. Always.

Worms.

"It's time for you to leave. Run away," he says. "You like to run. Run away."

Every day now, he is in the garden. The garden used to be so peaceful.

Now she is wearing a light blue dress. The gardener is back, digging another grave. She thinks she must hate him.

"You are fucking a Belgian banker," he says with contempt. "You can't hide anymore. Vacation is over. Run away."

She thinks she will run away from him, from the gardener, from the gh . . . she can't seem to finish her thought. Instead another thought fills her mind, then another time, another place.

There is a small girl in a big house. The French doors are open. They open out to a garden, out to acres upon acres of loneliness. And there is a gardener there as well . . .

"I'm not sorry I did it," he says. "You only knew him for one day."

"I'm number 421."

"Come off it. You only knew him for one day."

She is sure now that she hates him, the gardener, the ghoul. It's November. The weather has turned cold.

The gardener is dirty. He's dirty and he smells bad.

"You stink," she says.

There's a film of white frost on the lawn.

"You're shivering," he says. "Take my coat."

The house and the garden have turned into a prison. She finds four dead ducks by the creek bed—a new dead duck every day.

"Death is all around you," he says.

Why won't he leave her alone?

Worms.

She wants him to go away, but he won't. He comes every day for the garden.

The man says, "I like the job that gardener is doing."

What job? She wonders and pushes her hair back from her forehead.

"What have you written there?" asks the banker.

It's a number: 421.

They won't let her go outside anymore. The gate that opens out onto the street is locked. She has become a prisoner.

She is wearing the blue dress and it's cold outside. In the autumn garden, *he* is pruning the trees. Bare branches drop one by one.

She decides she will run away. She has the blue dress, his tweed coat. It smells bad.

There is no such thing as time in her world, but it's late, very late. There was a time when the dam broke in Amsterdam and the houseboat rained money and everyone was surprised about that.

The sun is like a persimmon. It's a fat, orange globe. It's setting behind the bare branches.

"Could you give me some water?" he asks. He stands at the blue kitchen door.

"Wait outside," the housekeeper grumbles. "Gypsy," she mutters in Flemish.

He is no gypsy. The woman is wrong.

I am wearing the blue dress and I smooth down the skirt. I have found my hands in the pockets of the coat and I use them. In the pocket of the tweed coat, I've also found a plane ticket. It is a ticket to Malaysia. I stand inside the blue door to the kitchen. Better. Myself again—at least more than I've been for some time.

There he is. There he is. I have my eye on him. He's not going to trick me again.

"I will leave the gate open," he whispers.

The housekeeper returns with the water. "Here's your water," she snaps at the gypsy gardener. "Back to bed with you, ma'am," she says.

I have my hand on the ticket. I remember how the dam burst in Amsterdam. It is all so terribly sad. Everyone said that it rained money.

Worms.

SHADOW PUPPETS

These people are like men, thirsting for sensual
pleasures, who live in a world of illusion; they do not
realize the magic hallucinations they see are not real.
—poet in King Airlangga's court

An incessant rain curtained Kuala Lumpur, cried into the Klang and the Gombak at the Y-shaped juncture of these rivers. In the City Center, the Petronas Twin Towers[22] pushed their eighty-eight floors up into the oily slick of haze and moisture that blanketed most of Malaysia. Indonesia was burning, Sumatra and Borneo giving up their forests, giving up their ghosts to industry, and the rainforests drifted over the Malay Peninsula as soot, as ash, as debris.

My eyes teared up, watering involuntarily, like the waterfalls that cascade down the limestone outcrops and cliffs that surround Kuala Lumpur. The waterfalls were tiny when I saw them from the window of the plane, the glint of a kris amid billowing clouds of green. They were lost when I landed.

In the pockets of the tweed overcoat I had found my hands and my hands found the other things he'd placed there: passage to Malaysia, to Kuala Lumpur; a photograph; and a passport. The passport contained the eighteen-year-old face of Erin Orison, U.S. citizen. She smiles in the picture. She is pretty. But I also have another photo. It seems to be of an entirely different woman. She is bleary-eyed, severe. She has a number written on her forehead—number 421. Behind her, in the photo, is a mirror. In the mirror one sees the photographer reflected, but the camera covers his face. In the window of the plane, I see myself. I see this woman's face framed in storm clouds. I see number 421.

The gardener, the gravedigger, the ghoul—he packed me off to Kuala Lumpur and I went . . . weak-willed being, what else could I do? Zombie, near zombie . . . on a journey that left me standing in Southeast Asia in the death rattle of a northeastern monsoon before it wasted over the Strait of Malacca. The tweed coat, which stank, was still in Belgium. I had only the light blue dress—the light blue dress, the passport, and the photo.

Taxis buzzed all around me like ferocious night wasps. Taxis and touts, but I had no ringgit, no money of any kind. Still, they tried to entice me into their cars until my abstracted manner made them worry. Then it all added up—no coat, no luggage, brooding silence and a snarl—to madness or possession by a maleficent spirit. Either way, I was no fare for a god-fearing driver, be he Muslim or Christian or Hindu or Buddhist.

"OK, lady. I give you ride."

The cabbie was a chestless brown man with a greasy mane of black hair that hung, thickly, down to his shoulders. "Come, come, get in cab. You wet and cold. Get in."

This one actually emerged from his vehicle, grimacing and wincing under the monsoon. He opened the door of the cab. "Get in, lady," he commanded. And I did.

The car was warm and thick with the smell of betel and booze, and we moved through the city in silence. I could see the man's eyes in the rearview mirror. Black eyes ringed in pink—they kept staring at me, not the road. We drove north. Kuala Lumpur fell away behind us and the jungle took over.

The north-south highway flowed. It flowed through Selangor past kampongs and plantations, muddy rivers and rubber trees twisting away from it, up into the hills and highlands where a canopy of cloud, a curtain of green closed around them. Where was he taking me, this fierce little man, teeth black and gums red from the betel? My dress was wet, the car hot and swampy so that the driver kept having to rise up slightly out of his seat to wipe the steam from the windows. The monsoon heaved buckets upon us. Chew, wipe, chew, wipe, drive, drive, drive—the windshield wipers were a metronome keeping time as we made our way through Malaysia. The road, the forest, the tin-thick earth turning to mud—it all had a derelict beauty. That beauty was a knife twisting into my heart. I hated it.

Sometimes it is better to feel nothing. A zombie should not have feelings. A zombie should be free, at least, from that. But something was wrong, and as the ghoul had correctly surmised, I had them. I was an abomination. He had screwed up whatever infernal experiment he'd made of me. My creator was an imbecile, damn him. Not a god, not even a man, and by his own admission, a renegade, and I was the victim of his ineptitude. I was not even blessed with the absence of pain. I was hurt. I was sad. I was lost.

But the driver wasn't. We were on the main road, motoring north toward Thailand, but that wasn't where he was going. We swerved from the highway just north of Tapah, turning northeast and into the mountains.

Rain was still falling heavily as we wound our way into the highlands, past recent mudslides, past waterfalls, waterlogged townships, and flooding jungle pools. It drummed down on the car in a cacophony of rattles and slaps. The landscape was changing, softening into a colonial Brigadoon of wet green hillsides topped with Tudor-style country homes, golf courses, and Swiss-style chalets. My driver plunged into this world of plantations and Surrey-like mansions on ever-tightening roadways until we arrived, at last, at the leafy perimeter of a huge tea estate.

It was strange. Fifteen-foot iron gates closed the road, but they swung from two pillars, one on each side of the roadway, like a freestanding door without walls. The driver chewed, spat and, cursing, got out of the car to open the gates, head bent, back bowed, trying to duck the rainfall. He was barefoot, and when he returned to the car, his feet were slick with orange mud.

He did not close the gates. They remained as he left them—wide flung and gaping—getaway gates ready for anyone wanting to beat a hasty retreat.

Once inside the gates he veered wildly from the road almost driving into the tea bushes before putting the car into reverse to turn it around. It was a whirling dervish maneuver that ended as abruptly as it had begun.

"OK, we here," he muttered to himself as he completed the process, the car now facing the direction from which we had come.

"You get out, lady," he demanded, and when I didn't move, he scrambled from the car, opened my door, took hold of my wrist and pulled me from my perch, slamming my door shut as soon as I exited and quickly driving away. I was left, standing there in the downpour, gasping like a fish, pushing water out of my face with one hand, passport and photo clutched in the other.

On either side of the road the tea bushes stretched out in an endless plantation of green. I quickly discovered why the driver had relinquished his footwear. My shoes were sucked into the mud, which rapidly filled them, and I had to step out of them if I wanted to move. I did not want to move and would undoubtedly still be there, wrinkled and rain-soaked, toes kneading mud, if a Chinese man hadn't emerged improbably from the acres of darjeeling.

The Chinese man was short and squat, a physique enhanced by the knee-high rubber boots and the layers of clothing in which he'd swathed his body, perhaps to discourage the rain. But it was wet and hot and he huffed and puffed as he made his way up through the bushes. He was monitoring how he was progressing, not where, so he didn't see me until he'd attained the road. He looked up with a start when he came upon me, but the surprise seemed to please him and he broke into bright, gold-capped laughter.

"You got me, you got me," he guffawed. Then he saw my shoes stuck in the mud and this set off fresh waves of laughter.

He tried to pick up one of the shoes, bending with some difficulty on account of the wet bulk of his clothing. The shoe wouldn't budge. Like a suction cup, it clung to its spot on the roadway. But this didn't dissuade the jolly Chinese man. He pulled and he pulled with all of his might till he lost his grip and went sprawling backward in the mud.

This sent him into further hysterics. "Who are you?" he managed to gasp between hiccupping bouts of laughter. He asked in Chinese, in Hindi, in Malay. Then he asked me in English. When I didn't answer, he pulled on a watery earlobe.

"Oh, from the clinic," he concluded with some glee. "Come on, come on. Let's go back."

He took my arm and steered me to the side of the roadway, which we followed, climbing deeper into the highlands. "I used to work at the clinic," he said. "They are crazy there. Yes. All crazy. My name is Ping," he said gazing sideways at me and nodding. "Ping Pong," he added. Then he burst again into laughter.

PING PONG XXVIII

We walked along for a short while in silence, Ping shuffling next to me, one hand guiding me by the elbow.

"You are very graceful," observed Ping. "I think you must be a dancer."

I attempted another poorly executed smile. Ping squinted at me then he broke into his own dazzling version.

"No, no, like this." He turned his face up to the rain, grinning widely, with a look that was clearly ecstatic.

I mimicked the expression, my clenched teeth slightly parted. Rainwater coursed into my mouth.

"Much better. You practice," said Ping and he gave my elbow a squeeze.

The roadway rose sharply and we stopped where it crested, looking down into a beautiful valley. The land dipped and rose softly in what looked like waves, the dark green tea bushes stretching for miles till they collided with the great wall of jungle. Our road came to an end in the middle of the valley in a shaved sweep of driveway, green lawns and flowery plantings. In the center of this oasis of control was an enormous edifice. It sprawled like a great white elephant between fruit trees and roses.

"Yes, the clinic," said Ping with a wink.

Saint Ali, as I was to discover the clinic was called, was shaped like a shallow, square-cornered U, the bottom of which was pointed in our direction. In the center of the U—I could see from our vantage point—was a courtyard. Behind it, at the mouth of the U, which formed a kind of back door to the structure, was a garden. The courtyard was intriguing, studded with small pools that, even under the storm-hung sky, sparkled like precious aquamarines. I counted five little pools: one circular, one square, one rectangular, and two small ovals. These were arranged, more or less, in a ring around a central domed structure prickly with blue minarets. Lacing all together were white walkways, green lawns, carefully tended gardens. It could have been the inner sanctum of a sultan's harem and it contrasted strangely with the sharp-cornered, straight-laced colonial lines of the edifice that embraced it.

The monsoon had dwindled to a sputter. Now the moisture seemed to rise up out of the ground, grabbing ankles, calves, knees, sliding humid hands up under my dress. I was panting.

"Cool down there," said Ping, clearly reading my mind.

We headed down to Saint Ali.

There was something old, tired, and a little off-kilter about Saint Ali, like an Englishman trying to recover from the end of the Raj. The bizarre juxtaposition of British colonial and Muslim elements lent it a whimsical quality that was further explained by its history. Originally built as a sanitarium in 1918 by the British, Saint Ali had served time as a hospital in the '40s when the Japanese had peninsular control. It maintained this identity through the postwar years of racial and political tension. In the optimistic '60s, with an infusion of cash from the Muslim monarchy, it morphed into an elegant spa and now, with so many of the local residents and well-to-do clientele attaining a doddering old age, it had turned back to its somewhat more medical roots, becoming a residence for the elderly and anyone else functioning on less than a full tank of gas. It was affectionately if not legally known as "the hospital" or Saint Ali, as it had been renamed in the '60's. The cumulative power of all of these roles seemed to have an effect on the property, for although the edifice's purpose had changed over the decades, the spirit of the building's earlier incarnations would not give up the ghost and it developed a fancifully patchwork identity mirrored in successive remodels, the end effect being that the present residents and staff were always a bit confused as to whether they inhabited a home for the sick, a retreat for sybarites, a house for the marginally insane or, as it would shortly be transformed, a refuge for the criminally inclined. Saint Ali was, in fact, a vortex of misrepresentation and, as such, it attracted and generated its own brand of insanity, serving as a gateway into a world of absolute relativity. Of course, I didn't know this at the time.

Ping knew it, however, and having an aura of hilarity all his own, should have fit right in, but the folks at Saint Ali, sadly, took themselves rather seriously . . . and Ping did not.

"Can't let them see me," said Ping, as we crept toward the back of the building. "They're mad."

Ping would reveal later that his last official act as a caregiver at the hospital was to take a number of the residents on an unauthorized outing, and that as a result of that outing an elderly British woman with Alzheimer's was lost. She was found sometime later in Thailand in the company of an old Chinese man who found her attractive in spite of her greatly diminished faculties and who had decided to make her his bride. Her family—she was a widow and the children had taken control—were outraged and threatened to sue. Ping was let go. Mrs. Parks was returned to Saint Ali, where she died within months, of a broken heart, long before she'd exhausted her fortune. Her heirs divided the spoils.

"I don't work at the hospital anymore," said Ping. "Now I mind the pigs in my village. They love me. Pigs, I mean, not the village. Sometimes Western people very greedy," Ping observed sagely. "Asian people greedy too," he added with lips pursed like a trumpeter's, hot laughter trapped in the air that ballooned his fat cheeks.

The Saint Ali courtyard was gated—the gate a heavy lacework of metal like the one on the road. It was locked, but Ping had a key. As we stepped into the courtyard, he seemed to forget his concern about being seen.

"Oh," he chirped merrily, "let's go for swim."

Ping proceeded to disrobe and I was surprised to see how many layers of clothing he was actually wearing. First the jacket came off, then the sweater, then the shirt, then the t-shirt, then the knee-high boots, then the mismatched woolen socks, then the pants. The underpants he kept on, first pulling out the elastic, taking a long look down the front and snapping back the cotton briefs with a smile. "Still there," he reported, and stretched his arms out in delight. Peeled like a grape, he was suddenly thin and fit in a childlike and puckish way.

"Come on," he invited, walking from one jewel-like pool to the next, sticking his toe in the water. "Ooooh, this one very nice . . . refreshing."

Ping took a deep breath at the edge of the circular pool before leaping in and submerging himself completely. When I didn't follow suit, he climbed out, walked over to me and took the photo and passport from my hand. He studied both carefully before setting them down on the ground.

"Ah, you are Elin," he said and the way he said it, turning the "r" into an "l," was familiar and, for some reason, pleasant.

Guiding me by the elbow again, Ping led me to the edge of the pool and pushed me in. I was shocked when I hit the water—shocked, then delighted. The water was warm, and it stroked off the monsoon's chilly touch, doused the humidity. The blue dress billowed out around me like the skirt of a jellyfish. I squatted on the watery bottom, watching my hands fin outward before me, my hair floating upward under the water like kelp, breath pearling upward also in fast bubbles. I could see the blued-tiled sides of the little pool. I could see the smooth bottom. Some of the tiles were chipped and cracked. Overhead I could see the dark outline of Ping as he gazed down at me on the bottom, above him the sky, like an oyster—nacreous and moist. The bubbles diminished, then stopped. The water rushed in and I choked as Ping reached down to pull me, coughing and spitting, to the surface. Then I felt it, the smile creeping over my face. Not some farcical copy of something I'd seen, but the kind of expression that finds its origin somewhere deep within you and ripples out into the world. I felt laughter, too, and Ping's hands just under my arms, supporting me lightly as I bobbed like a blue flower, the dress petalling around me on the water.

"See, I tell you. You practice, then you learn how," nodded Ping.

Now that I was truly smiling, I could not seem to stop, and I followed Ping like a puppy dripping my way from one pool to the next, sampling all the pleasures of the courtyard.

Perhaps they were watching us from the long windows that lined the two floors of the hospital. Once I looked up at the windows. There were sixteen windows on each side of the door, two floors of eight and eight, and they all seemed to have spies in them. It was as if Saint Ali were watching us. I thought I saw a figure draw quickly behind the sash. I thought I could see faces in each of the windows, pale faces swimming like lilies on ethereal stems. They swayed, plantlike, at the tops of their cottony shrouds, moving in an eerie, vegetal way.

What did they whisper to one another, those faces like lanterns in the long windows—that there was a strange woman in the courtyard, a strange woman who found them equally strange? What did they tell the staff?

"She follows the Chinese man from pool to pool."

Do they say this in between doses of the drugs that subdue them? Do they whine and insist on the truth of this vision until the orderlies quiet them? Does a doctor finally come to the window mistrusting their misinformation? He sees a woman in a blue dress, a Chinese man in his shorts. He turns away from the window.

"No, there is nothing out there," he says. Then he returns to the window.

I had removed my dress, which hung, heavy and wet; I left it next to one of the pools. Ping flashed another key, this one to the domed and turreted building around which the small pools were arrayed. It seemed sculpted of fine white sand or sugar, a diminutive Middle Eastern palace topped with its ice cream cone cupola and pointy minarets. The doors were glass with a grillwork like the gates and through them we could see the large, rectangular pool. Ping put the key in the lock. It worked. We slipped inside.

It was startlingly bright in the pool house. In the center of the ceiling, right above the pool, the dome rose in a rose-colored swirl of quartz-like glass that reflected the color of the sky. Much of the ceiling was glass and it was sequined with shimmering droplets from the rain, as if the monsoon had scattered diamonds upon it. The droplets made shadows that danced upon the smooth surface of the emerald-cut Olympic-sized swimming pool that floated beneath them. On the far end of the building, French windows let in shafts of more light from the courtyard. The room looked expectant, as if it had been set up for a gathering. The chaises longues carefully arranged around the pool were draped with fluffy white towels. On the tables next to every chaise were a book and a bottle of water. Ping stuck his pale and now prune-skinned foot into the quiescent blue. He grinned back at me and splashed into the pool. Moments later, I felt a draft, felt someone's tight grip upon me, rough hands grabbing my arms, pinning them at my back.

"Caught you," came the voice.

Then another pair of much softer hands took hold of my shoulder, grabbing my chin and twisting my head back as far as it could reasonably go without snapping my neck.

"Where is Ping? You were with him. Where did he go?"

The voice was soft and full. My chin was released and I was turned to find myself face to face with a tiny Asian woman in a white uniform and cap, her manner so starched, so erect, that she seemed more like a nun than a nurse. Her much larger companion, for there were two of them, loosened her grip on my arms. It remained that way as long as I made no effort to move.

"Who are you?" asked the diminutive nurse.

I hung my head.

"Ping let you in?" she persisted. I looked toward the pool. Ping was nowhere to be found, the French doors on the other end of the room, slightly ajar, the curtains kiting inward.

"Of course it was Ping," she answered herself. "We must change all the locks right away."

"The girl's shivering," said the other, the one behind me who had hold of my arms. "And naked. We should dress her."

"Yes, yes, first things first. Let's take her inside."

They steered me back through the courtyard where the pools stared wide-eyed up at the sky. I gazed furtively up at the windows. Not a single face beamed back at me from the tall rectangles.

Then I was inside Saint Ali, or "the hospital" as it was called in
resident shorthand. The hospital interior was an antique-looking
place, the floors of light wood polished shiny. The long multi-doored
corridors with their classroom-sized offices made it seem more like
a school. We were on the ground floor. Beneath us were the cellars;
above, the residents and their rooms. There were two large auditori-
ums, one on either end of the hall. These occupied the entire ground
floor wings. One auditorium was a lunchroom, the other a lecture hall.
The back door and the front, in the center of the building, opened into
an atrium space where the doors were flanked with glass cases that
held memorabilia from Saint Ali's checkered past. In one case there
were early microscopes, medicine bottles, and frightening electro-
therapy contraptions, testifying to the institution's sanitarium roots.
There were bullets and shrapnel and clamps and scalpels in another
case, bearing witness to its hospital duty during and after the Second
World War. Another vitrine held the special sponges and oils and
infusions from Saint Ali's days as a spa. And finally, there was a case
containing the inlaid cigarette cases, ivory canes, and jeweled combs of
recent residents—its terminally ill, celebrity clientele. On the walls of
this entryway and all along the halls were historical photos: pictures
of breaking ground at the turn of the century; of its colonial, pre-1920
appearance; of Japanese planes and soldiers during the occupation of
Malaysia; of the construction of the pool house circa 1965; and of the
long line of sultans and celebrities who were once spa guests. They all
ran together in continuous, albeit contradictory manner, thus anchor-
ing the confusing identity of Saint Ali firmly and definitively in the
present to the ongoing chagrin of current staff and residents.

The nurses marched me down this hall and into one of the offices
where a doctor stood with his back to the door. He was gazing out into
the courtyard.

"We had a visit from Ping," the tiny nurse announced. "He brought this girl along."

She had not bothered to clothe me and the doctor raised his eyebrows when he turned around and saw me standing, nude, in the doorway.

"She was naked." The nurse stated the obvious.

The doctor looked like a serious man. He had thinning blond hair and his eyes had the same watery and indefinite color as the courtyard pools and the sky.

"You should cover her up," he commanded, his slight British accent eroded by years spent in Asia, and as the larger nurse went to fetch clothing for me, he said, "Please sit down."

The remaining nurse steered me rather ungently toward a chair.

"So you were with Ping," mused the doctor. "Ping's a real character. How do you know Ping? What is your name?"

"She won't speak," the small nurse volunteered. "Something's wrong with her."

The doctor was studying me from his place by the window, hands crossed behind his back when the other nurse returned with a faded green hospital gown.

"Yes," said the doctor. "Seems so. Why not get her situated? I'll advise our administrator and the police, of course. I'm sure someone wants to find this lost girl. Then, I'll come around to see how she's doing."

"We found these in the courtyard," the smaller nurse added handing over my passport and the photo.

"I see," said the doctor. He looked closely at both. "American, eh? What will I do about Ping?" Then he turned back to the courtyard. "All right," he said. "Take her upstairs. I'll be along in a while."

A KISS IN THE DARK

My room was upstairs with a view of the courtyard, a quiet room with bright sunlight glaring in through the window. The walls were mint-green and calming, the sheets on the narrow bed crisp and pulled tight. Gita, the mean little nurse, was gone but not without warning that I should stay put. Where would I go? Why would I leave? I was still dressed only in the hospital gown. I sat down on the edge of the bed. Then, inexplicably, I started to cry—for the second time since I'd arrived in Kuala Lumpur. This time the tears were real. Earlier, laughter, now tears—all of this felt so strange to me. The teardrops—I have no idea what precipitated them—welled up in my eyes then spilled down my cheeks in a torrent. It felt like a tourniquet that was wrapped around my chest had been loosened. I was wracked with rib-jarring sobs. My lips shook, my nose, eyes and sinuses swelled, and still the tears kept pouring from me. I was drowning, caught in the pipeline of a huge wave of anguish. It carried me out to some tumultuous, wildly turbulent place then dashed me back again, emptied. Exhaustion and an enormous sense of relief overwhelmed me. I felt free. Was this happiness? I lay down on the bed and slept.

When I awoke, it was to darkness. At first I didn't know where I was. Outside my doorway, the world was in motion, a train of wrinkly, cotton-haired residents on patrol in the softly lit halls. They drifted from door to door in aimless and perpetual motion. Now here was a line of true zombies. I moved into the corridor and joined the parade. One sad little woman clung like a newborn macaque to the waist-high railing that ran down the carpeted hall. Another blue-veined granny wagged a crooked index finger at anyone who dared pass her. There was an old man dressed in a sweat suit who flapped his loose lips in imitation of a motor or engine, and there was a funny old gal who whooped like a crane if she managed to catch someone's eye. In a slow-moving conga-line they shuffled from bedroom to bedroom. The doors to the rooms were all open so that the ancient residents, with their terminally scrambled circadian rhythms, could walk. And they did—all night—under the watchful eye of a camera and the less watchful eyes of a night nurse whose attention wandered from the console to late-night British broadcast TV.

In a listless procession through the insomniac night, the aged and agitated population of Saint Ali traipsed through the halls until slumber caught them off guard.

In the darkened bedrooms, the small beds looked like coffins and their sleeping occupants looked like the dead. The ambulatory residents slipped in and out of the rooms. The sleeping ones shifted and snored. The hall was well lit, but the bedrooms were dark. Except for one. In that one a small cone of light illumined a corner where a silvery figure sat propped up in her pillows, the lamplight casting a pearly glow over her face. Shadows webbed the ceiling and walls all around her. She sat there, unmoving, an oasis of quiet and light in the midst of the shuffling darkness.

I later learned that Mrs. Soren-Schmidt had been at Saint Ali for seven years. She had Alzheimer's but she was still able to call out to me and to speak. Her cry was feeble, but impossible to ignore. I leaned into the room toward her.

"Oh, you're here now," she said, and smiled. "Isn't it lovely? It's sunshine. You'll be safe here."

I sat down on the bed next to hers.

"You look so tired," said Mrs. Soren-Schmidt. "I recognize tired when I see it. I'm tired, my dear, so I know what I'm talking about. You, you look so young to be tired." She extended her hand palm turned up. "Here, take my hand."

It was cold.

"I'm an ice bucket," she laughed. "Where's the champagne?" Then she sank back into the pillows, her head resting lightly against the wall.

"I am Mrs. Soren-Schmidt," she announced softly, "the only Schmidt left here in the Highlands. Why do women seem to live so much longer than men? Do you know how old I am, dear? No? Me neither, but I'd guess 1,000 years old. But it's nice here. I like it. The nurses and doctors are all troubled, poor souls, but for the most part, they leave us alone. Like roses," she said. "At Saint Ali we can rest." She closed her eyes as if trying to prove her point. I noticed how thin her eyelids were. Her eyelashes were wispy and white.

"We miss Ping," she moaned, eyelids lifting. "Do you know him? Who are you, dear? I don't believe we have met."

Mrs. Soren-Schmidt moved her hands through my hair, stroked my hand, her palsied fingers trembling like wind-shaken petals as they moved up my forearm toward my elbow. "We miss Ping, dear. But they leave us alone, don't they? And sometimes that's all that matters, especially when you're tired and all around you there are nothing but shadows.

"I used to dance out in the garden. It was quite a romance, I tell you. Then the next thing you know, all you want to do is to close your eyes. Look at those poor souls." She gestured out toward the corridor. "They can't rest. Those doctors and nurses, they are troubled. As for me, I just want to vanish. 'Don't hold onto me,' I say to them. 'I don't want to stay.' We are almost there, though. Trust me, this is as close as it gets. Dandelion. Romance. A soft kiss in the dark. Then nothing. It's lovely, you know. You just close your eyes. A soft kiss in the dark, then you're sleeping."

Mrs. Soren-Schmidt's hands still fluttered over my arms, lighting here and there, never resting. And while she spoke, a dark, black-haired figure slipped in through the doorway and began to tiptoe toward me.

I stiffened.

"Oh, don't worry, dear, that is Khalid. Poor Khalid is terribly troubled. Khalid, tell us what you want. Why have you come here to visit?"

Khalid, with his smooth brown skin and curly black hair was clearly not old like the others. His eyeballs were as white as cocktail onions, his irises like shiny black olives. His teeth flashed knife-bright in the half-light of the room and he pulled a glass jar from his pajamas.

"I'm going to catch her, once and for all," he said.

"Who?" asked my frail hostess.

"Her," he said pointing the jar toward me. "That one, the angel. I'll put her in my jar."

"Oh, Khalid," the old woman said, "That's a brilliant idea, but what did you do with the last one?"

"She has made a cocoon in the courtyard," said Khalid. "That's all right. This one is better. She is bigger."

"Your jar is too small, then," said Mrs. Soren-Schmidt. "Khalid, you must go fetch another."

"But she'll get away . . . "

"No, she won't, Khalid, I'll watch her."

Khalid looked from me to Mrs. Soren-Schmidt, considering the puzzle and his options.

"I'll watch her. Run along," advised Mrs. Soren-Schmidt. "But hurry if you want to keep her."

"He'll forget," said Mrs. Soren-Schmidt when Khalid left the room. "Poor Muslim boy, he's so troubled. He sees angels everywhere, not the Christian kind. His are like dakinis or divas or something of that sort. Now where were we, dear? You're a doctor, aren't you? We were going to play the piano."

Once again the sheer eyelids curtained her eyes and the fingers kept moving, this time like a shaky pianist's, up and down my arm, up and down. Outside in the hall the slumberless cavalcade continued.

I must have fallen asleep in Mrs. Soren-Schmidt's room. It was late in the morning when I woke up. Mrs. Soren-Schmidt seemed to be sleeping soundly. She had loosened her hold on me and her forearm stuck out from the side of the bed, palm upward, the fingers still slightly curled. I got up from the floor where I'd apparently dozed off and stepped warily back into the hall. The sunlight from the windows of the wide-open rooms filled the corridor with buttery light.

No sign of Khalid. No sign of anyone at all. I was still dressed only in the hospital gown, which was loosely tied in the back, hardly covering me at all. I ran down the hallway in the creamy morning light, the hospital gown flaring out around me. Gita, the head nurse, apprehended me. She was terribly fast and vigorous and seemed to come out of nowhere.

"There you are," she scolded as she steered me back to my room. "I think you have enjoyed enough celebrity. It's one thing to act up outside of the hospital, but here we manage differently. Sit down," she commanded.

I sat.

"Do you want your clothes back?" she asked regarding me with a look that I was certain was one of contempt.

I nodded.

"Then you have to behave," she said and seemed pleased when I did not react.

"Sit still," she said. "Stay right there until I come back."

She left. I sat without moving, believing that she hid just on the other side of the door ready to pounce on me should I move into the hall.

When she returned she did not have my dress over her arm. Instead she was carrying a simple blue chambray frock and white cotton underclothes and she had the doctor with her.

"Have a seat on the bed, there," said Doctor Hodge. He wore a white coat over his tan shirt and slacks. His eyes were a placid blue-gray. "Your documents," he said, offering me the passport and photo.

I looked away. If I hadn't, perhaps I would have seen him raise his eyebrows, throw his head back ever so slightly and exhale. I heard him exhale.

"As I thought," he said. "You have a problem. Maybe trauma, amnesia, shock, a reaction to drugs." He sighed. "Whatever the situation, we will endeavor to be of assistance. We are, frankly, confused about how you ended up on our doorstep, though it's clear that once more the ever-troublesome Ping has somehow gotten involved. No matter. I've phoned the authorities and the hospital's owners and I'm sure we'll have our answer before long. In the meantime, Ms. Orison—do you remember that name?—in the meantime, we will keep you safe and make attempts to diagnose your disorder. We cannot treat you without authority, but I suspect the police and our management will be able to locate your family."

Then he turned my head toward him—I didn't resist—and he used a little light to look into each of my eyes. Then he pushed the light thing up into each of my nostrils and peered into them. Then he looked into my ears.

As if he expected to find something there.

I could feel my lips curling back into something resembling a sneer.

"I do hope you'll cooperate and respect our rules," declared the doctor. "If you behave well, you may move about as the other residents do, without fear of restriction, until your family comes to your rescue. Otherwise we will have to find ways to restrain you."

This speech of his was really more for the nurse than me, wasn't it? She seemed pleased by it: nodding her head, her squinty eyes a pair of repeating horizontals.

I got up slowly and, turning my back to them, walked to the corner behind the bed. I felt the thin hospital gown billow out around me, chasing the hot, floozy breeze that came in through the open window. Who in the world invented this kind of clothing? I heard the nurse grumble something about my clothes. I turned to face them, narrowing my eyes and smiled a thin, canine smile. I must have looked like a trapped dog, panting.

"I'm glad you've decided," the doctor said tiredly. He pressed his fingertips to his temples. "Nurse, perhaps you should give her the clothes."

And that should have been that, but before he could leave, a nurse's assistant rushed into the room in a panic.

"Nurse Gita," she cried, "Doctor Hodge," I think we've lost one of the patients. "It's Loretta," she gasped. "I do believe she is dead."

It seemed that one of the hospital patients had died. The staff and other residents were quite absorbed by this for the remainder of the day. One would think that the death of its clientele would be quite commonplace in a facility devoted mainly to the aged, but this particular death caused a veritable uproar. It seemed the dead woman, whoever she was, was a favorite within their community. I took advantage of the situation by wandering about with abandon and that is how I noticed Ping at one of the pools in the courtyard.

It was as bright and clear that day as it had been rainy and dour the day before. There were clouds overhead but they looked like white frigate ships sailing on a wedgewood-blue sea. Under this gorgeous canopy Ping knelt in the courtyard beside the smaller circular pool. I could see from the window that he had something in his arms. That something was small and pink and it looked like an infant. As Ping dipped it in the pool and lifted it out, the little thing seemed to put up a tremendous struggle.

THIS LITTLE PIGGY

Ping's joy was contagious and impossible to disguise as he dipped his little bundle into the pool and tried to stifle its squeals. Like a priest performing a baptism, he would dunk the creature quickly then pull it out, smoothing its head with his free hand. The courtyard was empty, probably because of the death. There was quite a hubbub inside. It was easy, really, with all the distraction, to find my way out to the pool where Ping was performing his ministrations. He stood when he saw me approaching, tucking the struggling infant under his arm and squeezing it tight. Ping wore a Hawaiian shirt, shorts and old running shoes. His legs were so bowed you could toss a softball between them. As I drew nearer I saw that the creature he had tucked under his arm wasn't a child at all; it was a pig. Actually, a piglet—a squirming, pink, twenty-pound piglet, and Ping looked mighty pleased with himself and with it.

"Oh, Elin, I am glad to see you. This is my little pig. See. His name is Pitch Pipe," he added by way of introduction. "Pitch Pipe because he likes to squeal."

Pitch Pipe was not squealing, but he was snorting and snuffling and wriggling violently about, much to the delight of Ping.

"He is feisty," said Ping trying to maintain his hold. "That's why I love him. Look at how pink he is, how clean, how pretty. I have many pigs, but right now Pitch Pipe is my favorite."

As if understanding, Pitch Pipe stopped his furious motion for a moment and looked tenderly up into Ping's eyes and Ping gazed down on the little piglet with the pride of a new mother. Madonna and pig, that's what they resembled there in the white and blue courtyard, the towers and minarets of the pool house twisting up into the bright sky behind them. It was a salubrious moment. Then Ping held the pig out for me to hold. Its naked nosed twitched; it sniffed and snorted and sprayed the front of my recently cleaned dress with snot. I backed away.

"Oh, don't worry, he's a very clean pig," Ping insisted. "Pigs like to be clean. You come to my home and I'll show you. I have forty-two pigs. I take good care of them. You come with me. Let me show you." With his free hand Ping grabbed mine and led me toward the gate. "Hurry, hurry," he said, "They might spot me again—like yesterday. They're still very mad at me."

Things happen slowly in a place like Malaysia. It would be weeks before the powers at Saint Ali actually changed the locks. Meanwhile Ping was free to sneak in and out of the courtyard. When we passed through the gate, he hesitated, considering something closely. I watched his moon face cloud for a moment then he let go of my hand.

"Wait, Elin. I must lock the gate; if not, the patients escape."

He said it as if he were explaining something to a child, perhaps as it had once been explained to him. With Pitch Pipe still tucked under one arm, he turned and secured the gate. When he took my hand again he was trembling. He stood rooted on the spot, frowning, as if shaken by some great internal conflict.

"I don't like to lock them up," he said sadly. Then his wide smile returned. He readjusted Pitch Pipe for comfort and we set out toward his home.

Ping's compound, for it was more a small jungle fort than a home in the traditional sense, was hidden deep within the rainforest that pushed up against the tea plantation, on an old swidden or burnt space. In the center of the compound was a tiny, one-room house with cinder block walls and a roof of palm fronds. A concentric circle of fenced wooden pens surrounded it, each with an appended shelter. Here and there rainforest growth had returned—broad-leaf trees umbrellaed the periphery; lianas curled over the rotten fence posts—so that the run-down complex actually had a lushly paradisiacal quality. In one of the smaller pens, a few kinky, caramel-colored sheep stood in apparent reverie, their masticating jaws moving in unison. In another, a lone goat rubbed its bumpy little head on a trough. It trotted toward the guardrail at the sight of Ping and bleated an irritated welcome. The largest of the pens was filled with pigs. Pale brown, dark brown, spotted—they were enormous creatures and when they saw Ping they swarmed the fence like groupies rushing a rock star.

"Oh, piggy, piggy, piggy," cooed Ping to the legion of weaners and porkers. "Pigs are sweet and loving. See how they've missed me."

A host of pinkish-brown, mask-like noses shoved themselves through the fence, extended like hands wanting shaking. "Grunt, grunt, grunt, sniffle," they greeted their caretaker warmly. Meanwhile a raggedy chicken medley ran in from the compound's perimeter, gathering like empty-headed disciples at Ping's feet. White, red, brown—they pecked at the ground around him. He was the meal ticket, the roach coach, the lunch-mobile, and these little fryers were hungry.

Ping shifted Pitch Pipe's weight on his hip, and with his free hand, reached out to touch each and every snuffling, suspirating schnoz.

"See, see, this one is very happy I'm back," he beamed. "Oh, she is a big one. And this beauty, she is a very good mother. She gets angry when I take away one of her babies. I can't blame her," he added, shaking his head. "I watch the pigs for the village, because I love the pigs, but the villagers . . .

"Here, hold Pitch Pipe," he said cheerfully, thrusting the pig toward me. Pitch Pipe squealed and squirmed this way and that, but I held him tight while Ping went about feeding the animals. For the next forty minutes I held onto the defiant piglet, grappling heroically with his attempts to wriggle free of my embrace. Strange thing for a near-zombie to do, I know, but no stranger than the laughter that escaped from my mouth like a terrified hiccup and twirled up into the treetops. Can a zombie have a good time?

Ping looked up from his work and dropped his bucket, a look of utmost surprise on his face. The sound of my laughter was weird, it was mournful and crowing and wild, a new sound, unlike any other. Even the rainforest was silent for a moment as the sound announced its arrival and introduced itself to the world. It was a desperate sound, but a gay one, and every creature in the compound and the surrounding jungle seemed to stop to mark its generation. But just for a moment; then they all carried on.

I was probably the one most surprised by the sound that had come out of my mouth. More confusing still were the feelings that were fluttering around in my chest: great, bright, winged, uplifting feelings. They were jerking away at my stomach, heart, lungs. They were slamming against my ribcage. The outrageous cock-a-doodle-doo of pleasure burst forth from me again.

"Oh, you like the pigs, too," said Ping as he gently pried Pitch Pipe from my grip. "You see?" he murmured, tenderly petting the now-peaceful piglet. "You see why I can't let the villagers take them anymore. It's wrong," said Ping, turning his broad face toward mine, his sun- and wind-chapped cheeks bright as a pair of red peonies.

"How can I let someone eat you?" he asked the piglet, which responded with the soft push of its snout. "I'm going to release the pigs," he whispered conspiratorially. "Don't tell anyone, Elin. I'm going to set them all free."

It was impossible to tell if Ping's plan was indeed a plan or if he had stumbled upon the idea at that moment just as one might come upon an interesting and unexpected object at the side of the road—a short wave radio, a good pair of boots. In any case, he seemed very happy with himself. It had started to rain again, another of the monsoons that wash over Malaysia in the months between November and March. The clouds, fluffy and harmless only a short while ago, avalanched sheets of water. Within minutes the compound was awash in orange mud, the once-clean Pitch Pipe now rust-brown and wet. The penned animals headed for their respective shelters and Ping for his, herding me in through the door.

"No Saint Ali now," he assured me. "Not in the monsoon. We wait."

Inside Ping's house it was dark and warm. It had a dirt floor but the walls were covered with richly patterned carpets. In the center of the room was a beautiful ebony table, its legs turned and curved to perfection. Matching chairs were arranged around it and there was a sideboard against one wall full of elegant china and glass. A cabinet bed, its front elaborately carved, occupied another of the walls and a third wall formed the backdrop for his kitchen.

"My family," Ping winced apologetically. "A fool is a man who can lose everything. A wise man has nothing to lose. I was a fool. Now, I have nothing to lose."

I thought for a moment that Ping might be mad, but it didn't matter. He was happy. He walked to the stove, set a kettle to boil and tore up the leafy paku miding, for a salad. Among the other delicacies that graced Ping's table were bamboo shoots, lotus root, banana, fresh chilies, spicy pickles and coconut milk. These he arranged on fine china plates and placed on the table before us. The rain drummed hypnotically on the rooftop, fluted musically down from the eaves as we drank Ping's hot tea and feasted on the vegetable dishes and a deep bowl of custardy fruit that smelled like garbage but had a profoundly satisfying flavor.[23] The un-penned animals—chickens and ducks—crowded into the house for cover, along with a continuous parade of large and elaborate insects. Pitch Pipe stood on his hind legs, his forelegs on Ping's knees. Ping picked him up and placed him upon his lap. A gecko skittered across the room. Two macaques frolicked wildly at the lintel. Ping's home quickly filled up with a frowsy, malodorous aroma laced with the wet smell of jungle and blossom and rain.

Outside, in the dripping forest, breezes shook the trees, and birds like mynas and barbets called out. Inside we grew drowsy, climbed into the warm bed—Ping happily sandwiched between zombie girl and pig. Pitch Pipe nuzzled into Ping's stomach, trying to push his way through him toward me. I, too, snuggled up closer to Ping, pressing up against his backside. The rain continued its drippy lullaby and soon enough we all fell asleep.

I was awakened by a rooster crowing in the dawn. I was alone in the bed. The kitchen was clean. The food and china had been put away. Ping was gone. Pitch Pipe was gone. And when I went outdoors to investigate, I found all of the pigs were gone, too. I walked around the compound, walked around, walked around, like a second hand sweeping a clock face. Ducks quacked. Chickens pecked. The sheep, no longer penned up, munched on the elephant grass. The goat followed me neurotically around the deserted camp. I'm not sure how long I circled. In the end I sat on the threshold, waiting for Ping to return.

Morning crawled toward noon, the heat and humidity rising. Insects landed on my neck, legs and arms and feasted. The sheep grazed further and further afield, the distances between them multiplying. The goat, clearly annoyed, trotted off into the forest. On Ping's doorstep I grew drowsy and slept and woke until I was sure he was not coming home. Then, I stood up, smoothed out my dress and headed back toward Saint Ali.

THE TUNNEL OF LIGHT

The manicured front lawn of Saint Ali was crawling with big black vehicles. Daimlers, BMW and Mercedes sedans and SUVs—there must have been eight or nine of them parked like gargantuan beetles hunkering amid the rose bushes. I tiptoed around them and crept to the back of the building. Alas, the gate was locked, so I circled back to the front and found the main entrance wide open, the atrium space deserted except for a lone fellow with a camera and recorder, his nose pressed against one of the glass cases as if the better to ponder its contents.

The long corridors, too, were quiet, oddly so, but I heard noise at one end of the building where the passageway ran into the lecture hall that formed one of the arms of the "U." A crowd of white-haired residents was assembled at the door of the auditorium, and no one shooed them away so I joined them, peering out over the sea of cotton-topped craniums at a collection of men, women, microphones, and camera equipment engaged in what appeared to be a press conference.

On the stage in the front of the auditorium a table had been set up. Behind the table, decked out in a powder-blue cardigan sweater and shell set, her face dusted a disturbingly bright magenta shade, was a frail and much-changed Loretta Soren-Schmidt. Where once she was delicate, she now was brittle. Where once she'd been gentle, she seemed harsh. The silvery aura that had distinguished her seemed to have been transformed by some crude alchemy into lead. Understandable for a woman who had, as I was about to discover, recently come back from the dead.

To her right sat Dr. Hodge, to her left the mean little Gita. Staring up at the table, trailing wires and assistants, cameras, microphones and various recording devices extended, were the journalists.

"Dr. Hodge. Dr. Hodge. Are you certain that she was dead?"

"Of course we are certain."

"What was the time of death?"

"She died between three and four a.m. on the night of November 7th."

"Dr. Hodge, how long did you say she was dead?"

"Mrs. Soren-Schmidt was dead for thirty-four hours."

A hush filled the room, but only for an instant, and it exploded again into questions.

"Was she ill, Dr. Hodge? Who found her? Has her family been notified?"

"Mrs. Soren-Schmidt was the last of the Schmidts here in the Cameron Highlands. Distant relatives in Europe have been notified. Our head nurse found her in the morning," he lied. Gita sat up very straight and smiled. She beamed at the doctor.

"Of course, this is astounding," Hodge continued. "It is a medical and metaphysical miracle, if I may be so dramatic." Here he crossed some imaginary line. "Never before," he said gravely. "Never before have scientific and spiritual data been so perfectly co-joined as to give us absolute proof of an afterlife."

At this lofty proclamation, Mrs. Soren-Schmidt stirred. She threw back her head and stuck her arms up into the air like a puppet on the end of taut strings. "I was dead for thirty-four hours," she gasped in a wheezy and breathless falsetto. "It was marvelous, I tell you. Do not be afraid of your death."

"Mrs. Soren-Schmidt. Mrs. Soren-Schmidt . . ." The journalists turned their attention to her. "Were you conscious? Could you feel anything? What happened? What did you see?"

In tune with the drama of the moment, Mrs. Soren-Schmidt rose from her chair. She gazed out over the upturned and expectant faces with a look of superiority and relish. My elderly neighbors held their breaths, waiting for her pronouncements. She paused for a long time for affect and an eerie silence drifted in over the room.

"It was dark at first," the old lady began, standing ramrod straight, her arms extended before her now, like a woman walking in her sleep. "And I did not know I was dead."

She stopped her narrative and engaged the reporters and onlookers again, this time with a look of mystery.

"I was cold, very cold, but that feeling passed, and I felt as though I were floating, floating up in one corner of my room. Do you know what it feels like to be lifted ever so gently, like a feather on a breeze, up, up, and away? It was like it was when I was a child and my father took me up in his arms and carried me away to my bedroom and my slumbers. That is how it felt. Lovely. Safe.

"I could see myself on the bed below me." Mrs. Soren-Schmidt stared down at the table before her, as if she could see herself lying there. "I looked so tiny, so frail, and I felt an overwhelming compassion for the woman on the bed. 'Poor woman,' I thought, 'poor, poor woman. She has tried so hard and she's tired. She is so very tired.' I wanted to reach down and comfort the woman on the bed, but I couldn't. I didn't seem to have a body at all but I felt complete, fully sentient.

"Hospital staff came and went. I could see them all, running here and there, calling out to one another, so concerned. Doctor Hodge was so solicitous. I could feel his care. You were heroic, Dr. Hodge."

She turned to the doctor, who brightened at the compliment, saying humbly, but loud enough for recorders to catch, "I am a doctor. It is my calling to care."

"And the staff," Mrs. Soren-Schmidt added, "they were all so efficient."

The head nurse straightened and smiled.

"But they couldn't see me. All they saw was a dead woman there on the bed. I wanted to call out to them, tell them I was all right, but I couldn't. And that is what I want you to know," said Mrs. Soren-Schmidt, gazing out over the crowd. "I want you to know that the body dies, but you, the parts that make you who you are, live on."

She took a deep breath and beamed her message out to every being in the room, her eyes moving soulfully from one person to the next—the journalists, my elderly neighbors—searching each face until her gaze met mine and she stopped.

My throat constricted. My stomach turned.

"Yes. Now, where was I?" asked the much-pleased old woman.

"Oh, yes, I was floating above the dead woman and the staff, but I couldn't tell anyone I was there. Then I wondered, 'Am I a ghost? Is this what a ghost feels like? Am I doomed to float forever, alone and unnoticed in a disembodied limbo?' I'm sure you've all wondered about this. Wondered and worried. I was filled with a great melancholia."

Again, Mrs. Soren-Schmidt paused for affect, her cupped hand placed over her heart. She had arranged her visage into a look of profound sorrow, so profound as to be nearly comic.

"And then, as they wheeled my body away . . ."

"Mrs. Schmidt, you were ill weren't you? Alzheimer's, wasn't it? Isn't that what Dr. Hodge said? Late stage Alzheimer's?"

"Mrs. *Soren*-Schmidt," the old lady corrected. "You are far too impatient, young man, and rude to interrupt in that way. What are you trying to say, anyway? I am in the middle of telling my story."

Her mood changed dramatically. She became suddenly irritable, testy, but she calmed down a bit, put a hand to a brow and continued. "I wondered, *What will happen to me? Is this what death means? Is it an eternity of loneliness?* And that, my dears, is when I saw it. 'What?' you might ask. Why, a tunnel of light.

"They wheeled the body away and I felt abandoned, but just at that moment I saw, felt, came to know, what I can only describe as a tractor beam of warmth, light, and bliss. It opened above me. It was pulsating, too, as if it were alive, made of sentience, filled with love and compassion and every good thing I have ever imagined. And it was calling to me. Not in a voice, you understand, but in a language so pure and clear that it defied misapprehension. It was beauty and truth, and I knew that it was the center of my—of everyone's—highest good. 'Come, come,' the voices seemed to say, and I longed with all of my being to join them."

Mrs. Soren-Schmidt had us; we were all in her hands and she knew this as well, as surely as she knew what the voices desired. She closed her eyes—those thin-lidded eyes—her face suffused with satisfaction as she continued.

"Of course, this is the point we have all heard about. The point at which one must decide whether we want to live or move on. Many have come to this gateway, returned, and told others about the experience. But, you see, I didn't want to return. There was nothing left to bind me to this world: the worn-out husk of a body, an enfeebled mind. All my loved ones were dead. I was ready.

"So I did it. I let go, and when I did, I could feel myself being pulled—slowly, tenderly—right into the source of the light. What was it like? It was like the embrace of millions of arms, the touch of countless hands. I felt welcomed and loved and whole. I felt like I'd just been born. Soft centers of energy pressed up around me and I recognized them. One by one the entities made themselves known. Subtle greetings. There was a sound like a murmur, like a heart shushing blood, or the roar in the inside of a shell. I felt myself spreading, thin and wide and forever, like a blanket stretched out over the universe, and then I was the one embracing the others with compassion; they were all part of me."

Mrs. Soren-Schmidt opened her eyes. Hodge proffered a handkerchief and she brought it to her eyes. When she removed it, her eyes glistened with tears. They rolled down her rouged cheeks.

"There was warmth; there was light; there was movement. There were constant comings and goings and the excitement of souls embarking on new journeys and others coming back—such a sweet, single-celled celebration. Who knew?" she sniffled, dabbing her eyes again with the handkerchief. "And I'm back now, you see, to tell you about this. To tell you that there *is* a Heaven."

Mrs. Soren-Schmidt seemed to cave in at that point. She collapsed into the chair like a marionette, a creaky shell of a woman. Through much of her speech she'd been staring at me and the sour feeling in my gut had been growing. One moment she'd been animated, full of fire and intent, and the next she was broken and doll-like, like a battery-driven plaything run down. The end of her talk was greeted with a thunderous new round of questions.

"Mrs. Soren-Schmidt, what religion are you?"

"Is the Alzheimer's gone?"

"Did you want to come back?"

"How do you feel now?"

"Do you think there's a god?"

"Will you stay at Saint Ali?"

"Is there some way we can get an exclusive?"

"The patient is tired," said Dr. Hodge. "She has had a very big day . . . days, in fact," he corrected. "We must get her to bed, but of course I will stay. I'll be happy to answer your questions."

"I am just thankful," said Mrs. Soren-Schmidt, raising herself from her stupor, "to be able to bring back this news to you all, to allay your fears, calm your spirits."

The muscles in her face worked powerfully, as if holding back a huge wave of emotion. The ancient crowd at the door began moving forward, pushing their way into the room. The journalists yelled out more questions. Two certified medical technicians mounted the stage with a collapsible wheelchair, which they opened behind the old woman. The nurse seated at the table stood up to assist. Mrs. Soren-Schmidt threw one last glance over the room with its hopeful and attentive masses. She dismissed them all with a look of contempt, then her eyes caught mine and I knew that every word in the story she'd told was a lie, that this was not Mrs. Soren-Schmidt at all, but Clément, and that the emotion that he was holding back was not gratitude or reverence. It was laughter.

COLD CUTS XXXII

The cockroach skated around on the circle of egg, slipping and sliding on its journey across the flat, greasy surface. Ryu grimaced, mouth turning downward in his "unlucky" face. The breakfast buffet at the Holiday Inn in Kuala Lumpur was substandard, consisting of troughs full of rubbery eggs, fatty bacon, leathery ham, and watery, ketchup-soaked beans. The Asian offering was equally unappetizing. Ryu undoubtedly wished he were back in Tokyo where the food and the women were fresh.

Unlike his breakfast that morning, Ryu was amazingly fresh. Amazing because he had been on the road for weeks, starting with the late flight from Tokyo to Amsterdam on the day the story about Nakamura's murder appeared in the *Sports Mainichi*. I had escaped to Amsterdam thanks to Lou Lou and Clément, but the trail was already cold the next day when Ryu arrived in the Dutch city, and so was the photographer's corpse. Alain de la Cuisse, Lou Lou's half-brother, photographer, and the man I totally fell for, was found dead in a canal house shortly before the wheels of Ryu's plane touched the tarmac; and the police were again looking for me. Ryu knew that in spite of Albert's wild accusations, Alain's death was not my work. I'm sure he read a familiar signature in the scene. It was a suspicion confirmed when he received the furious phone calls from his yakuza superiors demanding the whereabouts of their infernal "courier." It had, after all, been Ryu's job to keep an eye on Clément, an assignment doomed to failure.

The cockroach discontinued its progress. It stood stock still on the pale yellow egg yolk, eating or shitting, it was hard to tell which. Ryu poured a short glass of beer, picked up the bottle of hot sauce on the table, dribbled a target around the insect and relaxed.

It was a classic double-cross. Someone else had been advised that the chip was in Amsterdam and in the photographer's possession. Unfortunately, the only delivery that Alain was aware of was his sister's friend and the little bonus of heroin tucked away in her bags.

Alain's murderers, however, were under the impression that he had knowingly taken possession of the chip. They thought they could intercept it. But Alain had no knowledge of this other contraband, and all the torture in the world couldn't get its whereabouts from him. Now he was dead, Clément and I were missing, and no one, including Ryu, had any earthly idea where the microchip was. So he followed the only trail he could, and it led him to Alain's houseboat.

The cockroach was on the move again, on a path that took it right through the peppery red moat. How tough are a cockroach's feet? The amber-colored insect sprinted through the spicy river and tangoed about on the egg. Did it feel things in the way that men did? Did it think? Did it suffer? Or, did it merely react?

Unfortunately there had been no houseboat by the time Ryu arrived at Nieuwe Doelenstraat, though there was still debris in the river. Alain's houseboat had been ransacked, presumably as part of a search, and then someone had blown it to bits. His carbonized photos had plumed upward in cinders that floated out over the fingers of water, out over the Amstel, out over the inland sea.

"You know, it rained money," the bewhiskered local had remarked from his spot canal-side, a few yards from Ryu. "Yes, lots of money on that boat."

Ryu picked up the plate and the egg slid to one side, the cockroach dangling for an instant at the greasy precipice before disappearing over the edge and scrambling beneath the plate.

That had been over a couple of months ago. Two months of waiting. Clément made it clear at once to all concerned that he was responsible for my flight, that Ryu was no more than a pawn, albeit an important one as Clément would deal with no one but him. Two months of waiting, hung out like a piece of rotting meat to attract the giant fly in the ointment. The photographer's friend, Albert, was missing. The other girl, Lou Lou, had also disappeared, so there was no getting any answers out of her. During that time, Clément sent Ryu tips—tips that led nowhere. Ryu engaged in a series of wild goose chases that confirmed for all that it was the ghoul's game. But for Ryu there was no going back. He would simply be glad when the "mission" was over. From the start he had hated working with Clément. He detested surprises and he hated being caught off guard. He knew he was no more than a patsy, a plaything, the mouse in a game of cat and mouse. Clément was toying with all of them; Ryu knew that. He wasn't sure why and he didn't particularly care; he just wanted to make it stop. His yakuza superiors were also tired of the ghoul's tricks. The Consortium was leaning on them. They wanted their info back. They would soon start punishing the failures.

Ryu's 'I spy a cockroach' expression hadn't changed. He took another sip of his beer, noting with some revulsion the stub of a missing pinky finger. So disgusting. Ryu despised imperfection, and now he was permanently stamped with it. Better to die, to be blown away in any number of gruesome ways than to become the object of your own contempt. The very thought of it made his head spin: but he had a job to do. He would finish it. Then he would find some way to make amends to himself. It would involve some killing, he was sure.

In fact, it was sure to be quite a bloodbath. The authorities had been notified of my re-emergence and with them, the Consortium, the yakuza, and everyone else with whom those in power secretly did business. They'd all be converging on Saint Ali. What a free-for-all it was going to become. But first, Ryu had decided to have breakfast. He'd already ID'd the Consortium lackeys there at the hotel. They were on the hunt too; they would try to reach me first. He needed to be fortified for the ensuing encounter.

Ryu put the plate down and finished his beer. From his suit breast pocket he pulled a brochure for a residence for the elderly in the Cameron Highlands. The photos made it look quite spectacular. One image featured several sapphire-blue pools in a sunlit and rose-studded courtyard that surrounded a palace-like edifice with swirling white towers and domes. Another picture featured a grand colonial façade—all columns and windows and wide, well-kept grounds. He turned the brochure over and noted the address, then he tucked the brochure back into his pocket. The Consortium men had already set out. No problem. It was usually not a good idea to be the first to arrive at a party.

He lifted the plate. The cockroach skittered out. He watched it make its way across the top of the table. It had ruined his breakfast, but fine; let it go. Why waste the effort? Soon enough he'd be up to his elbows in roaches.

DR. FRANKENSTEIN, I PRESUME

It must have taken a real miracle to get Mrs. Soren-Schmidt out of the auditorium, jammed as it was with the noisy masses, all of them delighted by the drama. How the nurse's assistants did it remains a mystery to me. I slipped away, looking for a place to hide, not wanting to be spotted by the doctors or nurses or any more crazy residents with jars. It was quiet up in the patients' rooms—everyone was in the downstairs halls. Looking for a refuge, I climbed the stairs, headed for the one place on the grounds that I'd actually found a moment of sanctuary.

Mrs. Soren-Schmidt's room was empty, the closet bare, the bed stripped. A sultry breeze blew in from the window, which looked out over the wide front lawns. It sent the thin curtains waving inward. It sighed through the room. It reminded me of Ping and a profound sense of longing overwhelmed me. That longing drew me to the window. That's when I saw them pull up—another black Daimler and several police cars. The vehicles came screeching into the drive. Almost immediately, I heard loud voices and a commotion in the entryway below.

I drew back from the window, threw my back against the wall only to encounter another grim surprise. There she was in the doorway, whey-faced and wobbly—Mrs. Soren-Schmidt. Only it was not the old lady at all—that much was clear. It was Clément.

Clément posed in the doorway, as though for a photo, one thin arm bracing himself against the lintel, the other crooked, his hand gently cupped against chin and cheek. The blue cardigan sweater and the pale blue lap blanket had fallen away and he stood, freakishly steady, on legs too thin to support the old woman. Not even the bright rouge of magenta could mask the darkening blue-gray hue of her lips and skin.

"Well, what did you think?" he asked proudly. "Quite a performance, eh? Don't you just love the way people cling to cliché?"

He swaggered into the room, took a seat on the unclothed bed. "Oh god, it's embarrassing. It's so *EASY*. All that stuff about god and love and everlasting life—what a crock, and they want to believe it. Human beings are so *literal*."

I was still standing, back to the wall, knees weak, any small sense of purpose leaking out of me. He seemed not to notice.

"Whatever happened to spirit? What happened to constant and unwavering faith? Why the big need for assurances? Weak, that's what man's faith is. If the truth came down and knocked on humanity's door, humanity would crucify it. Yes, and you've done just that, as a matter of fact, haven't you? It's completely appalling. Ludicrous," he concluded and sniffed, his eyes trapping mine, moving from them to my nose, my mouth, and then possessively down the length of my body, taking slow inventory.

"But enough of this. Do you know that you are in the gravest danger? I have come to warn you. You are in the hornet's nest, the lion's den. You are in a veritable snake pit, here, at Saint Ali. I thought you'd be safe here, far from prying eyes, but that damnable Hodge has set off the alarm. The police and consequently the yakuza, the Consortium and your father all know where you are. These are the very people who seek your demise. They need a dead girl. I, however, have my heart set on a live one or, more to the point, a live-dead one. My underworld trumps theirs, so I get what I want . . . well, almost.

"You know the game now. You know what's at risk. Call it high stakes blackmail. Call it gaming. Call it the double, triple, quadruple cross. Carlyle double-crossed Christian who stored information on the chip as insurance against his own organization, the Consortium. The yakuza are blackmailing the Consortium, who now know it exists, so Christian needs it back. I set this gambit in motion. How much is your life worth, Erin? Seven billion? More? You are as good as dead, only worth what you're holding; without it, worthless. Except to me.

"I don't want the money. Here is the real twist. All of this—this elaborate intrigue, the whole live-dead thing—is simply to make you mine. But you keep pushing me away, and I am the only means of your survival. I wish I could make you understand that. So, my dear, what do you say? Let me ask you again in these strange new circumstances. Won't you entrust me with your life? Come away with me now, I beseech you."

I could not have looked very approving, and Clément read my expression at once.

"Oh, right. You think I'm unappealing. Why? Because I feed on the dead? Who doesn't? Who doesn't? God, I hate that kind of hypocrisy. I don't see you living on air. I'm just honest about it. If I disgust anyone it's because I do exactly what they do, but without the denial, the falsehood, the untruth. I am what I am, and I don't pretend to be anything else. But you don't see that, do you? You don't care.

"So let me appeal instead, stupid girl, to your instinct for self-preservation. Let's ponder that for a moment. What exactly are your alternatives? You can stay here and let the police or the Consortium or the yakuza take you. None of those options ends well for you. Or, you can come with me. And don't for an instant think that you can find Ping. Ping has other priorities. He let those pigs out and he's on the wrong end of the villagers' wrath. He's wanted at Saint Ali. Remember Alain? Trust me, there'll be no help from Ping.

"So, let me invite you properly." The ghoulish old woman got down on her knees. "Come away with me, darling. Let me take you away."

I was tired, truly horrified, but what could I do? He'd set me up, made it impossible for me to escape without him. There was also the not-so-veiled threat in the allusion to Alain. How would he punish Ping? Clément rose from his knees, reached out, and with a sly smile that looked grotesque on Mrs. Soren-Schmidt's dead face, took my hand. I felt the old woman's fingers curl around mine imprisoning them, but I did not withdraw my hand.

OUT OF THE CLOSET

"Oh, please no more criticism," Clément hissed as he slipped into Hodge's office. He'd hidden me there when I accepted his proposal, just in time to avoid detection.

"Why is it always Judgment Day with you? Granted this," he indicated his current appearance, "is a rag, but that's what you get in the back alleys of Kuala Lumpur."

Clément had divested himself of the high profile corpse of Mrs. Soren-Schmidt. He was "dressed" instead as an ancient Malaysian man, rail-thin and bent nearly double.

"Short notice," he quipped dryly. "It's the outfit I arrived in."

The body was definitely worse for the wear after spending the last day and a half stashed somewhere on the grounds.

"They'll be looking for an old woman and a girl. You, we can't disguise, but I thought I'd just put on yesterday's outfit. Yes, it needs pressing. There's this fold in the middle. What can I say? No hangers in the janitor's closet."

Press were still buzzing around like wasps, while the police asked the administrators questions. Meanwhile, Consortium representatives with concealed firearms were conducting their own private search.

None of this was exactly furtive. In fact we could hear the noises in the corridor. They were coming closer and closer. There was a sudden commotion just outside the door. Clément brought a crooked old finger to his lips. "Sshhh," he warned.

I watched in horror as the doorknob turned, wondering how the skinny brown gnome beside me would be able to save us when the police or the yakuza or the evil Consortium goon squad or whoever was on the opposite side of the door busted in. Clément seemed oddly untroubled. We heard hurried shouts from down the hall, shouts full of directions.

The doorknob stopped turning, the footsteps moved away. Clément turned to me and flashed a toothless smile. "It seems our Consortium pals have arrived—to the dismay of their yakuza blackmailers. And I suspect that just about now, they've discovered the latest surprise. No Erin. No chip. Oh, they're going to be very upset." He twirled around like a nasty old troll and, sidling up to me, pawed at my arm with his days-dead hands.

"Don't worry, Princess," he whispered. "I'll protect you. But for once . . . ," he grew petulant, "you have to do just as I say."

"In a few minutes we are going to make our break. There'll be lots of confusion when the two forces meet. And just to complicate the tangle, I've led the villagers to believe that they can find Ping hiding here at the hospital, so they'll be here looking for their pigs as well. That's the set-up—plenty of chaos and your only chance; so follow me and don't look back."

He was fast, very fast. It was a grisly sight to see a cadaver moving with such speed. We could hear the melee in another part of the building and Clément, taking immediate advantage of the opportunity, dashed down the suddenly empty corridor and into the courtyard outside. In broad daylight, we flashed past white walks and sparkling blue pools, two fleeing shades in the sunlight.

I do know that only one set of eyes saw us go. Ryu watched us from the window of Dr. Hodge's office, his eyes steely and filled with his private and inscrutable resolve. He saw us leave and said nothing, going back upstairs, methodically stepping over the corpses.

GLOW, LITTLE GLOW WORM

There is a kind of beetle in Malaysia, one with shimmering capabilities—a firefly. Like many other fireflies, the female has a luminescent organ on the seventh segment of her thorax while the male has them on the sixth and seventh segments. These segments are endowed with a transparent cuticle that acts like the glass around a light filament. The bodies of these insects secrete an enzyme called luciferase which when supplied with oxygen from the creature's respiration ignites to create a light. But the beetles in some parts of India, Malaysia, the Philippines, and New Guinea are special. They synchronize their lights, so that they don't twinkle randomly but light up in a succession that resembles the flashing on a chain of Christmas tree lights. Clouds of these creatures buzzed and circled just below the forest canopy around the towering meranti, kapor, and keruing trees, winking off and on in a syncopated rhythm that was almost hypnotic. Beneath them the forest floor was bright, the broad-leafed ferns, spiky flowers, and twining creepers looking nearly neon underneath their gleam. Above them the umbrella of epiphyte-draped foliage hovered, dark and nearly impenetrable, and beyond that, night rolled out like the inside of a sock or glove, moonless and papered with wan stars.

It wasn't raining, and I was grateful. It was hard enough pushing deeper and deeper into the murky rainforest. There were the night rumblings—odd rustlings, whooshes, hoots: the kind of soft, subtle sounds that seem to ring out in the silence. There was also the sound of my breath, heavy and ragged. Clément had no breath at all, and I felt again the terrifying emptiness that had once followed me through the inky Tokyo streets.

Behind us there were people in pursuit. We had heard the villagers, seen them with their makeshift torches—glass jars filled with fireflies—swarming through the plantations, up and down the hillsides, into the forest—like fire ants—after their runaway pigs. With them, I assumed were policemen, Consortium lackeys, probably yakuza, and perhaps even a few reporters. Every so often, I would stop to listen to their voices, far away and unintelligible, flying up into the benighted sky. I would hang there, ears cocked, mouth open, lost in the sing-song of their anger and despair until Clément's dark tentacle would touch my arm, my shoulder, and chill me into motion.

"Don't dawdle," he whispered. "Hurry. Follow me."

The police, of course, had dogs. Bloodhounds. We had heard their baying earlier and they had frightened me. But the dogs had only my scent and Clément had carried me like a huge sack of rice a good part of the way so that we would not leave a trail. It had not seemed a simple thing for him to do, carrying the body of a largish woman across his scrawny shoulders. But the creature transporting me did not stagger under the weight or stumble as an ordinary human might. This walking corpse was tireless.

There was a point at which we stopped and Clément told me I could walk, but he watched me carefully as if I might sprint for freedom. Freedom? That was impossible. If I had any will, he had sapped me of it as surely as a parasitic wasp saps the strength of the unwilling caterpillar upon which its offspring will feed. My prison was my body; it was the almost listless entity he'd made of me. There was no escape from that.

"Let's wait here for a moment," he said.

The sounds of pursuit had dwindled off in the distance and then fallen away. We were in a small clearing walled in by the long smooth trunks of trees wreathed in curling creepers from the jungle floor and drooping lianas spilling down from the dark canopy overhead. Clément leaned his skinny dead body against a tree, the leafy trailers parting slightly before coming to rest on his narrow shoulders.

"I love the jungle at night," he sighed. "It's so alive."

He was not winded at all, though he had run quickly, carrying me for what must have been miles, and his voice had an otherworldly sound to it. It had become so clear and resonant, not the sharp scratching of sibilants that generally issued from the mouths of his various moldering incarnations.

"They will kill it though," he added. "Humanity. Like a great plague or a virulent infestation, man will devour the world. He will hack it to bits and set it on fire and cover it with his excrement. Even now, these trees, these very vines, are ghosts. I should know. I live on the refuse. I and the flies and the rats and the other vermin that man so despises, hypocrite that he is. Who, if he had this garden to walk in, would give it up, would kill it? What kind of fiend?"

Clément shook his head, gazed up at the blinking fireflies and down at the stiff and claw-like fingers of the dead Malaysian's hands. "If I had it, I would treasure it and worship it. I would never let it go."

He moved one hand toward me, pawed at my forearm with it.

"You are so beautiful, Erin, like this forest—so alive. I want to keep you, so I have made a net to imprison you. A faulty net, it seems, and full of holes."

He continued to poke at me with the stiff hand and fingers. He was all bones and skin. The old man's already meager flesh was loose and beginning to form gray blisters. This was a monster wooing me. I moved my arm—not much, just a bit—to put it out of reach. Clément spat out his fury.

"Still spurned like something horribly corrupt. All right, I'm a nose-to-the-ground, corpse-eating ghoul. But why can't I aspire for more than that? Why can't I break the rules? You do. You're a zombie. You're supposed to do my bidding, but you still behave like a vain human bitch. You're as grotesque as I am. More. You're an even bigger freak."

It was strange to see the little brown man rage, almost humorous, and I know that I was grinning because Clément narrowed his nearly hollow eyes and stepped back from me. He caught my gaze and held it, as if he saw his wrinkled, gnomish figure reflected there. Then, he paused.

My face was hot. My cheeks and eyelids beaded with a thin web of perspiration. Above us the fireflies continued to dance, flashing luminous messages at one another in their elaborate courting rituals.

Clément threw back his head and stretched the old Malaysian's neck until it looked like it would snap. "I am not this body!" he raged to the bright beetles overhead. "What am I, then, you might ask," he added turning a keen and evil glare toward me. "I am a sentient being just like you. Just like a cat, a dog, or a rat. Just like a flower, a tree. Just like anything that lives. I'm different, yes, but not inferior. And only with this body can I tell you how I feel. Trees, animals, all living things can communicate in a myriad of ways. You don't listen. I, a ghoul, can only do this when I have a corpse to project from. I am a prisoner, just like you are—sentience occupying an inadequate form.

"But that," he added suddenly calm, "is my problem, isn't it? And yours, Erin, is that you are stuck with me. Stuck because I want you, and I am willful, and I will not let you go."

The leer had long since dropped from my face. I didn't find him funny anymore. If I had any feelings, they were lost, hidden in the series of unimaginable options that surrounded me like distorting funhouse mirrors. He had me trapped. There was no way out. And so I did the only thing that I could possibly do at that moment, something dictated not by me, but by my body. I let out a long, slow, steady stream of urine. It rained down between my legs and made a little steaming pool on the damp rainforest floor.

Clément watched this first with a look of shock, then one of surprise. Then, he laughed.

"Pathetic zombie," he said, and shook his scrawny head. "Come on, let's go." And we continued on through the forest.

A POSSE OF PIGS

Everywhere they looked there were pigs. The rainforest was full of them: fat pink and brown porkers squealing around in the brush. This was, of course, very distracting to the dogs and an obstacle to the hunt. Between the canine trackers, the police, the remaining Consortium representative, recruits from the hospital staff, the angry villagers, and the pigs that Ping had released, the forest had morphed into a circus. At least, that is what Ryu must have thought as he fumbled along with the others trying to pick up our trail.

He hoped that this mob wouldn't find us. It wasn't so much that he wanted to protect me and Clément as that he had a sense of propriety, and a torch-bearing alliance of good citizens and bad seemed disorderly, undignified, and disgustingly unprofessional. He wanted to capture the quarry himself, to do it with grace and style and with intellectual relish. This was a free-for-all open to riff-raff not much better, as he saw it, than the creatures they were after. And there was me. I was carrying the microchip. Ryu had to make sure the yakuza got that back. And so he went along, more to ensure the safety of the pursued than the success of the pursuers.

He had watched us leave, had known we were hiding in Hodge's office. He could find Clément anywhere now. He had only to follow his nose. But he found it less than productive to discover us there at the hospital with a furious posse on hand to hijack the merchandise that it was his job to recover and trade. So he had sagely retreated, let us scamper away from the hospital while he went upstairs to further cut back on the competition.

In this he'd been rather successful. Hodge he dispatched in the hallway downstairs. The administrator was conducting his own furtive and timorous search after being advised by the authorities and his superiors that he had better find us and fast. It was a simple matter for Ryu to sneak up behind Hodge, put one arm around his chest, and run his knife across his throat. He did this with the grace of a cellist. It was quick. It was clean. No longer would the good doctor worry about his failing prospects or lament his wasted promise. He was at rest, his head, nearly severed from his neck, propped up against the corridor wall, his body sprawled out as though at leisure, like a man enjoying his music.

There were two Consortium gunmen upstairs, and for them Ryu had to resort to a firearm. He used a Ruger S.A. with a silencer, waiting for one of the men in a resident's bedroom and plugging him right between his raised eyebrows. The man had a look of surprise on his face, and Ryu couldn't help smiling as his finger pressed back on the trigger. Poof. Spliff. The gunman's mouth fell open in a gaping "oh," as the bullet hit his soft pillow of brain.

Ryu picked the other off near the stairwell, as the ruffian tried to interrogate one of the residents, a young Indian boy clutching a jar. Ryu shot this assassin first in the shoulder and then in the back of the knee. His first two targets had been too easily achieved. There was a lot to atone for. Ryu wanted to play slightly rough for a while. The man responded with fury, rising up like a baited bear and turning on the much shorter Japanese man. But Ryu was unruffled, delivering the next three shots with deliberate satisfaction. He shot the weapon out of the big man's hand, he shot out the second kneecap, and when the man crashed to the floor in a paroxysm of pain, he blew off the top of his head. Our favorite yakuza still made it a point to finish both gunmen off with his trusty blade. That way he could be certain the deed was done right. He didn't want any comebacks. He stepped over the Indian boy who had curled up, uninjured, in a fetal position at the top of the stairwell, his body wrapped tightly around the jar.

Ryu had counted a third Consortium assassin, but he opted to save him for later. The police were on hand and with them an angry collection of plaintiff villagers. His instincts told him to minimize damage, especially to anyone with no real idea of what was actually going on.

To the police, this was about an American girl accused of murder and smuggling. To the villagers, it was about their pigs. To the hospital staff, it was about a resident run wild. To the Consortium it was about obscene secrets that needed to be kept. To me it was about escape. I don't know what it was all about to Clément—I think about me. But to Ryu, it was about a mess, a mission out of control and a small spot of blood (he flashed back on they ladybug-sized stain on the Haitian desk clerk's white shirt) that was growing and growing and threatening to turn into an ocean.

Even before Ryu had dispatched some of the competition, the chase had moved to the rainforest. There the villagers fell upon the pigs as they found them, abandoning the search as soon as they'd secured an errant swine to call their own. The hospital workers, too, deserted early on, before the forest closed completely around them. The police, however, were determined and so were the dogs, but they couldn't pick up the scent. That's because they were trying to track a girl instead of a stinking ghoul. Ryu stayed just long enough to make sure that his quarry was not going to fall into the wrong hands. When he was certain of that, he made his exit. There was a big mess back at the hospital and he didn't want to get mixed up in that. He would find us, but this wasn't the way.

A STIFF DOSE OF REALITY

Any struggle was pointless. I could see this at last, caught fast as a fly in a spider's web as Clément wrapped his stratagems around me. We were at sea, the only passengers on a gas-leaking bumboat chugging into the waters of Riau Archipelago. Our escape was evidently no hastily planned affair. As we made our way through the rainforest, it became clear that my deliverer had planned every twist and turn of our flight. His markers were subtle: an odd-shaped pothole, the jagged gash in the trunk of a tree, two large stones set against one another, but they, and his behavior when he came upon them, were unmistakable. He had carefully mapped out the way. He moved very quickly from one cairn to the next, dragging me, pushing me, prodding me in whatever way he could to run faster.

As dawn broke, the forest thinned, letting in pearly light, then opening up to a bald patch dotted with spindly rubber trees, their trunks deeply scarred from latex-bleeding cuts.[24] On the other side of the torn veil of trees curved a narrow cart path, and upon this a taxicab waited. The driver stood outside the cab, leaning against the front driver's side door, puffing furiously on a damp cigarette, which he held between betel-stained lips. The skinny frame, the oily shoulder-length hair, the red-rimmed eyes were unmistakable. He was the same driver who'd picked me up when I deplaned in Kuala Lumpur. When he saw us, he threw down the butt end of his smoke and threw open the door of the cab. Clément pushed me toward the car.

"Get in, lady," the cabbie said to me for the very last time.

We drove south to Singapore, ultimately inching our way along in the long queue of vehicles and people that trickled across the border. I had been with Clément for over twenty-four hours. The muscular rigor that had gripped his body earlier seemed to have left him. Flies had found him in the jungle and he had grown maggoty, but the first instar hatchlings were tiny and concentrated mainly in the back of his head. Both Clément and the driver seemed unaware of their presence, but I could see them clearly from my place in the back seat directly behind Clément. They were in constant motion, seeming to multiply and fatten before my very eyes, dropping, like the flakes in a very bad case of dandruff, onto Clément's collar and shoulders. It wasn't until we were in central Singapore, the border well behind us, that the driver noticed the burgeoning numbers of rice-like worms dropping onto the seat and thrusting toward him, a development that sent the little man into a fit as he spat out his fury in a shower of betel-colored abuse before screeching to a halt and tossing us from his cab. He screamed at Clément as he tried to sweep the offending larvae from the car.

Clément seemed to take the mistreatment in stride. "You can never pay them enough," he said humorlessly, apparently irritated only by the fact that he had a new "situation" to address.

I saw, suddenly, the pitifully short leash upon which Clément's nature allowed him to play and the frustration of his existence, chained as he was to the brief and never-ending cycle of degeneration that measured out his lives—the maggots, the signs of the bloat that was beginning to balloon in his abdomen. "Right," he snarled, staring back at me with newly bulging eyes. "Not very pretty is it? A couple of days and I'm not fit to be seen in public." We were standing at the corner of Killeney and Orchard Roads, cars whizzing by, pedestrians, with more time for examination, turning their heads to stare.

"This is the part that sucks," he said. "Not bad alone—undignified, but manageable, but I can't very well crawl along in some culvert with you in tow. So, I am exposed."

He brushed at his shoulders and the back of his head, launching a throng of maggots out over Singapore's perfectly groomed sidewalk and street. "Obviously time for a change," he said irritably. "Execrable timing. Damn, I wish I had a hat."

Fortunately, Clément had the hypersensitivity of a pregnant blowfly where matters of death were concerned. He could locate a prospective corpse almost before the heart had stopped beating. So it was with quick and unerring certainty that he found a necrotic windfall.

He had also managed to locate a hat, which got us into the hospital without drawing much attention. With his wormy skull under wraps he could actually pass for the terminally ill. I had the distracted look of a totally disoriented companion or relation, so we had little trouble infiltrating the house of healing and finding our way to the morgue.

The room was large, quiet, and cold. The metal tables, the acridly chemical odor, the instrument trays and cabinets made me shiver. The smell of death was all around us, the first ptomaine sallies of decay's pungent gases masked under a formaldehyde pall. In a room like this, in just such a place, I was born or died—I wasn't sure which—a familiarity that raised the fine hairs on my neck and arms along with some serious existential questions.

"Oh," said Clément, noting my immediate reaction, "You're remembering how we first met."

He was already at the lockers, already going through drawers of cadavers.

I wasn't thinking about that at all. I was thinking about a life-size illustration of the human body, how it had seduced me with its exquisite architecture, how I had embraced its message. And now, in place of its pinks, reds, and blues, I had the black and white image of a girl on the run, a maze of black flies and white maggots, the colorblind visage of death.

There was a lull in the rattle of drawers and I looked over to see Clément bending over one of the newly departed. He looked like a poor man who had found a jewel, his rapidly deteriorating face suffused with a mixture of pleasure and awe that almost made it appealing.

The drawer was the third level up from the floor, around chest-height for Clément and I watched in fascination as, supporting himself on a dead man's splitting wrists, he pulled himself up to it with all the grace of a gymnast. I could not see the corpse from where I stood, but I could see Clément as he laid himself carefully upon it in what looked just like an embrace. Then I lost sight of Clément, but I could hear a faint and vaguely unpleasant sound coming from the drawer that held Clément and the cadaver. It sounded like kissing, but no, it was closer to sucking, yes, sucking and licking and a loud and gluttonous lip smacking.

The sound—it was such a disturbing sound—did not last very long, but in ways it seemed to go on forever. It was the kind of sound that one does not readily forget, like a catchy melody or a memorable lyric, a sound that one might call *haunting*. To me it is the sound of Clément, and if I am ever prone to feel pity for him, I have only to remember this sound to be reminded of the business that he is always about, a business that can only be repulsive. Clément is a ghoul. He battens on death. Like a flesh fly, a maggot, a crypt beetle, a moth—he's a creature unworthy of compassion.

As I said, the sound lasted no more than a minute or two, though it seemed to go on for hours. Then there was silence—the silence of a morgue—then a loud burping noise and a cough, and a new Clément—short, Chinese, male—climbed out of the temporary coffin.

It was cruel of Clément, I thought, to select that particular body.

"Remind you of someone?" he asked, his black humor very obviously refreshed. "Yes, like Ping," he said, answering for me. "Just like Ping, but not quite."

He was naked, of course, and his appendages—all of them—crimson madder and violet.

"I am a little stiff," quipped Clément as he shuffled toward a cabinet from which he retrieved a bottle or two of formaldehyde. He opened one up and took a deep swig. "This helps," he explained with a wink, and he tucked the bottles under one arm. Then he grabbed a thin coverlet from a stack on one of the counters and draping it around him like a toga, he took my hand in his cold one and pulled me into the corridor.

Clément's ability to animate dead bodies is amazing. He claims it's a skill. It's also a means of survival. It did not take him long to raid a patient's wardrobe, find a wheelchair and arrange himself in it.

"Push," he commanded, and when I resisted, "Look," he said, "I have no problem if I get caught. It's embarrassing, yes, but nothing I haven't handled time and again. But you, you have a lot more to lose. Push me, damn it."

So I did. I pushed him right out of the hospital.

AT SEA XXXVIII

"Ah, now we can relax."

Clément leaned back, happily it seemed, in his torn vinyl seat on the bumboat. Diesel fumes licked up from the engine and into the cabin in oily clouds. We were motoring through the Straits of Malacca and into the South China Sea, chugging along amid the 3,214 islands of the Riau Archipelago. I had no idea where we would land and, oddly, neither did Clément. More oddly still, he didn't seem to care. He had a new lease on life—literally, albeit temporarily—and he was in a jovial mood.

"Serendipity," he exclaimed, holding his wrists out before him as though they were cuffed, "I surrender." Then he threw back his head and laughed, more a honking actually. It was disconcerting to see the dead Chinese man laugh like that.

Less than an hour had elapsed since I'd wheeled Clément from the hospital. A short Singapore cab ride had taken us to the coast where we chartered the cheapest boat we could find to carry us out to sea, the cheapness being more a factor of the quality of the conveyance than the cost. It did not appear to be a particularly seaworthy vessel, but this did not bother Clément who was used to catch as catch can.

The bumboat rode low in the water. Aside from its greasy pilot, rows of dirty red and blue metal barrels, and mountain of sloppily stacked, tightly packed burlap bags, we were its only cargo. Cheerful and relaxing, Clément stood up and stretched, forcing any remaining rigor from the corpse in a series of cracks and pops, though the stiffness was probably due to wear off soon on its own. The clothes that he had stolen were a little tight. He wore ash-colored shorts and a crimson knit shirt that stretched across his bulging belly and made him look like an apple, a pomegranate, or some other kind of fat red fruit. His shoes were too large, but this clearly didn't matter to him. He moved about quickly and erratically with an animation that was cartoon-like and unnaturally spastic. I couldn't take my eyes off him. He was in constant motion and through this mesmerizing flurry of activity, he demanded unwavering attention. It was as though I were hypnotized.

"You know," he said soulfully as he performed a series of stiff-jointed Shaolin-like movements, his gaze never leaving my face, "I am the Dark Prince that you imagine, and while I did appear to assist in killing you—it seemed the only way to save you at the time—and while I did have a hand in planting the microchip, I did not sign your death warrant. For that you would have to look a little, shall we say, closer to home . . ."

I could actually feel my skin crawl, the extension points in his statement reaching creepily back into the convoluted past and an unimaginable future. He was going to divulge something, and I was certain I did not want to hear it.

"The sea, the sea," he said, changing narrative direction as unexpectedly as he shifted from one physical posture to the next, "it is a place of danger and promise." He opened his mouth wide in a yawn that exposed the black tongue and gums. "So many people are afraid of the sea," he continued. "Ocean gods are demanding. But then, that is the nature of gods. They crave sacrifice. Or is it the nature of man? Exquisite masochism, that's what I call it—a megalomaniacal elixir."

Leap and whirl. Leap and whirl. "The dragon swims to the depths," he pronounced sagely. Then, he sat down quietly next to me and took my hand in his. His hands were disconcertingly warm. He grinned at my surprise.

"So many stories and legends attached to the sea, so many myths and archetypes. But here is one that I know you will like. There once were two warring kingdoms: two warring kingdoms, exactly alike, separated by the sea, by a mirror. What to do? Why, there was no other solution but for one to destroy the other. So the ships set sail loaded with warriors full of purpose and the bloated, power-hungry kings. How did a girl come to be among them?

"Did they know, did they suspect that victory required the sacrifice of every vestige of humanity?

"Excuses. Justifications. Rhetoric. Humanity be damned, the war must go on! The king agrees to kill his daughter so that winds will blow.[25] Are you getting the parallel, Erin? That's you—the girl—only your father's a diplomat, not a king. But he's a greedy, power and money hungry bastard like all his friends in the Consortium, as avaricious and self-serving a group of robber barons as ever plundered the planet. They'll stoop to anything. Conspiracy. Terrorism. And Christian had it all captured on the microchip. It was his insurance. But when Carlyle stole it his secret was out, out and available to the highest bidder. Ah, that would be the Consortium. So, why not enlist the aid of a young and infinitely expendable lass to make sure *he* got the chip back. The yakuza would get their money; the Consortium would remain unexposed; and he would retain his power position. 'Keep it in the family,' that's what I say. Of course, there is also the little matter of your inheritance, which was his to control until you came of age. That sweetened the pot. And so you are dead. Consigned to the role of a carry-on by your own dear dad who will call for your corpse and the goods when all is delivered.

"It's horrifying isn't it, almost too terrible to imagine? So mercy, in the form of another powerful force, whisks our princess in the story away, transports her to a city on the Black Sea. She is saved, but not by a human hand, and she must live there in exile. You see how life imitates art? There you are on the verge of annihilation and I, the powerful hand of divinity, save you. I confound Christian, the yakuza, and the Consortium. I disguise you as dead and convey you to a place on a faraway island where you can live out your life in safety. It's touching isn't it? It almost brings tears to the eyes.

"And what matter," he continued, "that I have designs of my own, that I want you, too, in a different way? Isn't it perfect and elegant and just that my needs and yours should converge in this way, and that your salvation lies in my satisfaction? Oh, fate is a fabulous thing.

"And now, at last, our destinies conjoin. What god has united let no man tear asunder."

A monsoon let rip as Clément finished his speech, pummeling the windows of the bumboat, which now rocked crazily on the choppy waters. My mind was seesawing as well, grappling with the thought of betrayal by a father I couldn't even remember. He had controlled every aspect of my life, had virtually murdered my mother—though I saw now that part of her misery came from another, still more sinister presence—had kept me imprisoned in faraway schools where his spies had me under constant surveillance. But through it all, through the hurly-burly rattle and roll of the rain and the storm of confusion that Clément's revelations seemed to have let loose in me, I could see only one thing. One thing alone seemed to rise from the chaos of cloud and shadow as the imminent danger, the unfathomable outcome—garish, unavoidable, potent, and frighteningly omnipresent.

Clément.

I felt tears come to my eyes.

I believe he saw this change in me because he grew silent and, for a moment, stopped. It was as if a carousel had slammed to a halt. We could feel the pitch and roll of the boat, we could hear a cabin door slamming open and shut, open and shut.

Of course it was Clément who broke the silence. "So you see," he said softly, "we have come to this. It will be you and me in a world of my design. And maybe there will be something there for us," he whispered, leaning over so close that his mouth grazed my ear. "Something there for us, though I wouldn't dare to call it happiness."

SERENDIPITY XXXIX

And hand in hand on the edge of the sand
They danced by the light of the moon, the moon,
the moon . . .
—"The Owl and the Pussycat"

The beach, with its crescent of crystal sand and its fringe of palms, was a south sea cliché except for the sand flies that patrolled it. These flies swarmed Clément even before he had disembarked, though he paid them no heed.

"What land is this?" he muttered rhetorically, losing his too-big shoes to the sand, the dead skin on his feet shredding amid the pumicing dunes. He drove on toward a point in the distance, a place where a break in the line of palms created a natural gate into the surrounding jungle. Even here, in a place that he hadn't planned on, he seemed to know where he was going. I followed at a reluctant distance. I was very tired. I wanted nothing more than to sleep.

Clément paused at the frondy forest portal and waited for me to catch up with him.

"After you, my sweet," he murmured with a gentlemanly bow, "I wouldn't want to lose you."

The landscape was lush. The walls of trees with their thick liana- and orchid-fretted canopy made one feel as though this were a leafy house full of elaborately flowered rooms.

"Bower-like, isn't it?" smirked a much subdued Clément, taking my hand. "The perfect place for a honeymoon." He was joking of course, but when I gazed at him he looked away quickly, almost shyly, muttering, "onward" and pulling me along.

We plunged deeper into the forest and the rain began to fall again, lightly at first, then in the drenching sheets that characterize monsoons. The ground beneath us became slick, then viscous, and Clément began to lose the fleshier parts of his feet to the sucking mud. A few of the flies still buzzed around him, although most of them had been driven off by the downpour. It was amazingly quiet, the usual jungle cacophony silenced by the insistent splatter of rain. Water dominated the rainforest. Mist rose up all around us even as the torrent slapped through the treetops, sluiced down skinny trunks, and waterfalled from the fat, waxy platforms of leaves. Monkeys, insects, birds—all took shelter, hunkering down for the moment under leafy umbrellas. Clément forged on in spite of his rapidly deteriorating feet. A monsoon is not hard to outlast. Almost as quickly as the tap is turned on to full blast, it is shut. The rain stops; hoots and screeches once again fill the canopy; the creatures of the forest re-emerge.

I was drowsy, drugged by the low drone of the flies, which had returned with the end of the shower. I don't remember sitting down to rest, but we must have done so because the next thing I knew I was nodding awake, head bouncing on my chest, a thin line of drool casting a spidery line from the slack side of my mouth. Clément was seated beside me, his butt in the mud, picking at what was left of his feet.

"You are beautiful when you are sleeping," he said, looking at me sideways, smiling at the long thread of spit.

I blinked at him, closed my mouth and swallowed, exhausted all over again by his company. I opened my mouth as though ready to speak and nearly surprised myself with a verbal response, but Clément quickly shushed me.

"Shshshsh," he commanded, stifling my attempt at speech. "You can hear that, can't you?"

I could indeed. I heard voices and the rhythmic crash of gongs and cymbals coming from somewhere further along in the forest.

Clément was already standing. "Come on," he whispered pulling me to my feet. "This is good, very good. Let's see where this leads."

They were a motley procession. They marched along in single file: a man, a woman, a child, and an elephant. We were spying on them from behind a small tree. The first man in the procession was dressed like a clown—the world's largest clown. He was enormous, around six foot eight, and he wore bright yellow bloomers that failed to blouse out around his hammy thighs, curly toed shoes, and a sleeveless tank top that showcased biceps that bulged under the weight of a very large suitcase. The clown with the suitcase was followed by a veiled woman with something tied around her neck. She was carrying a boom box that was playing the gamelan music. Behind her waddled a fat, somewhat large-headed child leading an elephant pulling a colorful litter upon which was mounted a coffin.

"Jimor, are we nearly there? It's muddy and wet," groused the woman in veils in a voice that carried over the orchestra.

"Yes, very nearly," said the oversized clown in thickly accented English. "The gravesite is just around the bend."

Clément leaned forward in his hiding place next to mine. "Delightful. A corpse," he whispered. He had not taken his eyes off the casket on the bier, which was rapidly disappearing into the distance. "Come on, then. Let's follow," he directed. "My feet are a mess. This is just what the doctor ordered."

We tiptoed through the forest behind them, Clément totally noiseless in spite of the wet mud and his crumbling feet. He was the perfect stalker.

The large-headed child who, we discovered, was really a dwarf, kept looking back at the elephant and the coffin as if something were terribly wrong.

"Something smells bad," said the dwarf.

"Maybe it's Brent," the big clown replied. "Or Bila. I told you not to feed her any more bananas. You may have given her gas."

"Gas? I don't think so," the dwarf argued back. "I give her bananas all the time and she loves them. If you fed her once in a while you'd now that. Bananas don't give her gas."

I knew of course that it wasn't the elephant's fault. It was Clément who was stinking up the rear. I was used to the smell that surrounded him most of the time, but that didn't mean others were immune.

"Gas," muttered Clément, "I'll show them gas."

By this time the funeral procession was starting to unravel at the ends. The big clown was way up ahead and the dwarf and the elephant, only a few yards beyond us, though the dwarf couldn't actually see us. The elephant was in the way. If I'd been alone I would have run into them when they halted.

"OK, we're here," the clown announced, seemingly to his suitcase, as he set it down next to a hole in the ground. One by one the other members of the funeral procession arrived at the gravesite. Clément and I scuttled into the nearby bushes.

The suitcase fell over, opened itself, and a tiny Chinese girl unfolded herself from within it.

"Thanks for the ride," she said to the clown as she bent forward at the waist, hooked her elbows around her ankles, and stretched. Then she stood up, threw her thin arms to the heavens and, bending backward, placed her palms on the still-steaming ground. She wore a sparkly blue swimsuit and was only around four feet tall, though she looked even shorter next to the huge man who'd been carrying her around in the suitcase.

The clown nodded and stepped to the elephant's rear. He untied the litter, lifted the casket, and let it drop with a thud to the earth.

"This coffin business, what a chore," he complained.

"Yeah," said the dwarf. "I still say we should have cremated him."

"He was a Christian," said the little Chinese girl, putting one foot behind her head. "This is the way they like to be buried."

"And Muslims, minus the coffin," said the veiled woman, setting the music down and unwinding the thing around her neck. It repositioned itself, coiled its way up her arm. It was a very large snake.

"Whatever," said the dwarf, "Let's just put him in the ground. We don't need to bury him deep."

"We won't," said the clown, as he dragged the coffin toward a shallow pit apparently prepared for the purpose. "Bila," he called, "Bila, down." And the elephant pushed the box into the hole.

The clown, the dwarf, and the two women fell into silence. The woman with the veils kneeled, scooped up a handful of mud and tossed it into the hollow.

"Brent was a wonderful leader," she said.

"What will we do without him?" sighed the miniscule contortionist.

"A friend, a mentor, a talent," said the clown.

"The best trapeze artist in the Pacific," added the dwarf.

Then the veiled woman turned up the music and they all began dancing while the big clown spackled the hole in the ground with more mud.

"Very touching, but I wish they would leave," said Clément. The flies that buzzed around him seemed to have multiplied. He swatted at them with impatience.

By this time the woman had shed her veils and was dancing quite provocatively with the snake.

"I wish Brent were here to see that new dance," said the Chinese girl.

"He'd want Nidi to throw in a cobra," said the clown.

"And a poisonous adder," added the dwarf.

"Yes, I guess so," sighed the tiny contortionist.

Nidi said nothing. She was in her own world. She kept dancing until the clown finished covering the coffin. Then she rearranged the snake and her many veils and turned off the music.

"All right, that's enough," she said gruffly. "Let's go."

And with that, the troupe headed back through the forest.

Clément didn't wait long to come out of hiding. "About time," he grumbled, approaching the grave. "Here's where I take over."

Then he threw himself upon the freshly mounded earth, digging in frenzy, with claw-like hands. "Don't watch me," he hissed, bent over the gravesite and digging down, like a dog, throwing the wet dirt back over his shoulders. A finger or two flew back with it. When he got to the casket, he used what was left of his hands to pry open the lid, huffing and puffing and cursing. He wrenched the top off at last and stepped back clapping his palms together in glee.

"Ooooh," moaned Clément. "Oh, look. This is nice, so nice." He beckoned to me. "Erin, look. So fresh, nearly perfect, and, oh, what an outfit."

I inched toward him, and when I was within reach, he pulled me to his side and pointed with his remaining middle finger. "Do you like him, Erin?" he asked breathlessly. "Oh, he is lovely, isn't he?"

The man in the hole did not look dead. He appeared to be merely sleeping. His sun-streaked hair had a sleep-tousled quality, his handsome face flushed beneath a warm tan. He was not especially tall, but he did look very fit and his body, even lying cushioned in the casket, still exuded a powerful vigor. "A king of a corpse," as Clément might say, but I knew that the thing that most enamored my constant companion was not the man's physical composition, but his clothing.

Brent, the trapeze artist and ringleader to his recently departed cohorts, wore a turquoise jumpsuit with an Elvis-slick sparkle. It had trumpet sleeves, a deep V-neck and was made of a very sheer spandex. His broad shoulders were spangled in turquoise sequins. Gold threads traced the deep cleft of the neckline, arrowing down toward his waist. This accentuated a veritable codpiece of an erection, which further contributed to his lively presentation. He was dressed to perform, and as we stared down into his last resting place, we could almost see him up on his trapeze, knees hooked over the bar, arms stretched gracefully up over his head, ready to make a catch.

"Now that is a costume," Clément whistled admiringly, and he fell upon the body like a lover.

The body of the Chinese man sagged and seemed almost to pour off the corpse. The dead trapeze artist spasmed as though an electric current had hit him, then his mouth and eyes opened, he bolted upright, and he let out a low-pitched roar.

"Oh, god," gasped Clément, "that is so much better." He stood up, turned, and then stooped back over the grave. Once again I was treated to the oily suck, slurp, lip-smacking sound. He rose with a mouth full of offal. "Uuuh," he breathed, "that is so good. Sometimes I forget that I'm hungry."

I had not yet seen a ghoul feed on a corpse. It is a disgusting and mannerless thing. Like a ravenous turkey vulture, Clément had fallen upon the Chinese man's remains, gorging as though time were short. It didn't take long for him to consume a good piece of what was left in the casket. "Just like a stew," he said. "This stuff really sticks to the ribs. But check this out," he added, admiring his new physique. "I've definitely traded up." He gazed down at the penis that was still standing erect. "I have a hard-on, too."

I was squatting at the edge of the grave, my hands over my mouth.

"Help me out," he ordered and stretched out a hand.

I wished the grave had been deeper. If the grave had been deeper perhaps I could have left him there. Maybe I could have run off, tried to escape. But the grave was not much deeper than the casket was tall. Clément's demand for assistance was a mere formality, a way to exert his authority. If I didn't assist, he'd have easily climbed out. There was really no way to break free. So, I lent him a hand, and he pulled himself up. It was better to have no illusions.

"Well, what do you think?" asked Clément once he'd scrambled to my side, stretching himself to his full height, just shy of six feet. He stroked his chest in a downward motion, like a man trying on a new suit. "I like it," he said with a smile. "Brent," he declared, trying the name on for size as well. "Oh, god it's great to feel healthy."

He smiled the trapeze artist's smile, a little stiff perhaps, a little purple around the gums, but still quite passable. His arms were large and very strong, and I'd noted as I pulled him up out of the ground that his grip was firm and muscular. The trapeze artist had broad shoulders, slender hips, and a well-developed chest, and now, animated by Clément, he was crackling with animal magnetism in a way that seemed lascivious and appalling. It made me like him even less and fear him more.

"Come on," said Clément. "We've dallied too long. We have to catch up with our pals."

They hadn't gone far. It was, we discovered, a small and otherwise uninhabited island upon which the Breshtikowsky Circus (named after its founder, Brent Breshtikowsky) had erected headquarters.

Headquarters was a grand wooden house set on pillars in the Malay style with a sweeping saddleback roof; dramatic gables; brightly painted, pierced-wood-embellished eaves and balustrades and wide, split-bamboo verandas. A stone and tile double staircase led up to the second-story porch, and the many large windows were protected with shutters and capped by sheltering eaves.

"A palace," exclaimed Clément when we came upon it. "Fit for a prince. Shall I carry you over the threshold?"

I tossed my head and moved away from him.

"Your resistance never ceases to amaze me," he said. "Come along. Reunion is in the air."

The clown, Jimor, was the first to see us. His brown face blanched white and he let out a high shriek that brought the others running.

It was the dwarf, Snark, who spoke first.

"Impossible," he cried. "You're dead."

"Clearly not," declared Clément.

"But we buried you," insisted the dreamy little contortionist.

"Prematurely, it seems. I was buried alive and if this girl," he affectionately took my hand, "had not come along and heard my cries I would be still six feet underground."

"Four feet," corrected the clown.

"Three," said Nidi.

"Whatever," said Clément.

"Whatever," repeated the Chinese girl.

"Whatever," echoed the clown.

"You had a heart attack," the dwarf said bitterly. "I saw you die."

"Wrong. I'm very much alive. Alive and relieved and ready to jump right back into the saddle, to hit the road running, to take the bull by the horns."

"We're so glad you are back," sang the tiny contortionist, twisting sideways and backward and grabbing her left ankle with her left hand. "We missed you. We were just wondering how we were going to proceed without you."

"Yes, proceed," exclaimed Clément. "The show must go on. Now what exactly do we have on the agenda?"

"You should know," said Nidi.

"Yes, you should," agreed Jimor.

"Well, I don't," replied Clément. "You try remembering details when you're taken for dead and your cohorts have buried you alive."

This turned faces red, especially the dwarf's. "But we have a new plan," he said gruffly.

"No we don't," countered the contortionist. "Not now that Brent's back. We are scheduled for a month at Club Med on Bintan. It's our favorite engagement. Remember?"

"No, I'm sorry, I really can't say that I do."

"It's a great appointment," agreed Jimor. "Much better than the petty circus acts we perform for the villages. We only get to do it because you used to teach the Circus School there."

"What about our new act?" whined the dwarf. "You all liked that idea."

"Ach, that was a stupid plan," said Nidi.

"Yes," the Chinese girl added breathlessly. "We're glad Brent is back. Now things will go back to normal."

"Normal," huffed the dwarf. "What's normal to a bunch of freaks? I don't trust him. He's supposed to be dead. I'm not flying with you."

"Flying?" said Clément, a funny smile on his lips.

"Yes," said Nidi. "Snark's your trapeze partner."

"Oh, right, now I recall," lied Clément. "Well, I don't need him anymore. I have her." He held up my hand and introduced me.

"That board biscuit," sneered the dwarf. "What makes you think that girl can fly?"

"Oh, she can fly all right," said Clément, grinning at me. "Can't you, Erin? Let's show them how you fly."

DROP-DEAD GORGEOUS

The rig was set up behind the house: a swinging twenty-foot playground of poles, guy lines, platforms, flying frames. Jimor, Nidi, Snark, and the little contortionist who was called Blossom marched us up to it and Snark waddled up to the rope ladder and grabbed it.

"OK," he muttered, "let's see what you can do."

Clément pushed me toward the ladder then up, following close behind. I could feel him there just under my ass. "Now, I may be a bit rusty," he called over his shoulder to the gang on the ground as we ascended.

"It's sink or swim, darling," he mumbled into my skirt, and we clambered up onto the board, one of two platforms at either end of the rig. Then, without missing a beat, he grabbed the bar and swung out from our perch, back and forth, back and forth, gathering momentum, then flying like a demented lemur for the catch trap. Once he had hold of that bar he let go of the first, quickly throwing his legs up over the trapeze and dropping into a catcher's lock. "Come on, girl," he shouted on the back end of the swing, giving me no time to think—not that I would have anyway—"come on, girl. Fly."

I do not know if Erin had ever studied trapeze. I don't know if it were she or I or the fractured parts of the creature we'd become working in unison or if it was the ghoul and his provoking command that engendered the ensuing spectacle. All I can say is that the same uncanny grace that had characterized my drifting, skating, dancing path through the world since the day I awakened on a metal slab in that Tokyo morgue took over again.

I flew. I grabbed the bar that Clément sent sailing toward me and one, two, three, let go of it and flew toward him, grasping his wrists as he grasped mine. A gasp arose from the earthbound foursome and I knew that they'd seen what I felt. It was a leap of innocence, a leap of faith, like a leaf uncurling, a flower opening to the rain. It was a leap without any kind of plan, without effort—a perfect, heart-stopping, death-defying leap into the void. And for a moment, for one incredible moment, I felt free. Totally, completely, unalterably free. It was incredible. Then, I was looking up into Brent's dead face, into Clément's face and the smile that was cracking up the corners of my mouth plummeted downward.

"Very good," coaxed Clément, his hands locked around my wrists. "Very good, zombie-girl."

We were still soaring, swinging back and forth high above the net. "Hep," hollered Clément as he tossed me back toward the cutaway bar, which I caught in a single twist. I was back on one board, Clément on the other on the opposite side of the rig. I could see he was panting, a lunatic grin on his face.

"You see," he shouted down to the others. "You see; she is really quite good."

This was met with polite applause from everyone but the dwarf, who turned his back on the scene and toddled back toward the house.

"Demo over," said Clément, descending. They tried to talk me down. "She likes it up there," said Clément with a shrug, but I knew he was angry that I hadn't gone down with him. He was right. I liked it up high on the rig, on the board, on the bar, leaning into the ropes. I did other things—things that surprised me as well as my audience under the rig, though I had little interest in their reaction. Iron Cross. Inverted Crucifix. Mermaid. Half Angel. Isle of Man. Moon.

"Oh, enough," spat Clément, but I paid no attention to him.

It was exhilarating. But how long would it last? We would not be with the circus for long. Clément would eventually migrate to some other body and, with that new identity, some other profession. He was a metaphysical gypsy, and I could see that what for him signified freedom, for me signified the worst possible imprisonment. I didn't want to fight for a new place in the maelstrom of physical existence like a salmon fighting for reproductive rights. I wanted solitude, peace—things that, with Clément, would be unachievable. As obstreperous as he became, I became withdrawn, and I saw now the fearful medicine that the old bokor, Arnotine, had mixed up for us. I was Clément's polar opposite. Yes, I completed him like the second half of a locket in a Platonic wet dream, but with Clément I would be forever locked in tug of war toward equilibrium, and that was not how I wanted to spend eternity.

I don't know who cut the net. Perhaps it was Snark who seemed to be consumed with a jealousy of the dead man's leadership role. His antipathy toward the ringleader's second coming made him suspect, as did his poorly disguised attempts to wrest control. Nor, for that matter, was the manner in which Brent Breshtikowsky was called to his maker ever truly revealed. It could have easily been murder, and if it were, my money was on Snark. But what did that matter? The net was cut. Cleverly and discretely, the ropes slit and tied loosely back together in a way that guaranteed it would cave under so much as the weight of a kitten. I had noticed the mischief when Snark took hold of the rope ladder. The frayed ropes carelessly knotted. It was like an open door. I saw it, and I saw my escape.

It was, by now, late in the day. Clément was looking up at me, shading his eyes from the sun.

"Quite a performance," he yelled. "Are you coming down?" I continued to swing back and forth.

"Well," he shouted, "At last I've found something that you like."

I looked south, away from the front of the house, from the direction from which we'd come—south into the rainforest, into the leafy crowns of the trees, into the gathering storm clouds. The air was laced with hydroelectric force—lightning and rain preparing to fall upon us. I could smell the water in the sky, the water in the earth, the water surrounding the island. No, I wouldn't leave here. I was not going to follow Clément from one stinking corpse to the next, handmaiden to a ghoul, hapless, hopeless zombie. I'd die first.

I dropped into a Gazelle, then stretched into an Amazon.

Jimor and Nidi whistled.

"Well, if you can't beat 'em, join 'em," said Clément, and he climbed back up to the board. I remember his smile. It was wide and foolish, like the smile on the mouth of the painted carnival clown face through which you will throw the ball. I think he was truly happy, if a ghoul can experience that. I was taunting him, swinging back and forth on my bar, upside down, legs hooked loosely, arms hanging over my head like the martyr in a tarot deck. I knew that would tempt him. Clément stood on the board for a moment watching me, head cocked to one side, then he grabbed the bar and set himself in motion, still smiling, building up speed, matching his movement to mine. He was ready. I knew it.

"Hep," he said. "Hep."

In that moment I saw many things. I saw the forest, the house, the faces of Jimor, Nidi, and Blossom upside down, as though reflected in a still pool of water. I saw the clouds overhead, like fat purses of silver ready to shower us in diamonds. I saw my breasts, my hips, my long white thighs, knees curling the bar, defying gravity. I saw Clément, dazzling in turquoise, wrong side up like me, like mirror images caught in the eye of a camera, his blond hair rising from his head like a pale golden flame.

I pushed back, forward, back . . . and I jumped on the forward swing, arms outstretched, hands reaching toward Clément. I touched him. Touched his hands, the tips of my fingertips grazing his in farewell as I twisted to avoid his catch, somersaulted away and fell back into a bullet drop that took me down toward the net, toward the door, toward freedom, toward my escape from Clément.

MESSAGE IN A BOTTLE

So imagine Ryu's surprise when the letter arrived via DHL courier. He couldn't have known whether it was a distress call or a summons. He was used to messages from Clément, but he wondered how the ghoul had found him this time. *Erin*, he concluded. I was the only one who knew about his Hong Kong hideaway. He'd promised to take me there for the weekend—an empty promise. It seemed I had remembered.

Of course Clément hadn't used the usual yakuza delivery service. Understandably. The yakuza were very upset with him. He'd run off with the girl and the chip and he'd left quite a mess in his wake. The yakuza wanted him. The Consortium wanted him. Orison wanted him. The police wanted him too. And they all wanted me—or the product I was holding—including the police, who still thought me responsible for, or at least an accessory to, a long string of murders.

Ryu also wanted Clément. Clément had been playing them all for fools far too long. Now, without yakuza protection, Clément was fair game. All Ryu had to do was recover the chip and then he could deal with the ghoul. Clément, it seemed, was taunting him with just that prospect.

What was Ryu expecting when he tore open the box? A head? A

hand? A microchip and a note? He could feel his pulse racing as he contemplated the possibilities. A slight perspiration dotted his upper lip and brow. He felt a tingling in his groin. It was exciting, almost like fugu.

The box was only a little bit heavy—a kilo, maybe less—and this was explained when Ryu pulled back the packing material and the paper that carefully cradled its contents. A bottle. A dark green bottle filled with milky white liquor: sake—the best—and two beautiful cups . . . and a letter.

Fooled again and upset with himself, Ryu pushed aside the fancy contents and ripped open the letter. It was written in Japanese, in a childish but competent hand that Ryu instantly recognized as mine, though it was immediately apparent that the author of the message was Clément.

> *Dear Ryu,*
>
> *There has been an accident. It has brought me to my senses. I can only wonder what I have been thinking all this time. I see you for what you are now: a stalwart fellow—unsentimental, uncomplicated, and direct. Not a lying hypocrite like so many who pretend at decency. Therefore, I will deliver the microchip only to you. I am in Jakarta. Erin is with me, though no longer a captive. I am her captive. Her slave. You think I am raving. You must know by now that all of this: the microchip, the exchange, the method for delivering it, was all part of an elaborate plan—a plan to capture the girl as she had captured my imagination. For Erin, it was a misplaced belief in her father's rehabilitation and in your protection; for you, a chance to impress*

your yakuza bosses, for me, true love and a new lease
on life.

I can still remember the first time I saw her, as
an infant so many years ago: a child, Lizette's child,
the very image of her mother. She was so perfect, so
emotionally fragile. She took my breath away. It was
my interest in her, that led me to investigate her father's
alliances and activities, which naturally led me to the
Consortium. The yakuza, the Consortium, you, me—
Erin is the knot that ties us all together. I am Dante;
she is Beatrice, the poet and his muse.

How to get her? The microchip and information
that could change the world—if it could do this, it
could easily put her within my reach. And it did. With
a blackmail scheme I could mobilize the yakuza and
force the Consortium, and by association, Erin's father,
to play ball. Where do you think your "assignment"
came from? Who do you think suggested that they
should kill Erin? Her father surrendered her eagerly, as
I knew he would—anything to raise him in the esteem
of his power-hungry peers. But first a short research
trip to Haiti and a quick lesson in zombie powders. I
suggested the fugu. Remember? I didn't want her to
die, not really, that would have ruined my plans. Are
you following me? This is the shell game, Ryu. Just
keep your eye on the pearl. And what is that pearl?
Why, Erin, of course. She is the reason this game is in
motion. Pardon the unfettered romanticism, but this
game is really about love.

Well, I admit that, even for me, at first it was all

about power. I wanted to possess someone utterly—a
living someone. Don't we always want what we can't
seem to have? And when I saw Erin, she seemed the
perfect creature upon which to project my desires.

But things turn out oddly. The girl did not give up
easily, did not become the slave I wished her to be. And
then I began to have second thoughts. The object of my
fantasies became the subject of my dreams.

I can't say at what point my motives began to
turn inside out, at what point I began to identify so
completely with the girl, that her survival started to
become as important as my own, at what point I began
to believe that I, a ghoul, could find happiness, at what
point I began to hope. Maybe it was her tenacity, her
independence and a strength of character that not even
the witchdoctor's dark art was able to suppress that
won me over. Maybe that is when the first little threads
of real love began to knit themselves into my heart. A
ghoul's existence is predicated on the need to survive
at any cost, but Erin has convinced me that there are
things more important than mere survival.

Remember when I told you what it was like to
come back again and again; to be reborn over and over
into a meaningless void, alone, with no one to admit
that you even exist; to be isolated by the very nature
of your being? I thought I could find something more.
What can I say? I'm a breakout ghoul and I've had
too much truck with the living. It was a lark at first,
but I've fallen in love, and I believe that will be my
undoing. Come to me, Ryu, but come quickly. There

*isn't much time. You will find me with Erin, my own
true love. Not happy. No, that is impossible for me,
though I think Erin is happy, free at last from the
zombie spell. And me, I finally see what it means to be
human, how pleasure and pain are linked in the dance
of my own desire and my weakness.*

*But you have a job to do, Ryu. I respect that, and
I aim to help you complete it. And I have a job to do,
too. I was contracted to deliver a microchip. Perhaps
it is time for me to complete my assignment. Do I get
what I want? I'll let you be the judge. I will meet you
on the pier at Tanjung Priok Harbor. You may not
recognize me, but surely you'll know Erin on sight.
Find her and you will find me.*

Ryu sat down and lit a cigarette. Then he took the match to the
letter and burned it. He put the sake on ice. Later he would sit at the
window overlooking Kowloon Harbor and sip the beverage slowly. So
that was what the whole thing was about. It was as foolish as that.
And Clément, damn him, had won. He was sorry this chase was coming to an end, that the Consortium would get the microchip and that
Clément would get the girl. It would all end so predictably as things
generally did. That was, he decided, a shame.

DEADLINES

"Happiness is a chimera, eternity a farce." I write these words then pad into the kitchen, the kitchen I have no use for. Chen-nui is making tea. He turns when he hears me enter, the teapot in his hand. These days I never leave my room.

The teapot seems to have developed a life of its own. It wobbles like an old woman on rollerskates, kamikazes, but not without leaving a wide brown stain down the front of my houseboy's coat. I stand there with a little smirk on my face. Not my smirk, but *her* signature leer, still looking, I'm certain, even at this late date, fairly canine, hopeful, expectant.

The teapot hits the counter before it flashes to the floor, knocks down Chen's teacup. Slivers of china explode upward like shrapnel. Chen's hands go to his mouth and his eyes get so wide that he looks like a night-dwelling primate. Rain runs down all of the windows. Suddenly it is the only sound in the kitchen—the rain and the ticking clock.

I think for a moment that I ought to kill Chen. But I know that I won't. Killing is not in my nature. I know too much about the dead.

There is an island between Chen and me. It is made of wood and granite and it no longer has a teacup upon it. I suppose it is also a metaphorical island. We are from two different worlds, my houseboy and I, at least for now. His aversion to my world is apparent. I watch him back out of the ample kitchen, the large Western kitchen, the extravagant kitchen. I stoop to pick up the pieces of china—china chips. Not easy. There is not much left of my hand anymore, the flesh bloated, blackened, falling easily off the bone.

Friday was the last day I looked in a mirror. That was a week ago and I looked bad even then.

I hear the door slam. I know that Chen will not be back. He might tell others, go to the police, but that doesn't matter. I'm on the home stretch. I have to work faster. I have a very tangible deadline.

In the darkened bedroom, the cursor blinks on the computer screen. I've spent the past five days shut up in the room with the small table, the computer and, occasionally, the mirror. Five days working day and night, no rest, to get me to chapter thirty-six. Five days working hand-to-hand, mano-a-mano with the woman of my dreams, my citadel, my bride. This, then, is my deadline: putrefying flesh, deteriorating cartilage, crumbling bone. I am disgusted with myself. My hands are so rotten I can hardly type. But I have a non-negotiable deadline. It's made of dead flesh. I have to write like a bat out of hell, a house on fire. I have to finish:

Erin did not die right away.

She lay on the grassy sward beneath the rig, some twenty feet below her partner—beneath me—the pointless net spread around her like a mantle. Her eyes were open, an annoying look of victory on her face. I could have killed her, I was so angry. I could have torn off her head. I could still feel her fingertips brushing mine, my frantic reach finding nothing but air. Why had she done this? She'd been within my grasp.

The others stood around her, silent, stunned, mouths open. I climbed down, pushed past them, kneeled at her side.

"I loved you," I hissed. My mouth was dry. A temporary affair, I'd soon be awash in disintegration.

Erin said nothing, but she was communicating with me. Maybe it was that final baring of her teeth, the hideously ersatz smile, the self-righteous and preposterous moue of victory that had settled upon her countenance that made me do it, made me rush her, made me break another stupid rule. Rules—rules are made to be broken, and I have broken a lot of them. Yes, I have transgressed, and I have taken others along with me. How many sins have I committed? How many trespasses and crimes?

And so this time I broke Ghoul's Rule #1. I did not wait to take possession of the body. Dead bodies only—that is the ghoul's mantra, and although it may seem totally perverse, it's based on courtesy. Wait for the prior occupant to vacate before you move in. The gallant thing to do was obvious. And yet I couldn't do it. I was furious, and so I bullied my way into something other than a corpse. It was a brutal metaphysical exercise. There is a fight and it can be exhausting. And that is how I met her at the threshold of life and death: both of us fagged out from our little tug of war—me and my future, my bride.

How can I describe that meeting? If I had a heart, it would have been in my mouth choking me with imperatives, the kind that abstract existence and circumvent all that we invent. I was suffused with warmth, a feeling totally foreign to a creature accustomed only to the dead. That alone was pretty heady stuff. I felt emotion pumping through me, piston-like, intense. Was it because I had crossed over, snagged the at least partially undead, entered the world of the living? Or was it something else? Was it because I finally had her in my power: Erin, the fugitive other, the creature that I'd committed to possess?

It was so different from the inside. Different. She was neither woman nor zombie. She was none of that. She was much, much more. She was regal, fiercely righteous, spiritual; she was sacred. She was light, bright, winged, the most unphysical thing that I had ever encountered. I felt a warning reverberating all around me—a great reproach, a curse. Do you think that I paid any heed? No way. I jumped her holy, metaphysical bones.

Shall I tell you my fantasy? It is pathetic, the kind of desperate dream that only a dead thing might concoct. I thought we could move in together. You know, set up housekeeping like young lovers trying out their ties. Or at the very least, we could be liver and liver fluke, live oak and lichen, plant and parasite, embracing symbiosis, succoring each other, living off one another, but as one. In short, we'd marry. Hadn't I already taken up a kind of residence or at least established my control when I'd removed her will, made her into a zombie, though admittedly I'd failed to do it properly? That had been an attempt at union. But she had spurned me. Now, here I was, given another chance. How could I not snatch at it?

How do you embrace a soul? Cautiously? Firmly? Salaciously? There is no manual for this. I've mauled dead bodies many times and this was different, but I was not different, and so I was . . . salacious. I felt her struggle, just a flutter really, deep within her chest—my chest. I beat it down. I wouldn't let her go. Tokyo, Netherlands, Singapore, Malaysia, day-on-day—I'd worked too hard for this. I felt peevish, tired of the stupid game. She had no power anyway. What were we dickering about?

Oh, what it felt like to possess her! Every feeling she'd ever had, every sorrow, every joy, was—for a moment—mine! It was terrifying and thrilling, powerful and humbling. The tapestry of her life spread out for me in all its electricity and color. I held her fast and I felt the brightness burn down, like a candle. I had not realized that a soul is like a candle and that it can go out.

That's when she spoke to me. At least it felt like speech, although it seemed to come from within my own mind, from me.

"Come, then," she said, frantic. "This is where I jump. Follow me if you dare."

A taunt, an invitation from the beloved poised upon the very brink of oblivion, a suicide pact, so perfectly romantic. How could I refuse?

I almost did it, kicked the frame, leaped with her into annihilation. Did I? No way. What do I know of love? I'd like to count myself a hero for not giving in, but for a moment, it was irresistible—the dream of a candle, extinguished, two candles, actually, hers and mine. Although I couldn't share her life with her, I could have its opposite. I could share nothing with her, or "nothingness," as if that were a state of being. In the end, I made the ghoul's choice, opting for life—at any cost. No, I couldn't give up the generative and degenerating world. I gave up something else. It makes me sick to think on it. So I was left with candle wax, with melting fat wrapped round a dead wick. I had a chance at freedom and I blew it.

To say that the gang was surprised when Brent Breshtikowsky bent prince-like over Erin and kissed her and their precious ringmaster collapsed and the girl rose—whole and powerful—would be the grossest understatement. They were confounded, but I don't give a rat's ass what they thought. Not them or anybody else. It's over and I've got a book to finish, a mission to complete.

Haven't I killed love? Now, that is my real M.O.

Well, that's it. No ponderous revelations, just a story. A love story, actually—one that ends badly.

With any luck, Ryu has come to town. I have a date with him, and I mean to keep it. I'll keep it with this manuscript under my arm. I'm still not certain that I will hand over the microchip. I wonder: Will he recognize us after all these weeks? Part of her has escaped, to be sure, but part of her could not get away. We have been altered by our experience. Will he see me in Erin and Erin in me? Who knows with Ryu? We shall see.

NOTES

1   A Vodoun priest.

2   Yakuza are the Mafia, the Tong, the Triads of Japan.

3   A gathering of practitioners of the Vodoun rites.

4   The pantheon of Vodoun deities.

5   Zora Neale Hurston, *Tell My Horse: Voodoo and Life in Haiti and Jamaica* (New York: Perennial Library, 1990).

6   Wade Davis, *The Serpent and the Rainbow* (New York: Warner Books, 1985).

7   Wilfrid Doricent, who was examined in Port-au-Prince returned to Roche-a-Bateau "with no hope of ever regaining his mental faculties or living a normal life." Belavoix Doricent was sentenced to life imprisonment. Michel Lamisere, "Haiti: Where Zombies Are Real People," *San Francisco Examiner*, April 7, 1991.

8   Shibuya, Shinjuku, Ikebukuro, and Roppongi are districts or "wards" in Tokyo.

9   Guedeh, the irascible Loa of death, is often portrayed as a skeleton in a top hat and tails.

10   Allah Almighty says: "And I (Allah) created not the jinns and humans, except they should worship Me (Alone)." Adh-Dhariyat: 56.

11   For more information on ghuls, their dark origins and their amazing powers, go to the Persian *Epic of Kings*.

12   Fierce, highly stylized masculine poses assumed by male characters in Kabuki drama.

13   Fugu is the Japanese name for all fish of the family Tetraodontidae, class osteichthyes, order Tetraodontiformes, known in English as the blowfish or globefish. Highly poisonous, and at the same time very tasty, it has been the cause of many deaths over the centuries, including that of the famous Kabuki actor Mitsugoro Bando VIII in 1975. Japan consumes approximately 20,000 tons of blowfish yearly. The safest time to eat fugu is in the winter months. This scene takes place in August. Blowfish toxins, which block sodium channels

in nerve tissues, paralyze muscles, and induce respiratory arrest, have been identified as an ingredient in zombie powders.

14 Japanese cab drivers wear white gloves.

15 Only men are allowed to perform on the Kabuki stage—an old rule and a ridiculous one, based on a misconceived morality, though I have to admit it has yielded some amazing theater. They say that the very best *onnagata* actually live as women.

16 A member of the legendary feudal Japanese society of mercenary agents trained in martial arts and stealth whose assignments often included espionage, sabotage, and assassination.

17 It is a custom for family members to pick through the bones of the deceased with chopsticks after cremation. Key fragments are placed in a ceramic urn that is eventually inserted into the family grave.

18 The posthumous name assigned to the deceased for use in the other world.

19 Lou Lou, Alain, and Albert sometimes ran drugs in a casual, just-for-friends, pick-up-quick-cash manner. Albert was the business man and the driving force in this enterprise and although Lou Lou did hang out with a yakuza crowd, their small operation was independent and totally under the radar.

20 Today In de Waag, in addition to serving as popular gathering point, restaurant, and café, is the home of the Foundation of Old and New Media.

21 Exquisite Corpse is a game that was very popular with the surrealists in which each player creates one third of a figure without the benefit of seeing the other two segments. It is also the name of a magazine (www.corpse.org) created by Romanian poet Andrei Codrescu.

22 Completed in 1996 and named for Petroliam Nasional Bhd, Malaysia's national petroleum corporation, the twin towers in Kuala Lumpur City Center were built to be the world's tallest structure and are a symbol of Malaysian aspiration and ambition.

23 Durian is a smelly, albeit popular Southeast Asian treat.

24 Today around 90 percent of all rubber production comes from plantations of rubber trees in Southeast Asia.

25 The plight of the Greek forces at the Bay of Aulis is first mentioned in Homer's *Cypria*. Its next mention is in Aeschylus' play *The Libation Bearers* (c. 460 BCE). The priest, Calchis, tells the Greek king, Agamemnon, that he must sacrifice his daughter, Iphigenia, for a wind to carry his ships to Troy. Iphigenia is sent for, but before her execution the princess is transported to Taurus, a city on the Black Sea, and an animal is sacrificed in her place.

ACKNOWLEDGMENTS

Some years back, a crabby reviewer criticized my debut collection of short fiction for the number of people I acknowledged, which took up no more than a scant half page. Ridiculous! Everyone knows that most books are not published without a tremendous amount of help. This was definitely the case with *Dead Love*, which was very nearly consigned to a premature burial. So here, at the risk of further censure, is a very big thank you to just a few of the lovely people who were so generous with their time, energy, and support.

Thanks, first and foremost, to Lowry McFerrin, who has provided years of thoughtful editorial guidance, considerable handholding, and many a celebratory cocktail along the way. Thanks also to early readers Katsu Miyata, Christi Phillips, Lauren Cuthbert, Susan Brennan, Paul McHugh, Maureen Wheeler, Alison Biggar, Richard Passetti, Amelia Passetti, Jared McFerrin, Colleen McFerrin, Lucy Wu, Johanna Schupbach, and Mary Brent Cantarutti for their comments and encouragement, and to Rosemary James of the Pirate's Alley Faulkner Society for her love of literature and generosity of spirit.

I'm profoundly grateful to Peter Lang, Laurie McAndish King, Bradley Charbonneau, and Cheryl McLaughlin for their Internet and social media networking advice. Peter Goodman, Andy Ross, Ari, Linda, Maren, and Baba—many thanks for the creative and professional muscle (this includes lifting big boxes of books) that has finally seen this project to publication, and my admiration goes to Hikaru Sasahara, Evan Miller, and Botan Yamada for their terrific manga representation of the work. Thanks to Tim Cahill for being himself: a brilliant man you can count on. Finally, a very special thank you to Elaine and Bill Petrocelli, the entire staff at Book Passage, and the marvelous members of Left Coast Writers® for the constant company and enthusiasm for all things literary, and to all those who, like me, love and are fascinated by zombies.

LWM